Praise f

'The premise is simpl[...] [...]
Anna Karenina were a [...] [...] [...] [...]
that belonged to the crème de la crème of Russian society
of that time? Subtle and deeply intelligent... Delightful'
Los Angeles Review of Books

'A beautiful haunting novel...looking at a familiar London
through a frosty, snowy lens. Wonderful' Caryl Phillips

'*Monsieur Ka* is more than a sophisticated "what happened
next?" exercise... Goldsworthy is an elegant writer, skilful
at building atmosphere. Her fiction-within-fiction device is
clever and intriguing... The novel could hardly seem more
of the moment' *The Times*

'A wonderful novel, entirely original, and entirely absorbing...
The atmosphere she creates is exceptional' Carmen Callil

'It often takes an émigré to describe a country most clearly,
and Goldsworthy, who was born in Belgrade but has lived
in London for 30 years, is proving a most accomplished
poet of her adopted city... A delight' *Daily Mail*

'Mournful and evocative... It makes for compelling reading'
Book Oxygen

'In all three of her books, Goldsworthy has displayed a gift
for creating atmosphere... One of Goldsworthy's strengths is
the sensitivity with which she portrays the many marriages in
the book... Much of the pleasure of reading this remarkable
novel comes from its passionate dedication to the power of
stories' *Guardian*

Praise for *Gorsky*

'Evocative, captivating and acutely observed... Thrilling'
Sunday Times

'Written with such narrative elegance that you're led irresistibly on, as with some exquisite dish, from one perfect melting mouthful to the next' Michael Frayn

'This is the most enjoyable fiction I've come across this year. *Gorsky* is engaging and, best of all...manages to cast London in a new and softer light. I defy anyone who revelled in Fitzgerald's original not to have fun with Goldsworthy's attempt to transpose arguably the greatest American novel back to the old world' *Financial Times*

'An eternal, melancholy story which never fails to tug at the heartstrings' Lovereading

'The spell-binding story of a Russian billionaire setting up home in London's "Chelski". With wit and poetic verve, Vesna Goldsworthy explores our fascination with money, glamour, parties and sex and, ultimately, offers a haunting elegy to love' Sofka Zinovieff

'A glittering, glamorous novel' *Sunday Express*

'Entertaining and poignant, ironic and serious, *Gorsky* is both a literary homage and the work of a highly original imagination. Goldsworthy is brilliant on money, clothes. romantic love and decadent sex – and on various kinds of immigrant species. A *jeu d'esprit* with a heart and mind' Eva Hoffman

'Clever...entertaining...elegant' *The Times*

VESNA GOLDSWORTHY

Vesna Goldsworthy was born in Belgrade in 1961 and has lived in London since 1986. She writes in English, her third language. Her books include an internationally bestselling memoir, *Chernobyl Strawberries*, and a novel, *Gorsky*. A former BBC World Service journalist, she is currently professor in creative writing at the University of Exeter and at UEA.

ALSO BY VESNA GOLDSWORTHY

Gorsky
The Angel of Salonika
Chernobyl Strawberries
Inventing Ruritania

VESNA GOLDSWORTHY

Monsieur Ka

VINTAGE

1 3 5 7 9 10 8 6 4 2

Vintage
20 Vauxhall Bridge Road,
London SW1V 2SA

Vintage is part of the Penguin Random House group of companies
whose addresses can be found at global.penguinrandomhouse.com

Penguin
Random House
UK

First published in Vintage in 2019
First published in hardback by Chatto & Windus in 2018

penguin.co.uk/vintage

A CIP catalogue record for this book is available from the British
Library

ISBN 9781784704520

Printed and bound in Great Britain by Clays Ltd, Elcograf S.p.A.

Penguin Random House is committed to a sustainable future for our
business, our readers and our planet. This book is made from Forest
Stewardship Council® certified paper.

MIX
Paper from
responsible sources
FSC® C018179

To Vera

My God, if only someone could finish *Anna Karenina* for me! It's unbearable.

Tolstoy, *Letters*

Prologue

A Snapshot

'Unconditional love: people say it is the essence of motherhood. I was barely old enough to recognise it when suddenly she was no more, like a comet extinguished. To have a famous mother is a curse. To lose your mother at nine is a tragedy. I have lived my life in the shadow of these two misfortunes. It took a lifetime to comprehend the extent of the devastation they caused. There is no mother more famous than mine. Except the Holy Virgin, perhaps. Soon you will understand it all much better. We are now related, you and I, dear Albertine.'

The Count's face was lit by the familiar, lopsided smile. He said all this in Russian. I was so pleased with myself for finally understanding the words that I realised only later, when I was writing them down, that I had missed his meaning. He was using the familiar, informal *you* for the first time. *We are now related, you and I*, he said. My Russian is, still, barely passable. By electing to write his story in English, I chose a camera unable to capture the most significant detail in the snapshot. What did he mean? What did he know?

Monsieur Ka

Why do marriages end?

A better question may be: why do they ever begin?

'A triumph of hope over experience,' Albie would have said. He spoke like that, holding emotions at arm's length with the pincers and tweezers of clichés, like a bomb disposal expert. Years pass and I still don't know which live wire was to blame for the blast that blew us asunder. I hold myself culpable. Responsibility is easier to live with than ignorance.

Albie was not yet fully dressed. The long johns and the vest sagged around his knees and elbows and gathered under his armpits like old man's skin. A pair of suspenders hugged his calf muscles, holding his long grey socks in place. There was something incongruous and clown-like about the red and green regimental stripes of the elastic band, at odds with everything around us. His army days now lingered in vestiges like those.

'Ber,' he said, managing to extend the syllable into a mournful tune.

It was freezing, even indoors. The bathroom window was covered in fern frost. A faint glow beyond it suggested the arrival of a new morning – daybreak seems too strong, too definite a word. Albie pressed his forehead against the cistern, as though standing was an effort. A chain dangled to the right,

its white pull with a black rubber ring indecent in its plain-
ness, its no-nonsense utilitarianism. I was beginning to get
used to this island, the pride it took in the functional, in
making do. 'Mustn't grumble,' people said all the time. 'I'm
fine,' to mean they had had enough.

Albert and Albertine – an Englishman and a Frenchwoman,
if I could still call myself French. One might have concluded
from our names that we had been meant for each other, but
there was no deeper meaning behind the coincidence and
Albertine had nothing to do with Proust. I was a few days
older than the first volume of *À la recherche*. My father had
wanted a son to call after my grandfather: the name helped
overcome the disappointment of my gender. Albie's father
loved Queen Victoria. His mother did not approve of Albert
as a name. Too common, she thought. She had wanted to call
him Tristan; mine nearly plumped for Violetta. Patriarchal
authority gave us both a lucky escape.

He laughed when I called him Albie – fit for a Cockney
comedian, he said – but the nickname stuck. He used to call
me Bertie in Alexandria. Ber sounded like an English shiver.
It seemed apt, on mornings like this.

My nightdress offered little protection against the cold. The
mirror above the washbasin threw a misty reflection of its blue
stripes back at me. The pattern was unflattering, although I had
purchased the fabric and made the garment myself. It was ill-
chosen, or perhaps chosen all too well. I thought I knew what
I was doing as soon as I touched the flannel at the Army &
Navy Stores in Victoria, but I had miscalculated the effect. I had
assumed the stripes would suit a tomboyish garment, a witty,
wifely echo of Albie's longing for propriety. I took no notice of
the fact that it could make me look like a detainee, yet that is
what it had faded to, and so soon.

The sewing machine had been a wedding present from Albie's parents; a Singer, like my maiden name, or one version of it. On the day the gift was delivered, there was the clip-clop of horses' hooves outside. The livery of the coachman was as green as the cart and the big box from Harrods that it brought; the horses as black as the blackest night, with fetlocks from a gothic romance. I was green, too, new to the land where people sent expensive gifts by way of apology for not seeing you. We pretended that was normal, in England. Albie was used to communicating by parcel. The machine reminds me of those horses every time I open the lid. Friesians, Albie told me, a sight to behold. Graceful, dependable; foreign like me.

'Ber,' Albie said, 'you'll get used to London. You'll come to love it. I promise. Give it a couple of years.'

A couple more years, he should have said. It was eighteen months since our boat had docked in Southampton. It had been high summer then; 1945, the war just over. The train that took us to London cut through the Hampshire fields, parting waves of wheat as full of sunshine as the beaches we had left behind. London: the word still pealed like the chimes of wedding bells.

Before we left Alexandria for good, Albie and I had had a weekend by the water, west of the city, where the desert met the sea in luminous expanses. The Egyptian sand seeped from our hair and our clothes for weeks. I kept finding grains on pillowcases and felt them on the carpets under my feet well into that first autumn. Tiny, hard, grey specks; impossible to believe that, in their billions, they added up to something golden.

Albie joked that we had brought the dunes with us to our home in Earl's Court. It took a long time to learn how to

pronounce these two words well enough to make myself understood when I wanted to buy Underground tickets. The waves
closed behind me and the city took me in. Its size was overwhelming. I did not venture to its edges again until the end
of the second winter.

Albie combed some oil into his hair, then tidied his moustache with the same comb. He would soon put on a suit and
tie, button up his waistcoat so that it looked as stiff as a cuirass,
lace up his black shoes and finally throw his overcoat over his
shoulders, never once glancing in the mirror. He knew his
drill. Wrapped up and poker-straight, he was the very picture
of an officer in mufti – handsome, handsomer even than that
dusty, lithe creature in desert boots and shorts he had been
when I first met him – yet everything about him had stiffened,
become different, unreachable.

The young man who had teasingly boasted of defeating
Rommel now went to work in an office, eagerly and as early
as he could, often skipping breakfast. *Duty calls*, he'd say in a
sing-song voice, his face warming into a smile, as though duty
was a mistress, easier to please than a wife.

I knew little about Albie's work. Whitehall: that was what
he said when people asked where he worked. It sounded like
Whitelaw, his – our – family name. We had walked along
Whitehall, with its un-French, haphazard jumble of
commanding grey blocks, several times that first summer,
and he had pointed to the building which housed his office.
It was closer to Trafalgar Square than to the Houses of
Parliament; it had a shiny black door, with an even shinier
brass plate next to it bearing the name of an English county.
Sussex House, Cheshire House, Lancashire House: it could
have been any of these. I trusted Albie. I still do. Wives did
not ask in those days.

'Don't worry your pretty head, Ber. I'll keep bringing home the bacon.' That was his answer, and a hug, when I bothered to pose a question. It was such a funny phrase. I never doubted the essence of his promise. I felt lucky that he thought me pretty, that he had chosen me for a wife.

He was still on His Majesty's service, though no longer in uniform, and he no longer talked about his work. In our earlier days, he had often seemed unable to resist a boast. Chases along the wadi, madcap plots to snip apart Rommel's string of African successes: his yarns of military adventure were so riotous that I never believed any of them. He made the war sound like an English school sports day. Victory had turned out to be a more serious business. He even found it difficult to say whether he was hoping to be home for dinner. Every now and then he would pack a suitcase, leave it waiting in the hall and, in the morning, when an official car arrived to collect him, he would say, 'See you on Thursday or Friday' the way other husbands might have said, 'I'll be a bit late tonight, darling.'

I could guess where he had been on his return if a box of sweets appeared on the dining-room table – marrons glacés, calissons or bergamotes, leckerli, lebkuchen, the upturned boats of gianduotti or the sweet pillows of amaretti morbidi. Albie's gifts *from Europe*. He did not exactly hide his tracks, but that part of his life which related to the unfinished business of wartime victories was no longer mine, no longer a laughing matter.

In bed at night, he fell asleep within minutes. I counted hours, sheep, personal losses, depending on the mood I was in. Albie thought that happiness was a matter of pulling your socks up, making them stay there, by hook or by crook. I was beginning to think that perhaps I should become like him: bury the past, forget that which you can't bring back. Choose to be cheerful, stay cheerful, and happiness will follow. He himself seemed stuck at the second part of the proposition.

'You don't have to work, Ber, you know that. But if it would make you happy to go out into the world, meet people, please, Ber, I won't say no. I know it's difficult to stay at home when you have been used to working. Voluntary work, for example? A lot of ladies these days ...'

My stockings hung on the radiator like something vaguely prosthetic. I reached for them and stepped out of the bathroom. I could hear the hum of a motor outside. Albie started these conversations only when there was a way to end them quickly. Down in the square, the car was waiting to take him to Whitehall, a shiny black frog under the falling snow.

When he went to work, the day stretched emptily ahead. I had long ceased to pretend that the pieces of translation which Albie's people sent my way could keep me occupied. The brief communiqués that I conveyed into my most elegant French extolled the Allied war record and expressed optimism about the future. They were neither riveting nor revealing. I had no illusions about their importance. I was too un-English to be grateful for small mercies. Yet even these commissions were drying up. Treaties were being signed; war-crimes trials were being completed one by one.

I wasn't looking forward to the life of galleries and tearooms in which so many women frittered their afternoons over oils or china cups. When they thought no one was watching, I glimpsed the memory of war in their faces, the disorientation of a return to inconsequential civilities.

I would not have thought it possible to feel as homesick as I did when Albie was not around to distract me, although I knew I was homesick for places that no longer existed. The war took away Paris and Bucharest, and replaced them with a knowledge of their capacity for betrayal. I had arrived in Alexandria in 1941 and, while the world was at war, I felt at peace there for four years. I had a job. I polished my English as though I sensed my life would come to depend on it. I knew that Egypt was a temporary shelter, that the enforced largesse of the Arabs was not going to last. Now only London remained, yet I did not know how to love London. Albie was my way into the metropolis, but Albie had a country – a whole continent – to rebuild, a new world to defend. I had no such clarity of purpose. In the heart of a frozen city, on an island surrounded by icy grey waters, my insides felt frozen to the bone.

Every morning, after Albie left, I'd put on my coat and galoshes and walk to South Kensington to buy *Le Monde*, fresh off the ferry and a day late. To take some exercise, I cut through rows of mews and back streets at great speed, trying to look like someone who had to get somewhere in a hurry. It was a new habit, this new paper: *Le Monde*. I read it the way one reads fiction, as though France was a figment of my imagination, a country that no longer existed. I skimmed through the headlines over toast and coffee until it was close to noon, the day half gone, the thought consoling in itself.

'You're wishing your life away, Ber,' Albie had said when I told him how the best part of the day was always around 3 p.m. – when the light was almost spent. It was too late to start anything, close enough to his return from work to make me relish a bit of solitude – if he was in the country that is, and not, as so often, in Germany, France or Switzerland. When I had promised to have and to hold, there was no mention of a thousand temporary partings.

Europe, he called it.

'I'm off to Europe tomorrow, Ber. I won't be back until Thursday.'

'Isn't it perverse, Albie,' I had asked, 'isn't it perverse to wake up and look forward to three in the afternoon?'

'You're wishing your life away,' he had responded, spreading margarine on his toast, scraping it so thinly that the membranes of each cell crackled under the pressure of the knife.

'I am not. You are,' I said. I failed to grasp the meaning of the strange little phrase. I took *away* to mean *elsewhere*.

On one of those morning walks, I had spotted an advertisement in the window of the newsagent, offering light secretarial work to a lady fluent in French, two afternoons a week, or more. It had been typed out on a blue-lined index card. Someone had stuck a paper flag in the bottom right corner, a French flag, next to the telephone number, baiting the card to attract the Francophones left in the rock pools of South Kensington by the receding tide of the war.

It was the tricolour that had caught my eye. It made the card look like the advertisements people displayed on noticeboards in Alexandrian consulates and hospitals, hoping for news of family and friends. Now, when Albie mentioned work, I remembered the advertisement. Chiswick 9940 – I was not aware that I had memorised the number until I dialled it.

'My father is Russian,' a male voice explained, diffident, perhaps distinguished too, 'and *secretarial work* is not quite right. An occasional letter, maybe. Tidying the family archives, such as they are. A bit of reading. The sound of French. Company.

'We visit him often,' he continued, 'almost daily. But Father is bored. He was once a great walker; he now trips and falls so often. He used to read; now he complains that no light is bright enough. Company, yes, mainly company.'

The man gave his business address for the interview. It was less awkward that way, he explained, less disturbing for his father, in case I did not accept the job.

'I am sure it will be a formality, Mrs Whitelaw.' He sounded apologetic that he had to make me travel all the way to Chiswick. Apparently, I was the first – the only – person to respond. The temperature had been hovering around zero for weeks; a bad time to advertise anything, he added. He emitted a strangled little laugh. *Ha ha*: it did not sound so much like laughter as like someone reading the two short words from an unrehearsed script. I warmed to his shyness, his lack of self-confidence.

Fahrenheit, I thought when I put the receiver down. In Celsius, zero would be progress.

The following day I found myself in a vast office on the first floor of a Georgian terrace with bricks the colour of congealed blood and rows of black-framed windows reflecting the snow. The street sloped towards the Thames like a slide. There were the beginnings of an island at the bottom – an eyot, Albie later explained. Black stumps of reeds pierced layers of snow on its crest, and ducks paddled across patches of ice on the river's edge. The air was full of yeast, malt and smoke; the warm, pleasant smell of a medieval kitchen, as unexpected after a short ride from Earl's Court as the horse-drawn carts loaded with casks which emerged from a warehouse alongside the office and clattered away on icy cobbles, on a twin-track path cut through the snow. I had taken the Underground train, and – after half a dozen stops – emerged into a world teetering on the brink of the Industrial Revolution.

'Albertine Whitelaw,' I introduced myself as the secretary shut the double door behind me. 'How do you do?'

'Alexei Carr. I prefer to be called Alex.'

The man stood up from his desk and stepped forward to shake my hand. He was one of the directors of the brewery, he said. One of the oldest family-run breweries in London, he explained, gesturing at more buildings invisible behind the walls. I had glimpsed them as I approached the three-storey terrace that housed his office, a jumble of pitched roofs, clapboard towers and tall chimney stacks, like a walled city half-hidden from view.

'We brew the best beer in England,' he said.

'I will have to take your word for it,' I answered. 'I am not very fond of beer.'

He was considerably taller than me, and beanpole thin in his chalk-stripe suit. The coat looked double-breasted not by original design, but as though it had had to be taken in, as though it had originally belonged to someone much more solid. Behind the wire spectacles, his eyes were almond-shaped and slanted, a startling pairing with their clear Nordic blueness. I wondered if this was a Russian trait.

It was an odd job interview, as perfunctory as such a conversation could be. He seemed to wish no more than to set eyes on me. I tried to make sense of my chequered job history and the decade of dislocations that had followed my *agrégation*. I was the first in my family to go to university. I read English and French. Before the war broke out, I had intended to be a secondary-school teacher.

While Alex Carr stared at me, barely listening, I explained how I had left Paris in 1937 to teach French in a Bucharest lycée, on a whim; how this might well have saved my life although it had originally looked like a bad move; how I was evacuated to Greece, then to Egypt soon afterwards. I spent the war working at the British General Hospital in Alexandria and lodging with a Sephardic family, while losing touch with what passed for my own.

In Paris, I had lived with an aunt and her family for four years, I explained. Tante Julie, my mother's sister, ran a tailoring business with her husband, as my mother and father had done. We were tailors and dressmakers, as far back as memory stretches. My parents and my sister had died in a train crash outside Paris in 1933; a blessed year to die, it turns out, if you were Jewish. I was twenty – too old to be a proper orphan, too young not to feel like one. At least my mother had a sister, I said, someone to go to. For a long time, and until well after I had settled in London with my British husband, I was convinced that my aunt and uncle had made it to Montreal. That had been the plan, sketched on the last postcard I had received from them, just before I left Romania. Instead ...

Alex Carr's face remained expressionless throughout. He now raised his hand, as if to say *that will do*. There was no need to explain what happened *instead*. There were too many stories like mine to need telling again.

'Your husband?' he asked.

'We met in 1943.' I named Albie's regiment.

'I was in Palestine, around the corner,' he offered, although I had not asked.

'My father is Russian, I think I mentioned on the telephone,' he added. 'My mother was French, but not from France. One of St Petersburg's French. Father decided, when he was nine or ten, that he would never marry a Russian woman, although he is as Russian as they come. So was Mother, in a way. You will find him interesting.'

Carr did not sound Russian, but that was not surprising. Many people changed their names, to hide or to fit in. My own family had done the same, three times in the past hundred and fifty years. It did not help. We were not good at passing ourselves off, pretending to be what we were not. I recognised the deficiency in myself, the absence of will.

'Father suffered a stroke last year,' Alex Carr went on. 'He's recovering, but he can't do much and his days tend to get very long. That is why I thought of hiring someone to visit, to distract him. There is a housekeeper already, Mrs Jenkins. She is devoted, but not a companion, she can't be. Father speaks English to her, and he speaks Russian to me. He always spoke French to my mother. He still does sometimes ... although she is no longer around to hear.'

He took his spectacles off and proceeded to wipe them with a paisley handkerchief he pulled out of his pocket, while continuing to look at me. Without the glass barrier, his eyes seemed larger and younger.

A copy of a magazine was open at an article about the actress Vivien Leigh. It was illustrated with a photograph, the film star in a dark Victorian dress with a lace collar. Alex Carr followed the direction of my gaze, took a large brown envelope and covered the magazine with it. The awkwardness in his manner persisted. He was happier with long silences than me; happier than most people. There were papers on his desk, account books, invoices, pages covered with columns of numbers speaking of responsibility and tedium.

'Perhaps, if you are still keen, you could start with a visit to my father tomorrow, Mrs Whitelaw.'

He was implicitly declaring our conversation over, offering me the job.

'See how you get on. If you are free, that is.'

He dictated an address in Bedford Park.

An ice storm passed through the city overnight. The following afternoon, the streets looked shiny, as though everything on them had been sheathed in glass. Branches glistened darkly, clinking as they swayed. The tips of my fingers, my ear lobes and the flares of my nostrils tingled. The chill stung every inch of exposed skin the moment I stepped off the train. By the time I had left the station and crossed the road, my hands felt as dead as the branches.

I had memorised the route before I set off. I knew it would be too cold to pause to inspect a map, or to be certain that I would meet anyone en route to ask for directions. I passed a brick church half-buried amid the snowdrifts, then walked down a street lined with bare chestnut trees. If you ignored the temperature – if that were possible even for a moment – the scene could be idyllic. The gables and balustrades with their snow trimmings made the houses look like ornate dwellings in an ancient painting.

A garden suburb, Albie had said when I told him where I was going to spend my afternoon. I was building my English vocabulary with him like that, pausing when I did not recognise a term, asking him to explain concepts that were new to me. I was already used to the idea that suburbs meant something different in England, not dwellings for the poor, but pretty and quiet places away from the smog. *Rus in urbe*, Albie had said.

He was delighted at my news, helpful, almost irritatingly supportive. I was, at long last, following his advice. I was *pulling my socks up*. White Russians, he surmised when I repeated the scant details supplied by Alex Carr. Britain was frequently the last stage of a long journey. They had fled Russia after 1917, but they often arrived here after escaping Berlin, Paris or Prague, as recently as during the past decade, now doubly exiled and doubly impoverished. There were many in West London.

I had encountered these White Russians in Paris. There, too, they lived in the west of the city, while my people – the Ashkenazim – had settled in the east. The Russians came to my father to have their clothes repaired or relined. Between the layers of old fabric he sometimes found gold coins stitched into secret pockets, and once, behind a balding fur collar, wedged as interlining between whalebone stiffeners, a document containing the title deeds to twelve hundred *desyatinas* of Siberian land.

Father knew something of their world through stories brought over to France from godforsaken small towns in Poland where my ancestors had lived before they started escaping westwards. They had been powerful once, these members of the Russian gentry. Father pitied them and indulged them with old-fashioned deference, refusing large tips they could ill afford. I used to believe there was poetry in poverty and exile. I know better now.

It was strange to think of this employment by one of these White Russians as my first English job. They could not have done too badly in the end, I thought, escaping Russia for this quiet suburb. It was just past four, yet the lights were already on in many of the houses. Stained glass threw pastel illuminations onto the snow-covered gardens outside. I heard dogs barking as I went by, saw curtains twitching.

Mr Carr senior's house was no different from others on a street which curved in its attempt to emulate a village lane. Sticks poked out of the snow along the path to the front door, the stems of rose bushes pruned back for the winter. Gnarled branches of a dormant wisteria trailed above the porch. A woman opened the door, then left me for what seemed like hours in the hall, next to a coat stand decorated with beaten copper plates, reliefs showing plump pomegranates. Two coats hung on it: one male and exotic with grey astrakhan cuffs; another female, mossy in both colour and texture, with a rust-coloured woollen scarf falling out of its sleeve. Shoes and galoshes were arranged in a neat row underneath. From further inside came the smell of old books and furniture polish. Finally, there was a shuffle of slippers and an old man opened the inner door to beckon me further into the house. He had the same slanted blue eyes as his son.

'Madame Vitélo. It must be you. Sergei Carr. I am delighted.' He addressed me in French, and kissed my still-mittened hand. 'Please come in. Do let me take your coat.'

It took me a while to realise that he had uttered a version of Whitelaw, pronounced with playful French distortion. There is no sound more alien to French than that W with which my married name began and ended. I thought at first that he was hurrying me in.

'*Enchantée*, Monsieur Carr,' I responded, taking my coat off and stuffing my gloves into the pockets. I had been reading and translating, but I hadn't spoken French in months. It sounded strange on my lips, a secret code retrieved.

'Monsieur Ka,' he echoed aloud, as if amused by my accent. 'These English names of ours, Madame Whitelaw, they are not very pleasing to the Gallic ear, are they?'

He must have been in his early eighties and he was as tall and as slim as his son. High cheekbones and a leonine head of wavy white hair lent him an illustrious air. He could have been the conductor of an orchestra. He was dressed and combed with careful deliberation, yet signs of a loss of control were everywhere if you examined closely: a patch of beard missed in shaving, a fleck on the lapel of his tweed jacket, a cufflink holding only the insides of his double cuffs. The left side of his face sagged. It made him look as though he was on the verge of tears even when he smiled. His walking stick dragged along the tiles, the rubber tip leaving faint black trails as he moved ahead of me and into the library.

The interior – comfortable but far from lavish – was dotted with Russian objects: icons, a samovar on a side table, a few porcelain figurines of ice skaters and ballet dancers on the shelves. This, in a way, was what I expected. I did not expect to see watercolours, dozens and dozens of them, covering every available surface. One or two depicted the interiors we were passing through, creating the optical effect of infinite regression, a *mise en abyme*. For the most part they were images of flowers, individual blooms and countless bouquets in a variety of vases – lilacs and lilies, roses at different stages of their life cycle, chrysanthemums exploding like fireworks, fat bundles of hyacinths and narcissi, posies of sweet peas, violets and daisies – entire walls covered with fading flowers in near-identical thin frames. Some were verging on abstraction, consisting of two or three simple and elegant lines, others possessed an almost furious verisimilitude, parading the hours and hours of labour that had gone into them. Each picture, individually, might have been beautiful, but there was something overwhelming, depressing almost, about their cumulative effect.

'My wife,' said Monsieur Carr, lifting a shaky hand with its walking stick towards a picture of a bunch of anemones in a jam jar propped on the mantelpiece we were passing at that moment. He rolled his eyes in mock exasperation, as though his wife was in the room with us and she was able to register his displeasure with the clutter, but he said no more about the paintings. His voice echoed with a loneliness caused by something beyond physical absence, equalled by the loneliness emanating from the images on the walls.

There were no flowers in the library. Instead, in the gaps between the shelves loaded with hundreds of books hung a couple of framed documents in what I took to be Russian Cyrillic, and, above the fireplace, an unframed oil portrait of a couple. With its uneven edges and deep vertical furrow across the middle, the canvas appeared to have been hastily cut out of its original frame, folded flat for a long while, then stretched again over a new set of wooden bars. It depicted a severe, bald-headed man with strangely shaped ears. His raised eyebrows made him look as though he was about to ask the viewer a question. Next to him, by his side but not touching him – the distance emphasised by the awkward fold – was a younger woman whose shiny curls bled into a backdrop darkened with age. Her smile was directed sideways, at something or someone beyond the canvas. An elegant pale hand with several rings on the third finger was raised slightly away from her body, and away from the man, as if she was mid-gesture, reaching out for something. As a device to show off the painter's skill her pose could not be faulted, but it exposed something pent-up in her nature. In the entire household – or at least in those parts of it I had passed through – that woman alone seemed to exude a still unsubdued energy, an *élan vital*.

'My mother and father,' said Monsieur Carr, 'in St Petersburg, a month or two before I was born.'

Only when he said that did I notice the hint of a swollen belly under her severe black dress. Her modest décolletage seemed almost shocking: a milky throat amid so much darkness.

'The painter has caught my father's likeness, but *Maman*, I am not so sure,' continued Monsieur Carr. 'She died so young. I won't ask if you have ever visited St Petersburg. It's too late now anyway, has been too late for thirty years. The city exists no more.'

I shook my head. I knew so little of Russia. I could not imagine wanting to go to Leningrad, whatever now remained of it. Albie spoke of its siege as the worst episode of the war. Much worse than Dachau, he would say, much worse than Belsen. I refused the possibility of comparison, one infinity of suffering next to another.

'Poor city,' I said to Monsieur Carr. 'Things will get better soon, I hope.'

Platitudes, I know; it is one way to preserve sanity.

'No, not in my lifetime. Nor, dare I say, in yours,' Monsieur Carr responded.

His French was perfect.

The housekeeper brought in a vast silver tray: a teapot and two cups, a small jug of milk, a couple of plates with a single biscuit on each, a pair of folded linen napkins.

'Thank you, Mrs Jenkins. Please, feel free to take a break. We will have finished by six,' Monsieur Carr said as he dismissed her. His English was as good as his French; the English – almost – of a native speaker.

'And now, I am just going to close my eyes,' he said, switching back to French. 'It would be lovely to hear you read: from the start, why not?'

He took a copy of a book from the shelves, seemingly at random, and handed it to me having opened it at the first page, then sat in an armchair by the fireplace. His walking stick slid onto the carpet. He reached for the teacup and closed his eyes. I cleared my throat to the sound of clinking china.

'*Nous étions à l'Étude, quand le Proviseur entra, suivi d'un nouveau habillé en bourgeois et d'un garçon de classe qui portait un grand pupitre. Ceux qui dormaient se réveillèrent, et chacun se leva, comme surpris dans son travail ...*'

I paused to glance at the old man. He had placed his cup on the side table. His eyes were closed and his cheek was pressed against the wing of the armchair, pushing his lips further down into the lopsided smile. I had not bothered to check the title of the book before I started, but I no longer needed to.

I was fifteen when I first read *Madame Bovary*. All those stories of Cole Porter, Josephine Baker, Magritte, Dalí and Buñuel now make you think that Paris in 1928 was the centre of the world, but to me the 3rd arrondissement seemed much duller than nineteenth-century Rouen. I could almost re-enter my teenage body, sprawled on the bed with the book propped open against the pillow, the beams criss-crossing the eaves above me, the grey clouds sailing past the attic window of the equally grey city, while eight flights down my father and mother laboured in their clothing workshop and – on a floor halfway between us – Arlette, my younger sister, endlessly practised on her piano, trying to memorise her scores.

How could all that music vanish? Like Monsieur Carr speaking to his dead wife, I even now continued to compose letters to Arlette, explaining about Albie, making Earl's Court sound better than it was.

Whenever I paused, Monsieur Carr opened his right eye and waited for me to continue, closing it as soon as the flow resumed. And so I went on, in turn attentive to the words I read, then allowing my thoughts to wander away from the text, until I noticed Alex Carr, standing in the doorway, in his overcoat, listening. Outside, it was pitch-black.

The Underground station was empty when Alex Carr accompanied me to my train. I had tried to refuse his offer. It seemed no longer necessary, even a bit ridiculous in our new world, this old-fashioned courtesy, seeing a woman off safely to the station. He turned to me a couple of times to say something, but changed his mind. We stood for a long time by the small stove in an empty waiting room, looking down the platforms and along the tracks that stretched west, deeper into London's suburbs. The amber lights, like cats' eyes, were visible for the best part of a mile as the train approached through the falling snow.

'That was so kind of you, Mrs Whitelaw,' he said when the train came to a halt with a low whine of metal on metal. 'I could see how enormously my father enjoyed your reading. I hope you did too. I hope you will continue. A couple of times a week, more often if you wish, and please choose the days. It doesn't have to be reading. Anything you like. All sorts of joint projects you can think of.'

He made it sound as though his old man and I might be starting a business together.

'It would do him a world of good, take him out of himself,' he added.

'Me too . . .' I admitted. Without quite realising that I would do it until it happened, I raised myself on my toes and kissed his frozen cheek. In Paris, it would have been an unremarkable gesture. In Alexandria, an invitation. I still had no idea about London. I looked out of the window as my train pulled out of the station. He stood there, while snow accumulated on the rim of his hat.

At home, Albie had already laid the table for dinner. In the fireplace the gas fire had been lit; bluish flames licked fake coals behind the gothic tracery doors. The room was almost warm. Albie was beamingly expectant.

'Darling Ber,' he said as he ladled out the soup and lowered the bowl in front of me, smiling tentatively, proud of his cooking skills, clearly expecting a detailed report of my activities. 'I hope you have had a good day.'

The liquid was so startling in its vivid greenness that I burst into laughter and, almost immediately, into tears. I did not know how to respond to his efforts. There was a bunch of white flowers in a vase at the centre of the table, a yellow block of butter under a glass dome, a golden loaf of bread on the board. Its shape was even more startling than the colour of the soup: two balls of dough baked on top of each other, like a beheaded snowman.

'A cottage loaf, we call this,' Albie explained, pausing with the bread knife just above it. 'White. Still illegal, strictly speaking. For you, Ber.'

It was on sale only in Soho and Fitzrovia, he added, an Italian take on a traditional British recipe. He must have gone into the West End specially to buy it. He knew that I would recognise the gesture as a gift. Soft, like your *challah*, like your *brioche*, he said. The yeasty crown seemed to promise a new world in which food would again be fresh and abundant.

*

'You look happier today, Madame Vitélo,' Monsieur Carr said when I re-entered the library two days later, his face coloured by the reflection of the sun through the stained glass and divided into halves. The left was green and frozen in its image of sadness, the right rosy and smiling.

The side table was laid for tea. Instead of biscuits there were two slices of caraway cake. I picked up *Madame Bovary*, with its bookmark where I had left it last time, and prepared to read. Monsieur Carr's lopsided lips spread rightwards into a wide smile. He raised his hand to ask me to wait.

'I enjoyed your reading very much last time. I do hope you will continue to visit me. My son could not have given me a better present than your company. And I wonder if you would like to join me on an excursion soon. To Shepperton. It's just over an hour's drive from here. The film studios. I have had an invitation. They will be making a very special film this spring, and my grandson Gigi will be playing a unique part in it: me. Alexei will lend us a car and a driver.'

The reference to the grandson took me by surprise. I am not sure why. Alex Carr was in his forties; it was logical that he should be married, that he should have a child. Children, even. Several children. And that there should be a mother for those children. I had little time to wonder why anyone would want to make a film about Monsieur Carr. Our lives were strange, particularly at that time when London was so unsettled by the aftermath of war and turbulence on the Continent. The unusual life would be one without a drama, an uneventful life.

'Mrs Jenkins,' called Monsieur Carr, 'would you, please, bring that invitation from the dining table? I'd like to show Mrs Whitelaw what we have in mind for our outing.'

The housekeeper walked in holding the envelope, as though she had been waiting behind the door all that time. I stared at the address.

Prince Sergei Alexeievich Karenin,
20 Queen Anne's Grove,
Bedford Park,
London W4

'Open it, please, Mrs Whitelaw,' said Monsieur Carr. 'Do read the invitation. You will like this excursion. They are making a film about my mother.'

2

Air Street

The evening was an anniversary of sorts. Albie and I had been married for a year and a half. When a marriage is in its infancy we mark the small birthdays because the big ones seem impossibly far apart.

We dressed up for the occasion. Albie's new dinner jacket came from some allowance that had nothing to do with ration books and everything to do with the kind of international event he was now expected to attend from time to time. He was moving up in the world, representing Britain. I wore my best – my only – cocktail gown. Made by Tante Julie as a parting gift on the eve of my departure for Bucharest, it was a replica of a Schiaparelli frock, light enough to survive the dislocations that gave it a new audience for each infrequent outing. The Mediterranean sun could compete with it, subdue it even. In London, it glowed like a thousand-watt light bulb, shockingly pink against austerity tweed. Then there was the magic locked in a dozen precise cuts. My aunt was a mistress of her trade. She knew how to tame the silk, to make it flow and follow the skin without ever sticking to it. I couldn't wear the dress without thinking of my family, yet I had to stop thinking of them in order to do anything at all.

Albie caressed his moustache in a futile attempt to mask an expression of pleasure.

'Scarlett, my dear,' he said, mocking the accent of the Confederacy and pretending that he had never seen me in the dress before, although I had worn it on practically every occasion that deserved the name, including our one-night honeymoon at the Cecil in Alexandria.

'That – what do you call it? – is simply spectacular. You are on fire.'

Given the temperature inside the house, a reference to *Gaslight*, or some similar bleak and accented drama, would have been more appropriate than *Gone with the Wind*. Yet Albie's delight in my un-English looks was genuine. He relished hearing people talk about his 'European wife', as though our marriage represented a token of his goodwill towards the new, post-war world, a pledge to the work of its creation. In practice, he was much more European than me. Even the word – Europe – felt tainted to me. I would have preferred a new world altogether, where he and I looked alike, indistinguishable.

The taxi ride to St James's took longer than it would have taken us to walk there, but the weather was a good excuse for extravagance. The snow rasped underfoot. The silk hem of my dress felt stiff, like tent canvas. When we reached Piccadilly, I wound the car window down by a fraction and the smell of coal fires and rubble rushed in on the tip of an icy blade of air. Twenty-one months had gone since the Germans' unconditional surrender, yet warning signs and padlocks continued to guard the ruins, even in the heart of the city. St James's church was a roofless shell. The walls of the bank next to it had been lacerated by shrapnel. A hundred yards further on the left there had once stood a tearoom, the glass dome shattered by a bomb and now open to the elements.

'Forty-two people died here,' Albie said. 'I was in a bar on Air Street. I was killing time in London when I should've been killing the Eyeties in North Africa. I kept pestering my superiors, pleading to be sent to Alexandria.'

'You could so easily have died here,' I said, spying behind wooden hoardings a shard that projected upwards, propped up by a charred stump of a palm tree like the wing of a grand piano. 'You must have been less than a hundred yards away.'

'A hundred yards felt far enough. I ran to help with the rescue,' Albie said. 'There was an odd smell of burning sugar when the bombs hit Piccadilly that night. In the silence which descended after the masonry fell and the screams died out, I heard a sound, like an enormous sail flapping somewhere above. *The Angel of Mons*, said an old man while we were pulling a woman's body from under the rubble. I did not know if he meant the body or that sound above us.'

'Yet the ruins look so old now, under the snow,' I said. 'As though they have always been here. Like those ancient cities.'

'Not to me,' Albie said. 'I still feel that young woman's hair clinging to my coat and snagging on my buttons. A black line on the back of her calf was smeared at the ankle, where the man had lifted her. The line had been drawn carefully to emulate a seam on a stocking. It may have been done by a friend before they went out. But now the leg was twisted so strangely that you thought the girl could, almost, have drawn it herself.'

I had followed the progress of the Blitz from the other end of Europe, feeling, strangely, less and less afraid as Hitler's armies advanced. At the beginning of 1940 it was already becoming difficult to keep a teaching post in Bucharest. By late September, it was impossible to remain there, although the Germans were still a couple of countries away. I was evacuated to Salonika with a group of teachers from the Alliance Française, and I left them behind in Macedonia. They were trying to get back to France. I knew that France, for me, had become a bad idea. It had long fallen, and between Paris and Bucharest there was just deepening darkness. The news from Romania seemed monstrous and baffling. They were killing not just the Jews but their own, their greatest. I kept moving on, on ever smaller boats to ever smaller islands, further and further south and east, one less piece of luggage each time, until I was completely on my own and everything I owned fitted into a small rucksack.

In tavernas by the Aegean people spoke about *Tsortsil* as though he was some mythical creature, Menelaus or Agamemnon. In Crete, I remember, an old man pushed at a row of dominoes with an arthritic finger. When the last domino collapsed, he said: 'Romania, yes. Vulgaria, yes. Hellas, no. Anglia, never.' I nodded in agreement but I did not believe it.

'I was certain that London, too, would fall,' I said to Albie.

I caught the driver's glance in the rear-view mirror. He was dark and moustachioed, a fellow foreigner. London was full of people like us; many more people like us, it often seemed, than people like my husband.

'"Stop thinking about shrinking",' Albie read from an advertisement for Emu wool which took up the length of the bus creeping alongside us, as if to give me a sign that serious conversation was over for the evening. Above the cartoon of a jolly bird, we saw a man staring out of the bus window, visibly exhausted. His forehead was pressed flat against the glass, and his jet-black beard and strange hat made him look like an extra from an operetta, an officer of some vanquished East European army, a displaced person stuck in a miserable job somewhere in the West End, taking the bus home because it was cheaper than the Underground, because he was in no hurry to get back, because no one was waiting for him.

Albie raised my hand and kissed the triangle of skin exposed by the flared cuff of the glove. His moustache felt soft, like the touch of a baby seal. His eyes shone in the semi-darkness, the pupils so wide that they covered the rings of his irises; that blue-grey of the North Sea, the German Ocean. In his very English way, Albie seemed unaware of his own beauty, treating it as a fact of nature, like falling snow or clear skies.

He seemed distant, more unreal to me in London than he had been in Egypt, as though, at some unnoticed moment, an understudy had stepped in to take over his role, someone who had mastered all the lines to perfection but with whom I was no longer properly in touch. We talked a bit, we laughed, we made love, but I tended to inhabit a place several steps outside the body which inter-acted with his. The Alexandrian Albie would have noticed my distance and demanded that I account for it. The London Albie soldiered on regardless. I shared the pretence. I acted as though I still knew him.

The restaurant was hidden in the heart of St James's, in one of those narrow passages which seem forever enveloped in a film-maker's version of a London fog. An inconspicuous entrance opened up into a small reception area and a vestibule choked with coats, and then surprised you with one of the grandest flights of steps in London, a marble staircase that seemed better suited to a belle époque opera house than to a basement below Piccadilly. I noticed faces turning towards us as we entered, discreet nods of recognition for Albie, eyes briefly resting on me.

'You see, dearest, restaurants do keep their best tables for their most attractive customers,' Albie said as we followed the maître d'hôtel towards a central platform with the best view in the house. 'I never worry about having to sit next to the kitchen when I am with you.'

After the first sip of champagne, he produced a velvet box from his coat pocket. A wedding ring, I guessed, a replacement for the copper band around my ring finger which had served its purpose in Alexandria, as modest as the ceremony itself. There had been an unspoken expectation that it would be replaced at some point, when *things are back to normal*, whatever normal meant. I had chosen the ring in the bazaar and haggled over its pitiful price because the seller had expected us to, for good luck. It had since left a black imprint that no amount of soaking and scrubbing could erase. Old couples' fingers thicken around their wedding rings the way branches of wisteria grow around the metal that fastens them to the wall. My wedding ring left a tattoo.

Albie had noticed the black line while I was washing up. He had lifted the ring from the side of the sink, looked through it as though he was having trouble identifying the object, and promised – although it did not matter – that he would get a replacement. White gold, he suggested; much less flashy. In Egypt, we had grown weary of the dazzle.

'I hope you will like this, Ber.' He unhooked a fine latch and lifted the lid.

My guess had been wrong. Inside the box was a chain bracelet made of fine, interlocking gold links. Resting on a dark velvet cushion, it looked like a necklace for a baby or a doll.

'A Prince of Wales chain,' Albie explained. 'I bought it at an auction in Berlin.'

I tried not to think of the previous owner. I had never been to Germany. In my teenage years, I dreamed of summers in Spain or Italy, but rarely thought of Germany. All too soon, it would become impossible not to think of it.

'Now the Germans must suffer; it's their turn,' Albie sometimes said when the war was over, as though German suffering could comfort me, as though getting even had a bearing on anything. At such moments I glimpsed the advantages of his English birth. Not the silver spoon, anyone can have that, anywhere, but that particular sense of fair play, the staunch belief that life would deliver justice in the end.

'Berlin, darling, yes,' Albie said and raised his glass. 'I'll take you there soon, I promise.'

He seemed unable to grasp that I did not want to travel anywhere again. Least of all to Berlin. He hooked the chain around my wrist.

'It is beautiful, Albert. Thank you.' The bracelet felt too fragile to wear but it was strikingly elegant. He had an eye.

'I knew you'd love it.' He responded in an exaggerated Yankee accent. 'The moment I set eyes on it, baby, I saw it on your wrist.'

All the baby talk, yet we no longer mentioned actual babies. There was another box, not unlike a jewel case, in a drawer by my bedside, and in it a rubber dome, made in the USA, a circular spring tensing at night with unuttered questions.

'A child – having one, I mean – would be a point of no return,' Albie had said soon after we first made love. I agreed, all too readily, and never asked again. I knew that he spoke not of his commitment to us, which seemed unshakeable, but to life itself. I believed in fate, Albie believed in planning, but neither of us felt ready to become a parent. To hand it on, you had to be convinced that life was worth living. And that was tricky for both of us, for our different reasons, even when the world around was practically shouting yes to life. The papers were full of astonishing statistics, speaking of a humanity dedicated to the business of procreation with the same ardour with which it had devoted itself to destruction only a matter of months earlier.

After our glass of champagne Albie reverted to beer and what he described as his simple British tastes, although it was he who had chosen a restaurant full of crystal and red plush, so French and so old-fashioned that you could be forgiven for expecting Escoffier to walk out of the kitchens and greet his guests. The waiters busied themselves with silver cloches and pushed trolleys with paraffin lights and decanters of liqueur, ready to flambé the crêpes Suzette and the cherries jubilee the moment you asked. Albie was sipping his beer and talking about hop picking in Kent, or so I think, though I could not imagine why. The simplest monosyllables still defeated me on occasion. There were so many that the melody of language drowned in them, sounding instead like the noise of popping corn. Who could tell all those ales, porters and lagers apart? English had too many words for the drink that went best with fried potatoes and tasted of regret.

A group of ruddy-faced men recognised Albie and stood up from their tables to salute him. He raised his huge tumbler in response. The label on the bottle bore a picture of the familiar brewery by the river.

'I know this place,' I said, putting my finger on the image of that imposing Georgian terrace where I had first met Alex Carr. 'The best beer in England.'

'Lucky it's bitter,' Albie whispered, turning to me, and, with a nod of his head, he encouraged me to raise my glass to his acquaintances. London was full of young officers like him, demob-happy, appearing to believe that another victory party was about to begin. 'I'd look like a complete pansy if I still had that coupe of fizz in front of me,' he said.

'It would not do, would it?' I said and raised my glass.

It was I who decided that we must walk home. I felt giddy and bubble-headed.

'What is three miles between friends?' Albie said. 'I'll carry you all the way home, Ber, if need be.'

The moon hung full and low above us as we crossed the south side of Hyde Park. The snow crunched under our feet. My stockings emitted a dry, frozen rustle, and my ear lobes and my nostrils felt as thin as tissue paper. I had never felt so cold, yet I was too tipsy to care. Albie stopped and turned to face me in the shadow of his namesake's memorial. His hand found an opening between my coat buttons, sneaked under the edge of the thick woollen scarf and further in through the layers, past the silk dress and the frozen wires of my brassiere.

'*Soutien-gorge*' – he named the undergarment in French. His impossibly English accent made it sound as though we were staging a late-night language lesson for the blind. I pushed him away and he fell with slow deliberation, taking me with him onto a mound of virgin snow. The dark figure soared in the moonlight above us with the unrestrained joy of someone recently released from hiding; a German prince, protected by the British, even in the middle of the Blitz.

'It is outrageous, this monument,' Albie said, looking up. 'And I've never thought of that before. The sheer lunatic size of it. How could a woman build this for any one man? Would you, Ber? Would you erect something on this scale for your husband, when he is dead?'

'I would,' I said. 'And I would gild it, if I had the money.'

He kissed me. His lips tasted autumnal even amid so much snow; of tobacco and bitter. Albert of Saxe-Coburg and Gotha watched over us, his wide face that of a country groom.

Back home we fell into a late, deep sleep so that the alarm, when it woke us, felt as though it was only minutes later. I waited for Albie to turn it off, then stretched my arm towards the left side of the bed to find him no longer there. The bedding smelled of our lovemaking and his pillow was still warm, but he was already up, clean-shaven and ready to go, standing in the kitchen in his overcoat, a Gladstone bag waiting at his heel like a bulldog. He was taking the last sips from his teacup. Outside, the sky was as brightly starlit as when we came in.

'Go back to sleep, darling,' he said, kissing my parting on his way out. 'There's no reason to be up so early.'

I hugged him goodbye, gulped the remainder of his toast, washed the dishes and swept the kitchen floor, then went back to bed. It was going to snow later, as it had snowed most mornings since the beginning of the year. There was nothing else to do but sleep until late afternoon, until my appointment with Monsieur Carr.

I found the copy of *Madame Bovary* on the same footstool where I had left it, and proceeded to read aloud for some forty minutes, waiting for Monsieur Carr to interrupt me. Flaubert suddenly seemed too much, over the top, the prose almost delirious in its lack of restraint. Or was I, without even sensing it, becoming English?

Emma was attending a performance of *Lucia di Lammermoor*.

'She permitted herself to be lulled by the melodies and felt her entire being stirred as if the bows of violins were passing over her nerve-ends ...'

Entire being: what did that mean? It felt indecent, vaguely voyeuristic, reading about something so physical to an old man. His eyes were closed, and his lips moved in a soundless echo of the words. I kept my voice as inexpressive as possible. We would have been better off with Daudet, I thought.

'Please, Madame Whitelaw, I hope you don't mind, but I can't hear another word of *Madame Bovary* today,' said Monsieur Carr abruptly, as though he had guessed my thoughts. His fingers toyed with the fringe of the checked blanket covering his knees. He dragged one of his fallen slippers closer to the chair with the tip of his right foot, a thick maroon sock with a careful darn on the big toe, like a miniature spiderweb made of black wool.

'My little sister loved that book. She was an ugly little thing, Annie was, seven years younger than me. Strange, for both her parents were good-looking, as though nature had somehow wanted to revert to the mean when she was conceived. We had the same mother, but impossibly Annie resembled my own father more than I did. Yet she was charming, and no one would accuse him of charm. When she was little, she dreamed of becoming a ballerina. She remained in the old country after the Communists took over, I believe, and we had no idea of her whereabouts afterwards.'

'Since you mention your sister ... perhaps I may ask? That invitation, Monsieur Carr, I'd love to accompany you to the studios, but I don't understand … I know *Anna Karenina* – who doesn't? I love the novel, yet … I don't even know how to ask this. I thought … everyone does, of course … it is not history, not about real people … Are you really a prince? Are you really a Karenin?'

Our conversation had switched to English when he interrupted my reading. I always followed his lead.

'My dear girl, certainly not a prince – I am a count, a *Graf*, as we Russians would have it,' he said. 'The film people seem to think of all of us as princes. We changed the family name three times in the last hundred and fifty years, like our native city.'

'I am familiar with that,' I said. 'The need to change the name, I mean.'

'You think it important,' he continued. 'You think the name defines you, but then you find yourself re-imagined by Count Tolstoy. We were Russian and Orthodox, but the family was of German extraction. Hartung, we were called originally. An ugly German name few Russians could pronounce properly. The servants called us Kertung, Gartung, Karning. When the instalments of *Anna Karenina* started appearing, when it became clear that Tolstoy's story was about us, people began to call us Karenin behind our backs, to show that they knew, that the adulteress and her brood could never hide. I was a child still, and children were even less reticent about the link than adults. They called me little Karenin all the time. At first I answered to the name to spite my father. I liked Karenin better than Hartung anyway: it made me feel more Russian. Besides, Hartung was his name and I wanted nothing to do with him after she died.'

'After Anna died, you mean?' I asked.

'Anna, yes. That was my mother's real name. Father may not have been aware at first that people had made the connection. The gossipmongers had more pity for him than for her: they shielded him long after she was dead and buried. By the time we came to bury him, everyone in St Petersburg called me Karenin – the Karenin boy. The name was not inscribed on my father's tombstone, naturally, but it appeared in my Nansen passport, the document I travelled under after the Revolution, by what you could describe as a clerical mistake. I let it pass. The German original would have been an even greater liability by then. My father was dead, there was no need to worry about him.

'And so we reached Britain as Karenins, but we changed it again, soon afterwards, to Carr. I made that last one up – learning the lesson from your people – in order to become invisible among the English. I did not want to be a stranger in a strange land. You can hardly think of a less conspicuous name than Carr. I dropped the title too. The British don't care about our silly coronets any more than we care about theirs. Or than the Bolsheviks did. The film people love them, however. Many of them have purchased, or made up, titles and names considerably more fanciful than ours.'

'And how did they find you, Monsieur Carr?' I asked.

'Mr Kellner is to blame. Mr Korda, that is, or Mr Heart, if you will. Our dear Sir Alexander has even more avatars than I. His real name was Sándor – Hungarian for Alexander – Sándor Kellner – but that was not good enough. Kellner must have sounded too German, too prosaic in its meaning. He fashioned a new name for himself from *sursum corda*, he told me. *Lift up your hearts.* How much more odd than our name change is the case of a Jewish boy borrowing a name from the Holy Eucharist, yet you call Korda a real name? He changed the spelling to keep the initials,' Monsieur Carr said.

'A. K., like your mother, like the film he is producing,' I interrupted.

He paid no attention. 'Sir Alexander is to blame for our involvement. I was happy to end my days as a plain Mr Carr. He got to hear about us from an Englishwoman who had met Count Tolstoy back in Russia. Constance Garnett: "Garnet Stone", we used to call her. It was a childish pun, but it suited her. She was as hard as a stone. Churchill, of all people, recommended her as a consultant to Mr Kellner, to ensure the authenticity of the film. Authenticity, Mr Kellner, I remember asking when he approached me, what do we mean by authenticity here? How do you begin to know what authenticity stands for, dear Albertine, when you speak of *Anna Karenina*?'

'I sometimes feel that the life I lead is not real,' I said. 'That the real Albertine lives on somewhere else. The fictional lives we read about – your Anna, your Emma Bovary here – are so much more authentic than ours, and not just in the sense that they leave a deeper, more permanent mark on the world, while we, so-called real people, vanish without a trace. Is that it? Was that your question?'

'Perhaps,' he said. 'But the film people don't want to hear anything as knotty as that. They found their Russian prince. A scoop: that's what they would love me to become. I am more Karenin than anyone else, living or dead, and that's a fact, they say. No need to complicate matters.'

'And you do know more about Russia than your Garnet Stone,' I said.

'I would not be so sure, dear girl. The Englishwomen of her kind seem to know everything. But that is beside the point.

37

She could not take the consultancy, too far gone, practically blind, and a recluse,' he went on. 'She died last December, in fact, poor soul. I read her life story in the papers. I had no idea that she was part of an illustrious literary circle – an English *kruzhok*, a group of writers so famous that I had never heard of any of them.'

'Did you ever meet her?' I asked.

'She visited us once, Mrs Garnett, soon after we settled in London; as frail as you can imagine but full of the most unbelievable stories. Alexei can still imitate her Russian. It sounded so English, it took a while to realise she was even speaking it. And her yarns ... most of them sounded like pure fantasy. She had known Chiswick in the 1880s, she told us. Claimed she had learned her Russian from an anarchist assassin called Stepniak who lived around the corner here, on Woodstock Road. This Stepniak, Stone said, was run over by a train half a mile from where you and I are sitting now.

'You never knew what to believe. Not Mrs Garnett's fault, though, she told nothing but the truth, it turns out. This city is full of people with made-up names and made-up histories, and the real stories often sound the most fantastic. How the British can trust us at all, with so many tuppenny Munchausens going about, I am at a loss to make out. You know where you are with someone called Carr. I won't even ask you for your maiden name. Whitelaw seems real enough to me.'

'I was born a Singer,' I said. 'My family changed their name too ... three times. Kantor, originally, in Kraków. Singer in Strasbourg. We moved to Paris with it, when Alsace became French again. But my father thought that Cartier would be better for the clothes business, so we ended up as Cartier.'

'Carr and Cartier,' Monsieur Carr said. 'We are a fine pair, Madame Whitelaw.'

38

'There is nothing made-up about Whitelaw. There were Whitelaws in the North when the Normans came. My husband's people were never called anything other than Whitelaw. You know where you are with the Whitelaws too. Shrewdness enriches, says the family crest. English when sober, Scottish when drunk, my husband says.'

The memory of our drunken night made me blush.

'That sounds very Scottish to me,' the old man said, then, taking a vast white handkerchief from his pocket, wiped his eyes and his forehead and finally blew his nose, sonorously. His face was bright red too.

'Doesn't it, Mrs Jenkins?'

The housekeeper had just stepped in. The smell of food reaching the library was irresistible. Outside, the snow continued to fall.

'Would you join me for dinner, Mrs Whitelaw? I can only offer cabbage soup and pickled mushrooms, like a *muzhik*.'

We followed Mrs Jenkins into the dining room. The tureen on the table was hideously ornate. It was covered with poppies, roses, anemones and tulips. It had two large, yellow, leaf-shaped handles, like giant ears. A cherub sat on top of the lid in a matching yellow toga, holding a cornucopia from which bright fruits spilled into his lap. It wasn't hard to guess that this vernal riot had been chosen by the person who painted the watercolours hanging on the walls around us.

'My wife's possessions. Oh, dear,' said Monsieur Carr. 'She was not always like that. As a young woman she had subtle, impeccable taste. But something snapped after the Revolution. By the time we reached Chiswick, she had become a hoarder, a magpie, and, like a magpie, she went for bright, gaudy things. She had always been a quiet, with-drawn person, and she became practically mute towards the end. The less she said, the louder the objects with which she needed to surround herself.'

'But you kept it all,' I said.

'You would never believe, Mrs Whitelaw, how much I have always hated my wife's late taste in interior decoration, and how unable I was to remove a single thing after she died. Something similar happened to her taste in food. The older she got, the more elaborate it became, the sweeter her tooth. The millefeuilles, the croquants, the choux: I often asked if she was trying to kill me with them. Not that she deigned to respond. But I did stop eating French food when she died. English and Russian cooking are similar in many ways, medieval and honest – aren't they, Mrs Jenkins?'

'Of course, Mr Carr, how right you are,' said Mrs Jenkins as she ladled the soup without appearing to listen to his speech. She was wearing a pinafore whose flowery pattern was as riotous as that depicted on the dinner service, but its colourways were confined to a dozen shades of brown. Her food was relentlessly brown too. The soup and the mushrooms were coffee-coloured, and the bread as dark as the coal in the fireplace. The old man looked at me and nodded towards his plate with amused approval. He raised a thimbleful of vodka.

'For England, Mrs Whitelaw, for King George.' He downed the liquid in one gulp.

'The King-Emperor!' I said and took a tiny sip of mine. It tasted of cucumber and was as strong as absinthe.

I was wrong to be suspicious about the food. The cabbage was sweet and sour, and as delicious as anything I had ever tasted in England. The bread and the mushrooms were even better. I looked at Mrs Jenkins with astonishment and admiration. She noticed and straightened her pinafore.

'This is delicious. And I cannot imagine anything more Russian,' I said, trying to pay her a compliment.

'In spite of her highly misleading name, Mrs Jenkins is almost as Russian as I am,' Monsieur Carr intervened.

Her appearance suggested otherwise. Mrs Jenkins looked as English as it was possible to look, and I am saying that without prejudice. Englishwomen could be, and often were, impossibly beautiful. Some of the young secretaries from Albie's office who knocked on my door to deliver envelopes with translation work were stunning, their skin pale and glistening like porcelain. Although few would have described Mrs Jenkins as beautiful, she was unmistakably English, from the vast clump of hair on top of her head to the wide woollen slippers on her feet, so English that she merited an appellation d'origine. As if to confuse me further, she said something in Russian to Monsieur Carr and he nodded.

'The Countess, Mr Carr's mother, had a ward,' she said. 'A girl by the name of Hannah Wilson. She came to the Countess from the Vronsky household. The Countess took Hannah in, and looked after her whole family – Hannah's mother and brothers – when their father suffered from delirium tremens.

'My grandfather and Hannah Wilson's father worked in the Vronsky stables. Everyone knew these two men. They had brought the first Arabians from Aleppo to Russia. Count Vronsky loved his racehorses. He employed Englishmen to look after them, for no one knows more about the horses than the English. But Vronsky's Englishmen caused many problems too. They were fond of their drink, and in Russia they drank even more than they did at home.

'My family returned to Britain when I was a girl, after the Revolution, when the stables started disappearing. People were so hungry they used thoroughbreds for sausage meat. The

41

racehorses had all gone. The Wilsons were in London already, they helped us settle.'

'The Wilsons helped us as well,' said Monsieur Carr. 'They were the first to come back here; returned to England soon after my mother died. My father paid for their relocation. Handsomely, you could say, considering that they were Vronsky's staff. Who could have guessed when we fed the English that one day the English would feed us.'

'Oh no, Mr Carr, it was for such a short time. You mustn't mention it.' Mrs Jenkins collected the empty plates and disappeared into the kitchen. There was the sound of pots and pans moving and then a sweet smell of pancakes.

'After 1917, there was a small colony of British returnees from Russia in South-West London – language teachers, nannies and governesses, butlers, grooms, most of them, but merchants, bankers and industrialists too,' Monsieur Carr explained. 'One ran into familiar faces all the time. They, those St Petersburg English, did not always know what to say to you. Some crossed to the other side of the street to avoid having to talk.'

'And are you still in touch with the Wilsons?' I asked. 'Count Vronsky's groom and his people? His descendants, I mean.'

'But of course. We are related now. My son married Hannah Wilson's granddaughter,' said Monsieur Carr.

Mrs Jenkins returned to the dining room with a stack of pancakes on a green plate shaped like an enormous cabbage leaf.

'I suspect you know it, Madame Whitelaw, but it is Shrove Tuesday,' Monsieur Carr said. 'We must eat blinis now. Although the Lenten fast for us Orthodox is still some days ahead, and although I know that you are Jewish, Mrs Jenkins says we must eat blinis and honey and sweet cheese. She calls it Pancake Day.'

'Mardi Gras,' I said. I had forgotten. I did not think I could eat any more, but it seemed impossible to refuse.

'We will eat blinis on Forgiveness Sunday too, to see our Russian Clean Monday in,' Monsieur Carr said. 'Would you care to join us with your husband? I'd love to meet him. My son will be here, his family too. And you must meet Gigi, my grandson.'

'I would love to,' I said. 'I am not sure I believe in God, but I do believe in pancakes. Blinis, did you say?'

'You sound like a Bolshevik, Madame Whitelaw,' the old man said.

It was like a long forgotten childhood supper, this feast of pancakes and sweet cheese. It was hard to leave Monsieur Carr's house, to walk alone along the icy pavements. At the bottom of the street, on the green in front of the church, there was a queue of women and children wrapped tightly against the cold, waiting for water with huge canisters. In many places the pipes had been frozen for days. One saw such queues across London. A bobby hovered over them, like a benevolent bat in his dark cape. People shuffled from foot to foot to stave off the cold. The path before me was gritty and liquid. Someone had scattered a tray of hot ash onto a patch of ice. The smell of fried fish hit me in gusts. Only the rattle of a train on the embankment reminded that we were almost halfway through the twentieth century.

Back at Earl's Court, our house was as freezing as the streets outside. Albie's dinner jacket still hung on the back of the chair in the dining room, like a headless guest at the table, his black tie thrown over the right shoulder. I switched the wireless on and listened to the *Tuesday Serenade* in bed, a broadcast from the Wigmore Hall. The sound of the piano filled the room. The only other noise was the intermittent fall of footsteps in the street. The pianist was a woman of twenty-five, the announcer said, born and raised in Tel Aviv. She had studied at the Conservatoire in Paris before the war. She was sixteen when she graduated. During the war, she had performed to the British soldiers in Egypt and in Palestine. It could have been Arlette. For a moment, I imagined that it was. I saw my sister's hands and her profile above the keyboard.

'No Chopin,' Arlette would say when I begged her to play a nocturne or an étude for me. 'You can be such a sentimental fool, Albertine.' Yet when I was up in my room and she thought no one could hear her, she played Chopin all the time.

I knew the Wigmore Hall. Albert and I had been there once or twice, to listen to music on a Sunday morning. The painting in its cupola depicted the genius of harmony, a golden sphere which floated in the sky above, while human figures below extended their hands towards it through a tangle of thorns. The memory of those figures, forever thirsting, brought back the face of the man on the bus the night before, looking, with his black beard, like some sad, sad devil; the faces of waiters reflected in the silver cloches; Mrs Jenkins's face above the ochre shades of her pinafore; Monsieur Carr's face, redolent of a Byzantine saint even in its asymmetry; the face of Alex Carr under his snow-brimmed hat; then, finally, Albie's face, his hair oiled and carefully combed yet falling in strands above me; all of us striving for that golden sphere; Albie again on this same bed less than twenty-four hours ago, getting closer, moving away, falling towards me, moving away.

3

An Excursion to the Edge

I had never been outside London before, if you could call my trip to Shepperton with Monsieur Carr 'outside London', and if you did not count my not-so-grand entrance into the city in the summer of 1945. There had been no reason to leave the capital. I had not felt in the mood for pleasure trips, and Albie travelled all the time anyway.

Albie had a family: a childless older sister, married across the caste lines of the Raj to a tea planter, who wrote to him from Darjeeling; and parents in East Anglia who, after their wedding gift, had sent two tight-lipped little Christmas cards and who might easily have been living even further away than Darjeeling. They kept inventing reasons to postpone a meeting until I began to suspect that they might be hoping a divorce would render it redundant. Not that this troubled Albie. He had spent most of his childhood and youth away from his parents, at boarding school, then in the army. He protected himself by silence, and he probably assumed that he was protecting me too. Give them time to get used to the idea, he said. The British are spartan and this is the spartan way.

Nor did I long for the open country. I am an urban creature. London parks provided a more than ample supply of countryside. I remained sufficiently Parisian, even after a decade away, to prefer the rose garden in Regent's Park to the wild grasslands of Richmond, and I sometimes walked all the way from Earl's Court just to see the roses in bloom, to read their exotic names on black tags planted on stakes alongside the paths like little alien flowers. The streets of Paris, Bucharest and Alexandria were like sentences using the same grammar. They huddled inward against encroaching nature, whereas London opened up to it, allowed it to invade. London was a city created by people who didn't like cities, I had concluded, who in their hearts preferred villages but with the convenience of urban life. Albie agreed. He seemed puzzled one day when I said that I had spent my afternoon on a bench in the local park, reading. He asked where this park was.

'It's just a square, silly girl,' he said when I looked out of the window, towards Chelsea. A square. I couldn't see what the difference was. There were lawns in this square, benches and gravel paths under vast crowns of trees, nannies in beige uniforms pushing prams with huge, finely crafted wheels, office workers on the grass, taking their midday breaks, sandwiches wrapped in greaseproof paper in metal lunch boxes next to them, and young saleswomen, skirts pulled up high above the knee, sunning their legs in that eagerly joyful way only young Englishwomen do when the sun is out. How was the square not a park?

That was before this endless winter set in.

'We could be back in Russia,' Monsieur Carr said as our car headed westward, out of London. The world around us was still, wrapped in snowy silence. Snowdrifts were ten feet high in places, milky and yellow at the peaks where the sun touched them, bluish and solid like icebergs at the foothills. The road ahead was empty. Only an occasional lorry rattled by on snow chains, moving in the opposite direction, towards central

London. More often than not, the vehicles were olive green, covered with grey tarpaulin. They belonged to the army. It seemed, in the outer reaches of London, as though the war was not quite over.

The interior of our car was warm, too warm. I was fighting sleep, trying to see the outlying stretches of this strange city whose inhabitant I had become. It spread around us in undulating waves, in wider and wider necklaces of squat houses, until it appeared that there was no getting out of it, that the entire girth of southern England was just it: London, coast to coast.

We crossed the river twice for some reason, on bridges suspended above ice floes that glided slowly on murky water. I could never quite grasp the way the Thames looped through London, and I gradually lost even the last of my bearings in the tangle of suburban roads. After a while I had no idea whether we were driving east or west, north or south. The sun was to our left, then to the right, then left again. At times the houses thinned and it looked as though we were about to leave the city behind, but then the settlements coalesced around us again, entire high streets with queues of people huddling in front of butchers' shops and corner dairies; schools and churches; deserted squares; grand villas floating behind bare branches like cruise ships stranded at low tide. And everywhere there were bomb craters, dwellings missing from rows of identical facades like gaping holes left after tooth extractions.

At one point a cemetery straddled the road, and angels with snowy wings watched us go by. An iron bridge, black against white, connected the two parts of the graveyard. I could not imagine anyone using it. I noticed graves with unfamiliar white crosses, three bars on each. Monsieur Carr noticed them too, and crossed himself, thumb and the first two fingers in a point, up, down, right, left.

'We could be back in Russia,' he repeated and took my hand. I left it there, on the tartan blanket which covered his knees, in the bony cup of his fingers.

'My dear Madame Whitelaw ... Albertine,' he said. 'Allow me to call you Albertine. It is so good to have your company. We are survivors, you and I.'

'I am not sure, Monsieur Carr. You perhaps, yes ...'

'Oh yes, dear girl, you too. I can tell that in you. Just wait and see ...'

It seemed almost like a let-down when we finally arrived at our destination, a cluster of grim warehouses on the outskirts of Shepperton. Forklift trucks moved between them, loaded with rolls of canvas, and workmen carried ladders and toolboxes. From the outside, the site could equally have been a vast storage facility of some sort, a set of furniture warehouses. We were directed to the largest of the warehouses where, we were told, members of the crew waited for us. We must have looked like a strange pair as we entered an immense, echoing hangar: an old man in a black coat with an astrakhan trim and a matching fur hat on his white head, the beat of a silver-capped walking stick bouncing off corrugated walls, a dark-haired younger woman on his arm. My heavy winter clothes were British all right, but I was not sure if people could still tell that I was foreign, even before I opened my mouth.

'Welcome to the British Lion Studios, Prince Karenin. Julien Duvivier. I am not sure if you remember. We met at Claridge's last autumn.' The film director spoke in French-accented, American-inflected English. We were now standing with Duvivier on a set that represented a railway station's concourse covered with mounds of fake snow. The train tracks to our right narrowed sharply at one end, creating a false sense of perspective; at the other, they stopped before a camera crane. A railway engine stood on them, a real, life-size, black engine, with fake icicles hanging from its front lights. I was momentarily stunned by the surroundings: the presence of the film director whose French work I knew well, the scale of the scenery, the painstaking, detailed illusion of it all.

'We could be back in Russia,' Monsieur Carr repeated for the third time that day.

'But we could be anywhere in Europe,' I said finally, looking at the pillars, a grand, neoclassical facade that, but for the Cyrillic signs, had nothing distinctively Russian about it.

'Anywhere in Europe: precisely. That is how it should be,' said Monsieur Carr, making sure that Duvivier heard him. 'I feared that I would be greeted by onion domes and Baba Yaga huts. Then the next thing you'd see would be Miss Leigh in a peasant dress, with a kokoshnik on her head. At least the set designer knows his Russia better.

'And as for all the tons of fake snow,' he added, 'is it not bizarre to have to produce it, with so much of the real thing around us?'

Outside, on real snow, there were pieces of decoy aircraft, wooden tanks and gun emplacements painted to look like the real thing. It was hard to know if they had been left there from a war film, or from the war itself, as a trap for German bombers. Even the landscape connived in the trompe l'œil. The entrance to the studios faced an abrupt hill with a steep rise, flat-topped like an extinct volcano and behind an ornate fence, the kind of ironwork that had all but disappeared from the streets of London, where iron had been requisitioned and metal stumps continued to scar the streetscapes. The extinct volcano was a mirage too, a water reservoir, a raised lake.

'Mr Andrejew knows his Russia.' Duvivier seemed pleased by the old man's reaction. 'André Andrejew. He has worked with Pabst, with Reinhardt, with Brecht! He is one of the best things about this film. There is no better art director in the world just now. We are lucky to have him. He had a spot of bother in France after the war, because of a film he made in 1943: a great work, much misunderstood. That's France for you. Its loss is Hollywood's gain.'

Shepperton was not Hollywood, that much was obvious the moment you left the hangar. Monsieur Carr chose not to say so; nor did he show any sign of recognising André Andrejew's name, or any of the others the film director mentioned.

There was something conspiratorial in the way Duvivier gazed at us, his puckish expression at odds with his severe business suit. His eyebrows rose above then fell below the frames of his glasses, like strange little leaping fish. I knew his face from newspapers back in France, before the war. I had been looking forward to this meeting, thinking how surreal it was to come across a famous Frenchman in an anonymous London suburb, alongside this Russian count who was now my employer.

Monsieur Carr chatted to Duvivier as though he met French film directors every day, as though they were becoming a bit of a bore. He opined that he considered theatre by far the superior art, and that opera and ballet towered over both. There were so many versions of *Anna Karenina* already, he said – one wondered why the world needed a new one.

'They are all imperfect in one way or another,' Duvivier responded. 'We are making the definitive version. No one will dare to follow ours. You need a producer like Sir

Alexander, with a vision to match Tolstoy's, to do justice to such a big story.'

'*War and Peace* is a big story,' said Monsieur Carr. '*Anna Karenina* is a small story. The smaller you make it the better it will be.'

I was waiting to hear them switch to French so I could tell Monsieur Duvivier how much I enjoyed his films, how much I loved *Pépé le Moko*. In the run-up to the day I had imagined the kind of repartee he would remember me by. I dreamed of meeting Jean Gabin but I married Leslie Howard instead, and here I am, in Shepperton, I would say wryly. But the men carried on in English. Eventually, the director remembered I was there. He raised my hand to his lips and said:

'*Et vous, Mademoiselle ...?*'

'Albertine,' I introduced myself.

'*La Prisonnière?*' Duvivier referred to my Proustian namesake.

'*Pas du tout,*' I said.

'Albertine Whitelaw,' said Monsieur Carr in English. 'So inconsiderate of me not to have introduced you, Mrs Whitelaw.'

'*Vous ressemblez tellement Madame Vivien,*' Duvivier said. 'You look so much like Vivien, you left me all confused. I thought for a moment I was seeing our future Karenina when you approached.'

This was not the first time I had been told I looked like Vivien Leigh. Albie had said it too, but nobody else had ever observed the alleged similarity before. Albie also said I looked like Hedy Lamarr. I took neither comparison seriously. There was something, perhaps, in the set of my face which was vaguely reminiscent of Leigh, but I had assumed that pictures, even moving ones, were deceptive. I would never have guessed that someone who knew Vivien Leigh might make the same comparison. Perhaps I really look like her, I thought.

There was one major difference, however. My nose, small by the standards of my family, goyish almost, was nothing like Vivien Leigh's. The star's profile had a proud, royal curve. My nose was long, with deep, pinched nostrils, like something drawn by a mournful child. My mother used to call it 'noble', but she also used to go on about my beautiful hair when I was a girl and that is always a bit of a giveaway; she was like natives of countries with nothing but clean air to boast of. My face needed all the favourable angles it could get.

Two workmen carried a toy train past us. A woman approached but then just stood next to us, hugging a clipboard against her tweed-clad chest.

'Let me introduce you to Elizabeth Montagu, and see if she will spot the resemblance,' Duvivier said. 'What do you think, Elizabeth? Who does Madame Albertine remind you of?'

Without waiting to hear her answer, he returned to Monsieur Carr.

'Sir Alexander will be here in a moment.' He uttered the title *à la française*, Sér Alexandér, with an unnecessary rhyme and a dash of sarcasm.

'We have so much to talk about. Mr Andrejew will be here soon, too. I cannot wait to tell him how much you liked his sets. A lot has changed since we last met. I am not sure if you have had a chance to read the new script. Mr Morgan – Guy – has greatly improved Jean Anouilh's version, Sir Alexander believes.' The sarcasm was now palpable.

'The idea of moving the story to France seemed unnecessary to me,' said Monsieur Carr, choosing not to notice it. 'You would not have needed my advice anyway. I suspect that the British prefer the French to the Russians, but not by much.

And I shall have to believe you when you say that Monsieur Anouilh is illustrious in France. However, some stories don't travel so well. My parents were not bourgeois, not even haut bourgeois, and France has long got rid of their equivalents. The Vronskys' equivalents too. If the three main characters – my father, my mother and her lover – were to become French, the whole story could so easily have become a silly confection. Which is not to say it won't, even so.'

He took in the station building, the facade propped with supports and sandbags, and proclaimed it, again, very Russian indeed.

'Ah, I am delighted to see you, Prince Karenin,' said a tall man striding towards us. He shook Monsieur Carr's hand, then stared at me and finally back at Duvivier, who shrugged as if to say, yes, I can see the similarity.

'Korda,' the man said and grabbed my hand, holding it in both of his for a moment, then – still with both hands – raised it a fraction, bowed and kissed it, clicking his heels. Duvivier's eyebrows shot up above the rims of his glasses.

'Sir Alexander,' Elizabeth Montagu intervened, 'let me introduce Albertine Whitelaw. Count Karenin's assistant.' She alone used the correct title for Monsieur Carr.

Alexander Korda was an imposing figure, angular and owl like behind his thick spectacles, yet handsome and charismatic nonetheless. He was so dapper in his Prince of Wales check, his face under the carefully combed greying hair so English-looking, that it was impossible to think of him as a boy from a Hungarian village, a Jewish boy. The less you arrived in England with, the more freely you seemed able to reinvent yourself.

Korda excused himself and took Duvivier and Monsieur Carr to the far corner of the studio where rolls of paper were piled high on a trestle table. He started unrolling them, explaining and pointing at something here then there.

'I am the dialogue director here,' Elizabeth Montagu said to me, as we watched the men from afar. 'Although my job description means different things on different days. I am the only native speaker of English, but I also make an excellent cup of tea. I was at RADA with Vivien before the war. Hartley, she was then. Four years younger than me. You must be of a similar age.' She was friendly and unaffected but authority and even aristocratic grandeur lurked behind her nonchalance.

'The same age,' I responded, revealing that I had more than a passing interest in the star. 'We were born only weeks apart, Miss Leigh and I.'

'You do resemble her, but Duvivier exaggerates. Her eyes are blue, although most people think of them as green because of Scarlett O'Hara. They made them green in post-production. Yours are so dark, they seem to be all pupils. Vivien is a couple of inches shorter … and …' She slowed down.

'The nose, I am sure that's what you wanted to say,' I interrupted. She was too tactful to mention it.

'I meant something more complex than features. Vivien manages to look as though butter wouldn't melt in her mouth. But the nose too, I suppose.' Elizabeth traced the line of my nose with her index finger. 'Much more interesting than Vivien's, dare I say. You'd have been a better Cleopatra. And you are French, I take it, from your accent. Though it is barely noticeable: not like that lot there. Those men are often impossible to understand, especially when they speak English to each other. Duvivier speaks French to me most of the time. I was an ambulance driver in France at the start of the war. Mechanical Transport Corps.'

She paused as if to ponder recollections she was not going to share. I was silent too, confused by the unexpected touch of her hand.

'What a coup for the film,' Elizabeth said. 'I couldn't think of a better period consultant than Count Karenin. The people we have here – such a cosmopolitan gathering seems possible only in London. And I do hope we will be seeing more of you too, Mrs Whitelaw.'

We watched Monsieur Carr, Jean Duvivier and Alexander Korda as they talked to a series of men who came and went with papers and photographs, like military chiefs of staff hearing reports of distant battles. A young woman walked up to them, said something, then came over to us with the same news.

'We were hoping that Prince Karenin would meet Miss Leigh today, Miss Montagu,' she said. 'She was due in for a consultation with Miss Penfold and the hairdressing team, but she is not feeling very well, unfortunately. The girls have gone to her place instead.'

'How very sad,' Elizabeth Montagu said and they exchanged looks that suggested the news was not unexpected. 'There will be other occasions, Mrs Whitelaw, I'm sure. You are part of the film business now.'

It was mid-afternoon when we left the studios and settled in for our journey back to Chiswick.

'Mrs Jenkins will be expecting us with some proper food, Albertine. I hope you are not too hungry. I did not want us to have to have a meal with the film people, although they had offered. The food would probably have tasted of papier mâché,' he said.

'I was so fascinated by it all I forgot to feel hungry. I have never been anywhere near a film studio before. All those powerful men, so much money and so much thought going into something that looked like a child's game. I would have loved to see my husband's reaction to that toy train they brought in to show you.'

'And the station platform they created – they asked if it was anything like the real place where my mother died. "Just like it," I said. "It is as though I have stepped back in time." They seemed pleased, the film people.'

'How else do you begin to answer a question like that?'

'Well, I could have told them that my mother died at Obiralovka, a small suburban station outside Moscow, and that I assumed we were standing in the mock-up of St Petersburg, for example, but Andrejew will sort that out soon enough. He is an educated man, André Andrejew, he knew what he was talking about. He looked at me, shrugged, and said just "*Znayu*." *I know.* No one else paid any attention.'

'Obiralovka. Where is that?' I asked. I had read *Anna Karenina* in my late teens, and I remembered everyone shuttling between Moscow and St Petersburg when they were not going to their country estates. I was pretty sure this was the first time I had heard of Obiralovka.

'A small station outside Moscow, where the Vronskys had their country estate. They tell me that it is now called Zheleznodorozhny. The Steel Road Town. Very appropriate for this new world of ours.'

'But you should have complained,' I said. 'About Obi— I mean. I can't pronounce the name, I am afraid.'

'I don't complain. The Carrs are quiet people,' he said, then, after a brief pause, 'My mother and her lover produced enough excitement for the whole of the nineteenth century. And the twentieth. My son certainly seems to think so.'

'Did you hate her when you were a boy?' I asked. 'Do you hate her for the way she ended her life? I lost my family when I was twenty. I promised myself that I would not talk about their deaths. I know this is irrational but it seemed that by talking about their accident I was condemning them to die again and again. It was an act of God, people said, because there was nothing else to say. There is human error and there is bad luck. But your mother's ...'

I did not know what to call Anna's end in front of her son. She had wanted it.

'When Mother died, for a long while I could not even think of what happened. I wanted the event to unhappen, to be allowed to be ordinary, like other children. And you must remember that I lost her twice. My father, my awful, boring, dear old father, told me, lied to me, that she was dead because after she left him, he did not want me to see her ever again. But she came into the house on my birthday, secretly – my ninth birthday. I woke up and saw her and thought I was dreaming. She was a ghost. Then, so soon after I realised that it was really her, that she was alive, I lost her again.

'I had such a lonely, uncomprehending childhood, dear Albertine, in that bleak house. It was a mausoleum where we prayed for her sinning soul four, five times a day, with a procession of priests and monks who hovered around Father like vultures around a particularly juicy carcass. He converted my mother's dressing room into a chapel, had it consecrated. Father was fundamentally Orthodox, but there was this joyless Protestant side to him, a throwback to our German ancestry no doubt. He was interested in right and wrong, the rule of law; no music, no mystery, and no salvation unless the ledgers tot up. I couldn't wait to grow up, to escape from him and his joyless world, and I believe he felt the same about me in the end. He wanted me out and away. Physically, I may have resembled him as much as her, I am not sure, but finally, looking at me, he could see only her, and that other Alexei, Vronsky, who was everything he was not. I hated him and then I pitied him. I pitied him so much that even many years later I gave his name to my own son, my only child, blind to the fact that I was also naming him after my mother's lover. God forgive me.'

'But you left him anyway?' I asked. 'You left him behind long ago in Russia, I assume?'

'Yes, I did, well before the Revolution. I went abroad to study. That, at least, was my excuse. I came of age at the time of great expeditions and discoveries – the great Victorian era as the British like to think of it – when scholars and scientists risked their lives to cross deserts and climb mountains. I was sixteen when I went to hear General Przhevalsky at the Imperial Geographical Society in St Petersburg. He spoke about his journey into the Tibetan interior, places unvisited by Europeans since Marco Polo. I wanted to travel further, if that was possible. And long before I knew whether I wanted to be an archaeologist, or an explorer, or something else altogether, I dreamed of running away from my father.'

'And your father? Did he sense that? Did he try to stop you?'

'He was almost relieved when I chose Tübingen, happy to send me to Germany although there was no reason to go so far to study; our Russian universities were very good. Germany had united just over a decade earlier and, in theory at least, was an exciting place to be, but I wasn't interested in politics, wasn't interested in Bismarck. I was interested in ancient languages and scripts, pre-Christian and even pre-Greek, the older the better. It may well have been all those priests and confessors who, promising to save Father's soul, had damned my sister's soul and mine. Annie believed in God, I was not sure, but neither of us wanted anything to do with official religion. I became interested in the distant past, before the world as we knew it began, some place with different moral codes and different gods.'

He repeated the names of people and places several times, spelling them out for me as though I were taking dictation. Russia – nineteenth-century Russia – seemed a distant and incomprehensible place. Now this Russia no longer existed, and there was an enormous new country, the Soviet Union, that was our ally. Many English people spoke ill of it – it was a barbarous, Communist land, they said – though Albie rather admired the war-winning Soviets. Yet here I was, in a car in outer London, with a man whose world had been destroyed by the Soviets. But you could also argue that his world had in fact been shattered decades before the Soviet Union even existed, by his own mother.

'Before my mother died, everyone thought I was a technically minded boy, destined to be a great architect or engineer – a Russian Brunel,' he continued. 'After her death, I did not want to know about building anything. I became such a recluse that the family worried I would become a monk, withdraw from them and the world, see my life out in a hermitage on Mount Athos or on some other holy mountain. They were wrong. I hated even the thought of God. I just wanted to escape them all, to be left alone.

'In 1875, for my eleventh birthday, my uncle Stiva gave me a piece of parchment from St Catherine's Monastery in the Sinai. I had an epiphany then, found my vocation. I would spend my life deciphering old manuscripts; I would become a palaeographer. Stiva's piece of parchment – my parchment

– I learned, had a matching page in the collection of Freiherr von Gutschmid in Germany. I wanted to study with him. Father was happy to send me away. I was his son and heir, but I was also Anna's son and he couldn't forget that.

'Neither could I. I came to hate her because, when she couldn't have us both, she wanted that other man, my father's rival and namesake, more than she wanted me. For a long time I believed that her sin against me was more serious than her sin against my father. When you become a mother, Albertine, I am sure you will understand me better.'

'I am not sure that I will ever have children,' I said, trying to make it sound as though my childlessness was not a matter of anyone's choice. I did not want him to pity me, but pity was preferable to talking about Albie and me, to relaying the intimate conversations that Albie and I only ever half had.

'Oh, you will want a child, I know.' He appeared, perhaps deliberately, to misunderstand. 'Forgive me for speaking so directly. There will come a moment when you realise that you love someone so much that only having their child will do. Conception is the highest form of lovemaking: the only one that makes sense. My mother knew that in the end. I am not sure my father was capable of such love.'

I hoped that the driver did not understand French. I glanced into the rear-view mirror: the man's eyes were fixed on the road ahead. He was one of those short, wiry English types who could equally have been eighteen or thirty-eight. An ex-Tommy, probably, judging by the back of his head, covered by a close ginger crop. I wondered – you always did, about everyone – where he had spent the war.

'I remember my first journey to Tübingen in 1882,' Monsieur Carr continued. 'September it was. The night before, Father and I went to a concert. He had no understanding of music, no love for it; he just wanted to show me to the world before I left. I was taller than him, and I looked like him. Anyone could see that I was his child.

'Father was seventy-three when he died, ten years younger than I am now. Neither of us suspected that he would be dead before I completed my studies, or we might not have passed that last Russian evening together in stony silence. Rimsky-Korsakov was at the concert hall; spoke to Father at some length. Turkey and Bulgaria were mentioned. Some problems with Prince Alexander of Battenberg on which Father saw fit to opine. Everyone knew Father. There was the scandal, of course, but he had been part of the Establishment, and the Establishment closed around him to protect his honour and their own. Russia felt very small in those days, several dozen families, all connected.

'It was a strange year. I left Russia after the old Tsar was assassinated in 1881 and I was in Germany when the grand coronation of the new one took place in 1883. Father travelled to Moscow for that ceremony. There is a famous painting of it. You can see Father's bald head in the crowd at the Uspensky Sobor if you squint. No bigger than a sunflower seed. He was so proud.

'He had been a Slavophile, at heart, my papa, not a Westerniser. Like many Russian officials of German descent, he had believed all the more zealously in Russia's mission in the world. My mother's lover, Vronsky, somehow managed to be both, to be a Westerniser who died in Serbia for a great Slavophile cause. Now Father couldn't be either. He let himself be guided by the sort of people he would once have despised. He called himself Orthodox, yet he was seeing psychics and diviners. He was a lost soul.'

I looked to my right and saw the wide curve of the Thames and a hill rising from the meadows, a vast red-brick edifice on its brow, rows of lit windows and dark chimneys. Lower down, closer to us, there were Georgian villas, and cedar trees in elegant clusters. They spoke of gentler centuries, but that was a mirage. There had been no gentler times than ours, just times when the wars and the sorrow happened to take place elsewhere. To be spared: I no longer had a sense of what that meant.

'How confusing it must have been for your father,' I said. 'I am sure he loved you. Or believed that he ought to.'

'While I was in Tübingen, he wrote from time to time,' Monsieur Carr said. 'A father's instructions to the son: like a Russian Polonius or Chesterfield. Do not drink, do not gamble, do not duel. Be Russian and be proud of it, but be wary of other Russians. There were so many spoilt brats, frittering their family fortunes in the casinos of Baden-Baden, just forty miles away, that they were building a church there for them, with golden domes worthy of Yaroslavl.

'There was very little warmth in Father's letters. He wrote to me in French, but it did not sound like his French, it was as though someone was dictating the letters to him. As I studied ancient scripts during the day, so late at night I studied my father's handwriting. It was looking more and more like a cuneiform script: angular, sharp, as though he was scared of flourishes, of connections. He packed his lines tightly on the page, leaving no margins. If you saw the letters, you would have guessed that they came from a man unhinged in some way. I kept them in their envelopes, often without reading. When the news reached me of his death and I had to pack quickly to return to Russia for his funeral, I threw the letters into the stove in my room and slammed the fire door.'

Monsieur Carr fell silent and closed his eyes. I watched the houses along the road; in rooms here and there, people were already closing the curtains for the night. The moon sat low in the sky, unmoving and near enough to touch, like a picture painted on the window of the car.

4

Absence

I expected Mrs Jenkins to open the front door, but instead it was Alex Carr, in the same roomy suit I had seen him wearing at my job interview. He stooped down to kiss me on the doorstep, awkwardly and three times, in the Orthodox way, each kiss clumsier than the one before, all the while holding my hand in his between us, like a metal railing on the edge of a cliff. There was no intimacy in his action, no warmth, just something that suggested he had deliberated and decided on it as an appropriate response, a way of acknowledging that single, unpremeditated peck on the cheek I had given him at our first parting.

His movements were wooden, as though his body was a puppet or a toy horse, forced against its will to do the bidding of his mind. His height made his awkwardness more obvious. I felt almost protective towards him. I smiled and extolled the excitements of the day. I thanked him for his solicitousness in providing a driver, as though the Shepperton excursion had been my idea and not his father's.

Monsieur Carr remained close behind, removing the snow from his shoes with the boot scraper. He took no notice of our exchange. He was perhaps used to his son's gaucheness. He said something in Russian. Alex Carr responded briefly, then turned to me.

'Do stay on for tea if you can,' he said. 'The samovar is ready, there is plenty to eat with the tea, and the electric fires were turned on at four. We watch our meters as we are instructed to, but we don't shiver a moment longer than we have to. I am not sure how far people's patience with the government stretches in this weather. "Shiver with Shinwell": did you hear that one?'

And, when I did not respond:

'I hope you are not too exhausted by your excursion?'

He held my coat, then his father's, and we walked into the library. The samovar was steaming; platefuls of food waited on the table, some piled with cheese scones and sandwiches, others with small pastries dusted with icing sugar, like pyramids of tiny snowballs.

'Oh, you must stay, you must, dear Albertine,' said Monsieur Carr, then, pointing at the snowballs, 'You'll love these. Our famous Russian tea cakes. As the old joke goes, they are not Russian, have nothing to do with tea, but at least they are not cakes.'

We settled to a stream of Russian from the father, punctuated by now familiar names – Korda, Anouilh, Duvivier – and interwoven with dollops of French and English when they wanted to include me. Mrs Jenkins stood in the doorway and listened to the conversation, as fascinated by the film business as everyone else.

'It seems that my grandson won't be required in the studios more than half a dozen times, mostly during his Easter break and the summer half-term,' Monsieur Carr said to his son. 'By the summer most of the filming will have been completed. Strange how it takes years to set everything in motion, then it's all over in a blink.'

He was trying to talk his son into something, speaking English now as if to have me as his witness.

'I don't know, Father, I really don't know,' Alex Carr responded. 'Gigi does seem to have the talent, if school plays are anything to go by, but I would hate to see the boy want to become an actor, and worse, to be encouraged to think about family history, to see his Russianness, in the context of this film. To learn about our past by drinking a glass of Hollywood lemonade. It's all frippery.'

'It's not Hollywood, and the film business is in a different universe from ours, Alexei,' said the old man. 'It is the future. One day young Etonians will queue up to become film stars. What would you like Gigi to do, become an accountant, like you? This is not St Petersburg and there is no shame for us in the film, none at all.'

'I don't mean to forbid this film part, Father,' Alex Carr intervened, 'and you know it. So long as Diana is willing to chaperone him and so long as it is just that once. Let me say it again: I really do not want Gigi to become an actor. Or a film director, for that matter. And neither does Diana. We want him to have a respectable career.'

'Oh, Alexei, you are so boring sometimes,' the old man said.

Judging by his expression, Alex Carr took this as a compliment. He turned to me and asked me if I had enjoyed the day. I nodded vigorously and told him how fascinating it had all seemed, how much I had learned.

'And I mean it,' I added. 'without witnessing the shooting of a single scene. I would love to see Gigi transformed from a modern, 1940s child, into one from the 1870s. It would give the boy something to remember later in life. And his children too: people will go to the cinema to see him long after we are all dead and buried.'

'But the reasons for wanting to see him will not be something to take pride in,' he said. He looked disappointed in me. I was not taking his side.

He was standing up to leave, to make his apologies. I stood up too, to shake his hand, worrying that another triptych of those awkward kisses might be forthcoming.

'Thank you for all your help, Mrs Whitelaw,' he said. 'I am glad you were with my old father today. If you could talk some sense into him about Gigi and this film business, in spite of your present enthusiasm, I would be most grateful. He's got Gigi all excited. The boy talks about earning ten guineas a day as though that is going to change my mind. I am sure my old man put him up to it. We want the boy to be a lawyer or a doctor when he grows up, not Rudolph Valentino.'

'And just what would be wrong with Valentino?' Monsieur Carr interjected from his seat. 'Our Gigi might grow up to make an even more devastating sheikh.'

'Oh, Father. Have you lost all sense of dignity and gravitas? Our ancestors would be turning in their graves,' Alex Carr said.

With that he left us to our tea. We heard first the front door and then the gate close behind him.

'I have held on to my dignity and gravitas for much too long,' Monsieur Carr said. 'I've let life pass me by, because of my mother and father. I don't blame them; it was my choice, but I was wrong. Let's be childish, Albertine. Let's eat the Russian tea cakes and talk about Valentino. I noticed that you know much more about film than you affect. My son seemed so disappointed in you.'

But I liked Alex Carr. There was something fragile about his very English propriety. It was acquired and hard-earned. There was not the easy assurance I was familiar with from Albie and his circle; in its stead there was a sense that everything you had could be snatched away just like that, without notice. I knew that feeling well. Strangely, it was not there in Monsieur Carr. In spite of all his losses, he had the childish optimism of someone who expected the gods to be on his side.

He pointed at the food and urged me to help myself.

'Will you be mother?' he asked. 'My hands are too shaky but I did not want to detain Mrs Jenkins. It's the Russian Caravan today. A present from Sir Alexander. He claimed that it came in fact from Miss Leigh, that she brought a box of it from Paris especially for me. She went over for a costume fitting with Cecil Beaton just last week, he said. I don't believe any of it for a moment. If it is true, then it must have been some poor assistant getting a dozen boxes in one of the large department stores, for a dozen old fools like me.'

The tea was syrupy, smoky and as black as coffee. I poured it from a small teapot into glasses in gilded silver holders, then added hot water from the samovar and finally sweetened it with a spoonful of rose syrup. That was the way Monsieur Carr liked his Russian tea: he had guided me through the process.

'*Voilà*, you are almost Russian now,' he said. There was a Clark Gable moustache of icing sugar on his upper lip. 'The roses for the syrup came from our garden. Mrs Jenkins does not waste a petal. While Tonya was alive, those two used to sugar violets and pansies. Tonya believed you had to pick the flowers at five in the morning, soon after they opened, but before the sun was properly out. We used to pick the violets in the meadows by the Thames sometimes. And nettles and sorrel, too. Can you imagine what the English thought? How hungry, how desperate these Russians must be ...'

'Ha, I remember being asked something similar about the French by one of the British soldiers who guarded the hospital where I worked in Alexandria,' I said. 'Is it true that we French eat snails because we are so poor? Then someone told him I was Jewish and he came back to ask me if snails were kosher. I was the first Jewish person he had ever knowingly spoken to, he admitted. There weren't many Jews in Shropshire, he said. That is where he was from. But I knew even less about Shropshire than he knew about the Jews.'

'And what if we manage to procure some caviar for that party we are planning?' Monsieur Carr asked, as though the subject of my diet had not crossed his mind before I mentioned the snails. 'Do you eat fish roe?'

'I don't keep kosher,' I said. 'I have never tasted caviar and I hope there will be some, particularly now that you conceded I am almost Russian. I take it as a great compliment. What would it take to become fully Russian?'

'You will need to learn to speak Russian. I am sure we will achieve that. If little Gigi can, Albertine can too,' he said. 'You are a linguist, my dear, aren't you?'

I was preparing to leave and I assumed that Mrs Jenkins had gone home, but she stepped out of the kitchen with a string bag and two jars in it, wrapped in pages from an English newspaper.

'Pickled mushrooms,' she said, 'and a jar of rose petal jam. I heard you speaking about it. Not syrup, mind you, thick, proper jam: don't go putting this in your tea. For you and your husband.'

'There must be a duct of some kind connecting each room with the kitchen,' Monsieur Carr said. 'Mrs Jenkins hears everything. Be careful what you say to me, Albertine.'

It was late when I returned to Earl's Court. I heard the telephone ringing well before I opened the front door, a metallic sound echoing in the hall as though it had been going on for days.

'Ber, darling, you had me worried.' There were sounds of jazz alongside Albert's voice on the line, somewhere further back, as though the music was reaching whatever space he was calling from through an open window.

'It's been a long day,' he said, sounding tired but not unhappy. 'I wanted to hear your sweet voice before I retire. How was Shepperton?'

He chipped in with explanations as I related the events of the day, giving me details of Elizabeth Montagu's family, saying that Alexander Korda had employed Churchill at some stage before the war. He seemed to know everything about everyone.

'He's a plausible chap, your Korda,' he said. 'An immense commercial talent.' Plausible: it was a strange adjective. I could not quite guess what he meant. How plausible were we, all of us?

Then I started relaying the detail of our impromptu tea party – the pros and cons of a film career for Gigi. There was no interruption from Albie for a while as I spoke and I thought he had fallen asleep, but I realised that the sound of music had vanished too, that I had been speaking to no one. That happened often; lines went dead mid-sentence. I waited for him to ring back but the phone remained silent. There was just the hum of London in the dark, a distant crunch of tyres on icy roads, and closer by, inside the house, that cracking of beams shrinking in the cold.

I gave up waiting and went into the kitchen. The breakfast dishes were still in the sink, bathed in moonshine. There was a glint of ice over them. I boiled some water and washed up, watching the plumes of steam rise around me, and then I took a mop and cleaned the floor, moving on to the hall, carrying on without thinking, mopping and wiping and sweeping and dusting, without properly seeing the dust in the weak light of a succession of twenty-five-watt bulbs, ceasing to feel the cold, without noticing, as I finished, that there was grey light in the windows and the first sound of horses' hooves, a milk cart in the street below. The snow had started falling again.

I was woken up late by the winter sun streaming through chinks in the curtains. I had already decided to spend the afternoon making cushion covers for our bed; the deepest blue velvet, with two wine-coloured appliqué As, one bottom left, one bottom right, mirror images of each other. I had dreamed up the design on the Underground, returning from Chiswick, then sketched the pattern for the As on the back of one of Albie's large Manila envelopes. I thought of the vague point-lessness of the task even as I cut out the paper letters and pinned them to the blue squares, to test out the look before the formal commitment of the lock stitch. I wondered, for the first time ever, what Albie must have written about me to his parents to make them choose a sewing machine as our wedding present.

'A girl I met in Egypt,' I imagined. 'A university graduate, and a seamstress.' Or the other way round. I wondered which came first, which seemed more fitting: the linguist or the dressmaker?

'You are the only woman I have ever wanted to marry, Albertine,' Albie told me soon after he proposed.

'Why?' I asked bluntly. Why might that be? was the meaning I intended. I tried to avoid unnecessary verbs in those early days. My conditionals were shaky; *may* and *might* seemed interchangeable.

'Because you question everything,' he said. 'You'll keep me young.'

Whenever I thought of Egypt, I chose to remember only Albie's days on leave, the few days taken here and there lodged luminously amid the months of his absence and my anxiety, strung close together by memory like a pearl choker, without the bitter knots of worry that separated them. I feared that I might never see him again, that I would be left guessing if he had died or reneged on his promise. I was certain that he would, simply, disappear one day, because things and people did. Death seemed the less likely possibility; I was convinced that I had had my allotted share of it.

I wound the bobbin, threaded the machine, put my right – my stronger – foot on the treadle and rocked it gently like a seesaw. When I refused piano classes with Arlette, pleading an absence of talent, my mother had given me sewing lessons instead. She was determined to demonstrate that life offered no easy options, no escape into the garret and the company of books. The stitch ran along the edges of the soft blue squares. I soon found the rhythm of the movement I had known since I was a young girl.

The steady sound of the machine – the punch of the needle piercing fabric, and the beat of the cast-iron base – was not unlike the sound of a railway engine. I followed the lines of the pattern, joined the surfaces together, made sure not to stitch the appliqué through to the back of the cushion.

The motion became unconscious. Time passed. The beat was soothing and the concentration it required was demanding enough to hold every other thought at bay, to keep me away from myself. This sense of absence was perhaps the purest form of happiness I knew. Yet to maintain it, to make it last for an hour or two, I needed to be persuaded that what I was doing was necessary, and so often I found that almost impossible. When I finished the cushions, I put them on our bed and sat in the window facing them for a while: Albie's A on the left, mine on the right, their symmetrical flourishes like faces in the mirror, the background as pretty and as blue as midnight.

5

Orphans

We were sitting opposite each other, Monsieur Carr and I, on the seat that followed the shape of the bay window in his library, like passengers in a railway compartment.

'Tell me about Albert,' he said. 'Where did you meet?'

'In Egypt,' I said. 'I was working in a hospital, an administrative job. Boring, you could say, but people like me wanted jobs just like that; the more boring the better it seemed in those days. Albie was part of a small group of English soldiers, wounded somewhere in the desert. They were like young gods, he and his fellow officers, when I first glimpsed them through an open door of their ward. They were lean and sun-bleached. When the nurses gave them their baths, their naked torsos looked as though they had been dipped in cocoa: white where their khaki uniforms had covered their bodies, dark where the rays had caught them. They asked to be given those baths, although many of them could have bathed themselves.'

'I am sure they asked,' Monsieur Carr said.

'The nurses would oblige, at first,' I continued, hoping to convey that peculiarly Alexandrian mixture of hardship and poetry to the old man. 'These men were the walking wounded: a bandaged shoulder, a limb in plaster, the permanent smell of iodine about them, from the sea outside and from the tinctures in the hospital vials. The windows of their ward remained wide open throughout the Mediterranean nights, like the windows of all our rooms, as though the buildings of Alexandria were shells, there to offer shade but otherwise almost unnecessary. The swifts screeched and swooped low against the stone walls, the sea was on its endless roll, and the whole wide horseshoe of the bay hummed with the never-ending collision of the waves. The calls to prayer reached us from the hinterland at their regular hours. "God is great," they repeated. "God is great."

'Above all those sounds, the English gods laughed. Their laughter was as sonorous, and as self-confident, as they were handsome. What did they have to laugh about, we wondered, all of us others, when the war is closing in, when they had so many dead comrades on the mortuary slabs and in the desert sands, what did they have to laugh about? Only the English nurses giggled giddily, coming back from the wards, as though they were in on some secret the rest of us did not share.

'I had seen Englishmen before, in Paris, and very occasionally in Bucharest, but these men were of a different kind. Now that I had seen these men, I knew, long before I could say it to anyone else, that there was no way that Britain could lose the war.

'On the day he, one of these young gods, was discharged from hospital, he knocked on my office door, an open door, holding a card of some kind, asking me to note something down on it. He needed to take the note back to his unit. I could barely understand what he was saying. I was thirty, not some inexperienced young thing, yet I looked at him and blushed like a girl of fifteen.

'"Lieutenant Colonel Whitelaw."

'It sounded as though he was repeating his name for the second or third time, and I still had no idea what he wanted from me, this half colonel, as they called them. I took his card and looked at it, hoping to get some clue from the writing, but the letters swam before my eyes. Away from his friends, in uniform, standing before me, he was not a laughing young god any more. There were wrinkles etched by the sun on his forehead. I noticed tobacco stains on the insides of his second and third fingers, where he held the card. I felt, though it was impossible, that I had met this man before, that I knew him. This close by, he was even more handsome.

'"Lieutenant Colonel Albert Whitelaw," he said again, now exasperated and a bit worried. He stepped back and read the name on my office door to make sure that he had come to the right place.

'"Miss Cartier, yes?" he asked.

'"Albertine. Albertine Cartier," I said at last, and offered my hand, as though I had finally understood something, as though he was just introducing himself and not about to explode with irritation.

'For some reason his anger was diffused by the sound of my name and he laughed instead. He shook my hand so firmly that I still felt the squeeze ten or fifteen minutes later.

'"Albertine, did you say?" That laugh of the gods, at last, with me or at me, I knew not and I cared less. I nodded. He laughed again.

'"Well, my dear Miss Cartier, Albertine indeed, if I may, I am asking you to complete this form here. And you must keep a copy for your files," he said. He jabbed the card I was now holding, then looked at the rows of metal drawers full of identical index cards. He pulled the one labelled W–Z out by several inches.

'"You can't do that," I said, and put my hand out. "It is not allowed."

'"Oh, yes I can. Let's see how many Xs and Ys you've got there, Miss Cartier, in your no doubt excellent filing system."

'"You can't," I repeated and pushed the drawer back in by a fraction, trying not to trap his fingers.

'Albie took out a random card, held it up in his tobacco-stained fingers.

'"Yeast, Mike," he started to read. "Christ."

'I snatched the card from him.

'"You misspell diarrhoea, Mademoiselle Cartier. An error like that and the whole system goes down the drain, so to speak."'

'Charming,' Monsieur Carr laughed, 'absolutely charming.'

'Anyway, that was our first conversation as I remember it, more or less verbatim, since you asked,' I said. 'Later that month he returned to hospital with a bundle of jasmine branches and a triangular piece of metal mounted on a silver chain.

'"They open at night," Albie said, pointing at the buds. "They are white inside."

'A flowerless bunch and a souvenir of what nearly killed him. I still have that piece of shrapnel.' I pulled the chain out from under my shirt collar, unhooked it and handed it over, a piece of black metal the size of a monkey nut, encased in a filigree silver thread as a pendant.

'You could have that sort of thing made in Alexandria for next to no money and overnight,' I said. 'Albie said that he was putting his luck in my hands.'

Monsieur Carr held the metal in his palm. The chain dangled below.

'A small thing,' he said, 'and it looks so harmless.'

'It was lodged in Albie's right shoulder. It was blisteringly hot when it hit.

'"I am afraid I have a puncture," Albie had told the matron when he arrived. Semi-conscious and in pain, he still spoke in understatements. They had irrigated the wound out in the field and sent him on to advanced care, because the shrapnel was too awkwardly embedded to handle on the spot. He has a diagonal scar on his shoulder blade, as though he had been trying unsuccessfully to grow wings, he jokes. They say it will fade away in time. It is barely visible already, but it gets angry sometimes, and then it shines bright red. I beg Albie not to scrub it when he has his bath. Perhaps that's not it. I don't know enough about wounds.'

I looked at the portrait of Monsieur Carr's mother and father, and it seemed, in the reflection the fire was throwing against the wall from the fireplace, that there were dancing shadows in the backdrop, that the painter had painted other people and then covered them in tar-black oil. Monsieur Carr looked like a creature from an era that pre-dated his parents. His white hair and his rough white jumper, which could have been knitted by one of the family serfs long ago, would not have been out of place in a medieval wall painting. The asymmetry gave his face a plaintive, Byzantine aspect.

'A fisherman's jumper,' he said, following my eyes and touching the fabric of his garment. 'From the Outer Hebrides. Have you heard of the archipelago? A present from Alexei, our Russian Allenby. He loves Scottish things. What a confusing world we live in, Albertine. One day, our grand-children will look at our lives and think, our poor ancestors, so many trails, so many countries, so many wars.'

'I told you my story; you promised yours,' I said. 'You were going to tell me what happened after your father died. After you returned to Russia.'

He looked out of the window into the wintry garden and buttoned up his fisherman's jumper at the shoulder, as though he was bracing himself against the cold.

'My return to Russia was in 1892,' he said. 'It felt like a short visit at first, but I had preserved the sense that Russia was my home. No other place has ever felt like that. Not even England now, after twenty-three years. An entire decade passed in Germany and I never even thought of it as a place of permanent residence, let alone a home.

'I assumed that Russia would always be there, that I would always be able to return. First, I wanted Russia to forget my mother. Until that happened, I would remain in Tübingen. People spoke of Anna – Tolstoy's Anna – in Germany too, but they did not know that it was the story of my mother's life; they did not know me, or ask themselves what I was doing in their country. I was just another Russian youth at the university which had educated Hegel and Hölderlin. Who would not study at Tübingen, given half the chance? In the ten years I spent there, my landlady never once asked why I chose Germany, so obvious was the answer.

'The library was my refuge. I believed that nothing bad could happen to me behind a palisade of books. How naive I was, dear Albertine. I studied dead languages and deciphered manuscripts late into the night, and hiked, alone, in the hills or along the Neckar on Sundays. Latin, Greek, Church Slavonic, one could perhaps have expected me to want to study those, but not Assyrian, Egyptian, Sumerian. Yet I slowly mastered them. In 1892, ten years after I first set foot on German soil and crossed the threshold of Tübingen's philology department, I defended my doctorate. My teachers wanted to keep me in Tübingen. I had no self-confidence, at least not enough of it to believe their praise.

'"Count Karenin," my tutor, Freiherr von Gutschmid, told me early on, "Germany will be kinder to you than Russia will be. It is a more civilised country."

'I loved Russia, I was proud of being Russian, and, although Gutschmid was thirty years older than me, I refused to believe that he knew what he was talking about. You cannot grasp Russia with your mind, the poet Tyutchev said. Gutschmid was pure mind.'

'Could you tell that they felt superior to you, the Germans, simply because you were Russian?' I asked. 'Is that why you chose London in the end?'

'In Germany, however polite people were – however convincing the veneer of social niceties – there was always an apprehensiveness about Slavs, the looming threat from the East. My distant Teutonic ancestry did not signify,' he said. 'That vanished in England, where we became just another category of foreigners from faraway lands, but, in the dying years of the last century, no one could have guessed that I would end up in England. I am not sure if I was ever fully aware of the choice I was making as a student. For someone like me, with a scholarly bent, there was Russia and there was Germany. Austria-Hungary too, perhaps, but Vienna was not so different from Germany in its attitudes to Slavs.

'Later on I wondered if I had made a mistake by not staying in Tübingen. I look at those German years, and I see my father looming over them, his money, his patronage, his purchase of the distance between us. When I was still a boy and he a recent widower, Father hired only the best tutors for me. He read textbooks in pedagogy to find out how to bring me up. His parenting was like that: mechanical, correct, devoid of anything instinctive. He wanted the best for his son, but I felt no warmth from him.

'My late wife was interested in the workings of the human psyche. She read a lot of psychology, and she tut-tutted whenever my father was mentioned. High intelligence, she would say, but a failure of empathy, an inability to interpret emotion. She cited a paper by a Soviet woman psychiatrist someone gave her to read, and she urged me to look at it too.

'"It describes your father and his kind," she said. "There is more than a touch of him in you and even in our son."

'I laughed and threw the paper into the sitting-room fire. Perhaps there was a bit of my father in me after all. She was at the other extreme, my wife, so highly tuned into others that she forgot to think about herself.'

'According to Tolstoy's retelling of events,' I said, 'I seem to remember that most Russians took your father's side at first.'

'You are right, Albertine. We are all like Tonya now; we put our feelings first and are inclined to blame my father and not my mother for their shared tragedy. In my boyhood, it was the opposite. She was the goddess of destruction. He had never achieved his potential, and for that, too, my mother was to blame, everyone said.

'After her death Father worked for a long while in the Ministry of Finance under a minister who was both younger and of lowlier birth than him. He remained superior only in humility. He took on the permanent mask of a man who had suffered an unjust blow, who had been tested beyond human strength. Not a cuckold but a martyr. And this did not change in the two decades he endured as a widower. Only when a terrible famine struck Russia in the early nineties did he seem to wake up, to realise that there were greater tragedies in the world than his own. He worked tirelessly, and seemed finally to have found a sense of purpose, a kind of peace. Twenty years, almost, after mother died, and months, practically, before he did. A sad, late display of what he might have been all along had he had more generosity of spirit. Who knows why we don't have it, my dear child? We harm no one but ourselves by feeling slighted; we carry acid in our soul even when it eats nothing but the vessel it is stored in.'

He stood up from his seat and looked out of the window. He held his right hand in his left behind his back, palm over hand, like an officer surveying troops in the field. In contrast to his determined pose, his body seemed frail and ancient. His jumper and trousers hung loosely off a skinny frame, his shoulders were stooped and he wobbled slightly as he stood there, as if harvesting the memory from the weather outside. Then he turned, faced me again, and sat next to me. We were now side by side, both facing his parents' portrait.

'But I have all that about Father second-hand, from other people,' he said. 'From our cousins, the Oblonskys, the Galitzines, the Levins. Father came to visit me in Germany for the first and only time when I was twenty, on my birthday. Mother had been dead eleven years. He stayed at the Brenners in Baden-Baden and I travelled to meet him. He looked like a raven, all in black, his black beard covering much of his face, his bald head covered with a black hat. He walked slowly and noisily, click-clacking on the cobbles in his heavy, English-made shoes, and he seemed so old and so Russian that I was embarrassed to be seen with him. Not because of his Russianness, but because of his evident, alien difference, which called attention to itself when all I wanted was to be invisible. The Germans stared at him wherever we went, the waiters and the coachmen expected tips in gold coins, and everyone spoke slowly, waiting for me to interpret. No one dared address him directly. Father's German was fluent enough, his French was perfect, and he had more than a smattering of English, but he avoided eye contact, he made no effort to speak.

'We walked, and took waters, and talked, yet remained distant from each other. He would have preferred me to study law or even philosophy. My studies meant little to him. He understood well enough that their endless continuation had as much to do with forgetting as it had with my thirst for knowledge. He was similar in that respect, more interested in the religious disputes among Russian Orthodox philosophers than in me, our wider family, or even Russian politics. There were women around him back home, I later heard, circling like birds of prey, mothering him, telling him what to do, hoping that he would remarry. Devoutly Orthodox as he was, he seemed to be toying with spiritualism. He talked about it as though it was some kind of exact science, a way of getting in touch with the hereafter. I now wonder if he was trying to contact my mother, God forbid. She deserved peace over there at least, poor soul.

'We were equally unhappy, perhaps, father and son, wedded to each other as we were, till death did us part. One suicide was enough for the Karenins.'

Monsieur Carr paused again and now stared at the pattern in the carpet. For a moment the silence around us was complete. We were in London, but we could have been almost anywhere on this earth. Paris was so densely populated that you always knew you were in it; there was always someone shouting in the street, the sounds of conversation or love-making seeping through party walls or open windows. In my London home, when Albert was not in it, there was often, as now in Monsieur Carr's house, complete silence. It tempted you to speak aloud to yourself.

The word suicide echoed. It was the first time he had used it. Suicide was against religion, and against the law, even in Britain now, against the Crown. In last century's Russia, it would have been an even graver sin. I was still not sure how to ask about Anna's death.

'After he left Germany, Father wrote to me less and less,' Monsieur Carr continued. 'When news of his death reached me, I was twenty-eight and we had not seen each other in eight years. They wanted to bury him as fast as possible, as the Orthodox rite dictates. Yet they postponed the obsequies to give me – his only child and heir – the time to get back to St Petersburg. I would not have regretted missing the occasion, the days of condolences and obligatory feasting required of me to mark the first week, the forty days, the first full year after his death day. Orthodoxy may lift your soul closer to God than any other faith, but it can be atavistic in its attitude to the body. I was unprepared. I had not even known he was ill. The pancreas, apparently: too much bile, the doctors said. If anyone could die from too much bile, it was my father.'

'And what does the Orthodox Church have to say of suicides?' I asked, pursuing my own train of thought.

'You are thinking of my mother,' he said. 'She had been distressed, and high on opium most likely. She took opium with increasing regularity, they said; it was an acceptable painkiller in those days. It was easiest for everyone concerned to conclude that Anna was of unsound mind at the moment she took her own life, even as they condemned her act. The Church preferred it that way. Yet there was little doubt as to the real, scandalous implication of her demise. I had left for Germany in order not to have to share its long aftermath with my father. Now that he was dead too, I was no longer sure where I wanted to be. His death had rendered us both free from slavery to hers.

'On the way back to St Petersburg for his funeral I vowed that the train journey would be my final long voyage, whatever happened. How wrong I was, what distances lay ahead. I remember a procession of German towns and villages, the peasants on the platforms selling cups of water, pretzels stacked high on long sticks, paper cones of redcurrants and late cherries. The fruit was shrivelled, insanely sweet from the sun. The bread was decorated with zigzags of salt. It made you want to drink gallons, so you parted with your last coins for enamel cups handed through the train windows. We stood for hours in Berlin. When we crossed the Imperial Russian border and stopped in Warsaw I felt I was already at home, yet home was still hundreds of miles away. One forgets the vastness of Russia, how small it makes other countries feel.

'It was only June, but the plains were so parched that the whole world seemed to be on the verge of some great, all-consuming fire. I felt a searing pain when I first noticed Cyrillic inscriptions on station platforms, a sense of years lost, of having missed a Russian youth, something I did not even think I had wanted. Russia was arid and dusty, halfway through what turned into five rainless months. Evenings melted away as we moved north, until at night there was just a continuous dusky, rosy light. I had not seen it in such a long time that I had forgotten what it was. White nights, I half whispered, as the memory returned. White nights, summer heat, and my father is no more, on ice somewhere in St Petersburg.

'The funeral went on for hours, the liturgy, the speeches, finally, for some unknown reason, even a military band, its sound tinny and desolate in the heat. There was a honeyed smell of lime trees high above the grave, the buzz of bees. On the ground, just the tang of melting candles. Everything felt sticky and thirsty at the cemetery that day. St Petersburg: there is no better place in the world in which to be dead. But the living sweltered. The wreaths were shrivelling before our eyes, white turning yellow, red turning rust, as though an invisible fire was consuming us all. It was impossible to mourn my father while all eyes were on me. Instead, I planned a letter to Gutschmid wrapping up my affairs in Tübingen. I knew already I was not going back to Germany, although I had left everything and everyone there expecting a temporary absence.

'My father's coffin was open.

'"Accept, O Lord, the soul of your slave Alexei," chanted the priestly choir, voices plumbing the depths that only the Russian basses seem capable of. I looked at my father's waxen face, his grey beard, his stern features. I bent down to kiss his hand when instructed. His skin was warm, not from life but from the heat.

'Annie, my dear little sister, bent down to kiss my father's hand too, and sobbed although he was nothing to her, although he had been responsible for her own father's death. The Vronskys had not wanted to know her. My father took her in, in the first flush of his martyrdom, but then left her to the nuns. She came to look like a nun too. She was twenty one and should have been married for three or four years already, according to the Russian custom. Marriage seemed unlikely now.

'Then the casket was closed and he was no more.

'"We have only a little time to please the living. But all eternity to love the dead," Annie whispered, throwing a handful of dust onto the roses which shrouded the descending coffin, then wiping her gloves against her long black skirt. I had not wanted to please him while he was living and I certainly did not intend to love him dead, not for an eternity, not for a minute. Pity, yes, always, for the three of them, as for the two of us. I squeezed Annie's hand. She and I now had only each other, and her life, whatever happened, was marked out to be more difficult than mine, for, cruelly, my half-sister was a bastard and I was not.'

'And afterwards?' I asked. 'You stayed on in Russia because of Annie?'

'Not just because of her. A kind of inertia, perhaps: I could not move on. But I did feel a sense of duty for Annie, and guilt that I had never thought of her in Germany. We stayed on the Oblonskys' country estate that summer and moved back to my father's house when the rains finally came. I took a modest job at the Imperial Public Library. I looked after the manuscripts in the collections established by Count Korff, while Annie looked after the household. Some years later, already in her late twenties and an old spinster, she married a country doctor called Zaytsev, a friend of an acquaintance of mine. Dr Hare – not an aristocratic name.

'It was matchmaking, pure and simple, but Annie was happy to go. Her Hare took her to Suzdal of all places. I think she had three sons and a daughter, but we lost touch. The little Hares, descendants of Anna and Vronsky, that other Alexei. Isn't it strange, dear Albertine, to think that they may still be somewhere in the old country, that they may be suffering or making others suffer? When you read about Russia nowadays, there seems to be no other option.'

He paused. I wondered if he was going to say something about present-day Russia. In the letters pages of *The Times* and *Le Monde* people argued endlessly about Communism, about Stalin. Some said he was a dictator, worse than Hitler.

There were also many Communists in Britain who saw the Soviet Union as a model society, the only way ahead. Not as many as there were in France.

'I find it impossible to hate them, these Soviets, these new Russians,' Monsieur Carr said. 'I saw footage of the Victory Parade in Moscow in June 1945. Alexei took Gigi and me to the Electric on the High Road to see a film and before it, in the newsreels, there was the Kremlin, Red Square, the soldiers, mere boys with their wide, familiar Russian faces, marching. My mind whispered that they were Bolsheviks, but my heart saw the faces of my people, after all these years, only my people. Even the marches were familiar: the cymbals were striking the Russian beat. Red stars on their hats, yes, but my people. Do you feel this about the French, Albertine?'

'The only face I see when I say *my people* is my husband's. I do think of Paris sometimes. But I have no one there any more and I am growing to like London,' I said, buying time, out of wishful thinking more than conviction. 'I like the resilience and the modesty of the English. It is strange to think that I am married to an Englishman, odd, but not totally unexpected in this new Europe of ours.'

'You don't have to answer my question, but are you happy here?' he asked.

'I feel disoriented,' I said. 'What does my happiness matter? I feel I owe it to my husband. I mean I owe it to him to be happy. So many people have lost everything in the past eight years. So many have died.'

'You survived,' Monsieur Carr said. 'I thought of that after I had this stroke. The value of survival. At first, I couldn't walk and I could barely talk, but my languages came back, even the languages I will never need again.

Things do get better. The only correct thing to say in the face of death is: not today.'

I continued to think about our conversation on the train home. In its lingering fragments it revealed itself as much more important than I had thought as we sat in that bay window and the sun slowly dropped behind the roofs of Bedford Park. I went straight to Albie's study when I returned to Earl's Court. Taking off just my gloves, still in my overcoat, I took his typewriter out of its case and positioned it among the piles of memoranda and official letters: *On His Majesty's Service*, over and over again.

A heavy, upright machine – an Imperial 50 – it was the very model, in war paint rather than black, on which I used to type up hundreds of case histories on index cards at the hospital in Alexandria. Even in the midst of conflict, the British maintained a perfect bureaucracy. There were some advantages to it, I thought; it had brought me to my husband.

I tightened the ribbon, shifting the carriage-return lever. There it was again, the familiar sound of the bell that had measured, with its steady beat, so many of my Alexandrian afternoons. I inserted a clean sheet of paper and started typing. Soon it was like sewing, a tick-tock, an immersion, but now with a kind of euphoria behind it. The writing felt like something that I alone could do.

I noted everything Monsieur Carr told me, in English, as fast as I could, while I still remembered it. I would polish the words, worry about spelling later. At some stage we might continue to read *Madame Bovary* again, but this business seemed so much more pressing. I would write his memoir for him.

Halfway through my typing there was a blackout. Power cuts were so regular that I ceased to register them as interruptions. I took a candle out of the top drawer of Albie's desk. We had them at the ready, with boxes of matches, in every room. I continued as the air around me grew colder, until I typed that phrase 'You survived.' I shifted the lever and covered the two words with a line of crosses, writing myself out of the story.

6

The Wild Mane

It was only when I went into the bedroom hours later that I knew Albie had returned. There was the curve of his hip under the eiderdown, the sound of slow breathing. He appeared to be asleep, but raised the cover to beckon me under when I approached. He let out a little yelp when he felt my hands, fingers as cold as blocks of ice. I tried to embrace him, but he caught my palms under his upper arms and squeezed them.

'I did not mean to wake you up,' I said. 'I had no idea you were back.'

'It's not me,' Albie said. 'It's a burglar. Didn't you see his overcoat in the entrance hall?'

He turned on his back and we rested as an occasional crescent of light illuminated the ceiling whenever a car passed in the street below. My hands grew warmer. I felt the slimness of his body, the parallel lines of his ribs. We tended to forget how thin we were under the many layers of clothing we wore all the time. His face was etched by exhaustion, his eyes sunken. He reached for the alarm clock on the bedside table and fiddled with it.

'I won't be needing this tomorrow,' he said.

'How was Berlin?' I asked. 'If it was Berlin.'

'The flight was awful,' Albie said. 'I think I was the only person on board who wasn't sick. And that includes the crew. So much turbulence, we thought we were going down over the North Sea, the whole shebang. The landing was, if anything, even worse. And it took longer to drive up from Croydon than to fly over from Europe. My car broke down halfway, and I sat inside it for an hour waiting for it to be fixed, on a slip road above the railway line, watching a unit clearing the line into Victoria, poor buggers. Soldiers, prisoners of war with them. I heard the orders passed on in German and Italian. Balham, Streatham, Tooting, don't even ask where I was, Ber. I'm sick of snow, sick of this bloody war.'

'But Berlin?' I persisted, not bothering to correct him. Not saying that it was twenty-one months since the war had ended. I counted them always, counted the months.

'Ah, Berlin, Ber, my dear' Albert said. 'Like London but worse. Rubble everywhere. Everyone hungry, although the black market is thriving there too, better than here: German efficiency. And everywhere these pathetic allotments. I saw women using ice picks to dig a few potatoes out of the frozen soil of the Tiergarten. And so many people whisper that it was better under Hitler. Even to me, an Englishman, in a jazz club, after a few drinks. Can you imagine what they say to each other when we are not listening?'

'What about you?' I said. 'I don't care about the Germans. How was your work?'

'So much of it is just tedious administrative stuff, endless meetings full of jargon and acronyms, details you think are of little consequence, and then suddenly the Russians or the bloody French take offence and all hell breaks loose. Barricades go up, permits are revoked or someone threatens to let one damn obersturmführer or another slip away to Spain or Argentina. And you realise that the boring stuff is important, that you are walking a bloody tightrope – one wrong word, not even your word, a wrong nuance chosen by the interpreter, and the entire thing collapses. Bang. The whole of Germany is like that. The Russians don't trust us; they want to run it. The French don't want any Germany at all. They'd rather see it in pieces, as it was before Bismarck. Five wars in eighty years, they say. A country which starts five wars in eighty years forfeits the right to exist. The Americans have more patience with the Krauts than any of us, but it's easy for them, fat buggers. Why am I telling you all this? What were you typing in that room? A secret memorandum to Stalin? On my typewriter?'

'I was writing up Monsieur Carr's story. I have this plan, silly perhaps, to write his memoir for him. For his descendants, I mean. In the first person. Does that make sense? In French, we call an invisible writer, such as I would like to be in this case, a *nègre littéraire*.'

'A ghostwriter,' Albie suggested. 'I believe that is what they call them now, in America.'

'I prefer the English version to the French. A ghost, yes.'

I started sketching the details of Monsieur Carr's life. Albie listened for a while but then his breathing slowed down and he was asleep again. The circles under his eyes were darker than the darkness in the room. His skin was dry and pale, all the Egyptian light washed out of it, but so was mine, so was everyone's. So many Londoners who had had exotic wars were now pallid and looked more strained than they had in wartime. We survived, Monsieur Carr had said. Was it so important to survive? I had doubted this, before.

Outside, London was eerily quiet, nursing its own ruins, its own scars. In the morning, when the city started moving again, there would be men like Albie on every street, in every train. If their sleeves or trouser legs were empty, you could begin to guess the wounds they carried.

I did not tell Monsieur Carr about my plan when we next met. Not yet, I thought. If he knew what I was planning, he could become self-conscious, censor himself, tell his story differently. I asked what had happened when Annie left and he found himself living alone in his father's house.

'Let me tell you about London first,' he said. 'I have been mulling over that night at the Electric Cinema since we parted. I have forgotten the film – it could have been any old comedy – but I cannot forget the Pathé News that came before the main feature: the national anthem, that parade from Moscow, then a report about a terrorist attack in Jerusalem. Alexei had just returned from Palestine. There were bombings there all the time, though the worst – the King David Hotel – had not happened at that stage. You could see that Palestine had changed Alexei. He and I talked about exile when we came out of the cinema; the meaning of a homeland.

'"I am the only English person here," Gigi said suddenly as we were walking along the High Road. He had, until that moment, been kicking a bottle top along the way.

'That made me sad, Albertine, and I could not quite understand why. The child was half English and only a quarter Russian, and I was to blame for the fact that he had an English surname, yet I wanted my grandson to feel all Russian. Is that not perverse?

'Alexei could see that I was about to say something, and he jumped in.

'"So you are, Gigi. You are the only one without even a trace of an accent. But you are also a citizen of the world.

When you grow up, one's nationality will not be nearly as important as it seems now."

'Hearing himself described as a citizen of the world, the boy beamed with visible pride and looked at me for approval. I nodded. I liked this cosmopolitan ideal, yet I still wanted him to feel Russian first. I felt very old, and defeated in some odd, intangible way. Can you begin to understand this, Albertine?'

'I am not sure I can,' I said. 'I agree with your son. Albie talks about Europe, but I find even that claustrophobic. Citizen of the world seems so much better. The only way to raise a child.'

'Perhaps I am too old to change. I was sixty when we arrived in England in 1924,' Monsieur Carr said. 'Too late to begin a new life, too early to die, I thought already on our strange ferry crossing from Ostend. My wife was forty-four, Alexei had just turned twenty. He was tall, my son, lanky like a stick insect, and with the brittle, evanescent smile of someone who had known suffering too young. I worried that I could soon become a burden to him.

'Our little family, the three of us, sat on the ferry to Dover – the *Ville de Liège*, the boat was called – at a metal table screwed to the floor, a circle of battered suitcases around us on the deck, like the collapsing ruins of a pagan temple. We shared a single egg sandwich and a cup of beef tea, the cheapest meal available in the ship canteen. It tasted like infirmary food. Perhaps it was; the vessel had been a hospital ship. My wife took a single bite and chewed it for long minutes, staring ahead as though she had the task of spotting land.

'Everything around us was grey: the sea, the sleet, the screeching gulls, the sky above. It was January, but nothing that a Russian would recognise as winter, not like this one now. An English January, kind to the body, cruel to the soul. I did not know English winters then. Even those famous white cliffs of Dover, when they finally emerged in the drizzly mist, were grey and forbidding, so that you wondered what kind of world lay up there, enveloped in layers of fog, as though we were arriving at the opening lines of some version of *Jack and the Beanstalk* created especially for the survivors of the Soviet Revolution.

'We had little money and a lot of worthless papers, and we persisted in thinking – seven years after the first shots were fired from the *Aurora* at the Winter Palace – that we were going back to Russia soon, within a year or two at the most. Our fellow passengers looked at us, sometimes enquired about the strange language we were speaking and, when we said it was Russian, nodded without surprise. We were not even the only Russians among some hundred-odd passengers on board. As we sailed towards England, a small, bird-like man, a Russian Jew from Riga, came up to inform us that Lenin had died, that Lenin's body was, as he spoke, on the train from Gorki to Moscow.

'"Believe me, *cher* Prince," the man said to me in the canteen while I waited for our meagre ration, "in two or three years it will all be over, this experiment. The Soviet state will vanish, will seem like a bad dream, and your people will be back in power, back in the red fort."

'He must have heard us speaking French and Russian to each other, yet I am not sure why he had decided that I was a prince, or who he thought my "people" were. I don't think he could have deduced anything from the look of our small, exhausted trio. Our clothes were worn and we were permanently hungry, not because we had no money but because we did not dare spend what little we had. And although we were not spending it, money seemed to be melting away. The only treasure we possessed was an address in Kingston, that of Hannah Wilson, my mother's ward, my daughter-in-law's grandmother. Mrs Jenkins told you about her.'

'So you stayed in touch?' I asked. 'It must have been – what? – half a century since she left Russia ... and she was a small girl when she left.'

'For a long time after my mother died and Hannah was sent to England by my father, she used to write to us once or twice a year: a Christmas card, a short letter in Russian just so as not to forget the language and the alphabet. She married and changed her family name; she had children of her own, but she still signed herself Hannah Wilson, anxious that we might have forgotten her. The last card we carried with us in 1924 was old, fifteen years old at least. The chances that Hannah would still be living at the same address were infinitesimal we thought, but it was as good a place to start in this new exile as any. We had other addresses in London, but no more reason to believe in their usefulness. No one here owed us anything, except Hannah Wilson, perhaps.

'But I rush ahead again, dear girl. You asked how I coped alone after my sister Annie married. That is a much lovelier story. I met Tonya. I met my wife.'

'How old were you then?' I asked. We would return to England, I knew.

'Thirty-four, almost. It was in 1898, my fifth year at the library. I was probably the first person in my family, in God knows how many generations, to look for a job rather than be offered a paid sinecure on a silver salver, certainly the first not to see that as a personal tragedy. Long before the Revolution, I was an aspirant bourgeois. It's neither the proletariat nor the aristocracy, but the professional middle classes that will inherit the earth. I saw that in Germany.'

'It is so poignant, funny almost, to think of Anna Karenina's son as a librarian,' I said. 'Although it sounds like a modest way to describe what you did, the kinds of books and manuscripts you were handling.'

'I prefer librarian to curator or palaeographer, although both of those might be more appropriate,' he said. 'The library treasures were such that they made the Tübingen collections look provincial and meagre by comparison, as if to contradict von Gutschmid. The manuscript holdings alone ran to thousands of pages in every language and alphabet imaginable – enough work to keep generations of palaeographers busy. I spent my days deciphering, copying and dating, happy to think of this work as my destiny.

'Not far from the Tsarskoye Selo railway station, there was a printing press run by a Frenchman by the name of Angevin. His family had come to Russia during the reign of Catherine the Great. Work took me to him several times a month, sometimes for several hours at a time. The library had commissioned a print edition of an early Russian chronicle. The line setting was laborious. You had to possess a steady hand to insert a metal sort in the right place, a sharp eye to spot an error, and you had to be a pedant to enjoy all this. I certainly was. The work suited and soothed me. I took hours poring over each forme, over each page.

'Angevin was convinced I had printing in my blood. One of the earliest printing presses in St Petersburg was Hartung's, like our original family name. This was a coincidence, but a meaningful one. I would have been happy as a printer, away from political turbulence and from the storms men and women create for each other. There might also have been something of my father in me, the thirst for the safety of dead things, for the mastery you can achieve only over that which doesn't change, doesn't move. You find it in people who collect stamps, coins or butterflies, or who paint lead models of soldiers. Indeed, they are usually men, such people, bright, intelligent, decent men, not at their ease in the world of women.'

'I understand that,' I said. 'The wish for safety, I mean. Like my hospital index cards. You must have been so lonely, nonetheless.'

I did not want to ask a direct question about women, about love, but my meaning was clear. Whatever damage his mother had inflicted, she could not have extinguished all desire.

'It might not surprise you, and forgive the openness of an old man,' he said, 'to hear that I was still a virgin at thirty-three.'

He had understood me well. The admission was shocking. From the speed with which he rushed to explain it, I could see that he knew.

'I did not find women unattractive,' he said. 'I did not grow up to hate them because of my mother's transgression. I did not wish to punish any woman for my mother's sins, nor was I one of those men who seek to have their prejudices confirmed in brothels.

'I fell ill soon after I saw mother that last time, on my ninth birthday. I developed a raging, delusional fever which lasted for days. In that time, I seem to have repressed my memory of her – my first-hand memory, I mean – only to replace it subsequently with other people's accounts, with false histories. She died, I was told, in a tragic accident. No one ever mentioned suicide. I was not allowed to attend her funeral and I never knew the location of her grave. I don't know it to this day. Although I missed her, I can't say that I mourned her. At first there were moments when I thought that she was still alive, that her death was another lie told by my father. By the time I was fourteen, I could no longer recall the sound of her voice or the image of her living face.

'Others would have forgotten her too, I am sure, but for Count Tolstoy and his novel. "Was there a real Anna?" people asked, as though they had every right to know. "Was it your mother?" It was impossible to offer an answer that would satisfy. If I said "Yes, it was my mother," they laughed it off as a presumption, a denial of Tolstoy's genius. If I said "No, Tolstoy's Anna is someone quite different," they kept finding more and more parallels between my mother and Anna Karenina, until they had proved that there was no significant difference between reality and fiction. You should not be surprised that I preferred to spend every hour in the library, away from the chattering of the intelligentsia. You would have thought there were more important things to keep them preoccupied.

'I often walked after work, to clear my head, to fill my lungs with fresh air. Many cities are called the Venice of the North, but St Petersburg alone deserves the title. I particularly liked the Fontanka embankments and the reflections of palaces in water. The Yusupovs, the Sheremetevs, the Mikhailovskys, the Beloselsky-Belozerskys: their buildings were stunning, surpassing perhaps even those built by the Venetians. And their names represented my father's Russia. Alexei Karenin knew them all, but this was no longer my world. I doubt if any of these old princes, if they happened to look out of their silk-lined coaches, would have guessed who I was.

'One day, while I was crossing the Anichkov Bridge, I found myself walking behind a woman with a little boy. He was holding an ice cream, tilted so precariously that I became transfixed by the sight, expecting the scoops to drop any moment.

'"Dear Kutik," I heard the woman say, "be careful with that cone – hold it up or the strawberry ice will stain your suit."

'I used to have an almost identical little sailor suit. I remembered it well. In the sixties, such suits for boys were still a strange quirk of fashion brought over from England. My mother spoke English and liked the English ways, but I was embarrassed when adults enquired about my costume, when they complimented her on the fine serge collar or the hat, which I hated even more than the suit itself, when they pinched my cheek and called me the little Prince of Wales. I had no idea where this Wales was. I wanted to dress like all the other children.

'"Kutik": that is what Mother used to call me. The two syllables surfaced from some recess of my memory and pierced my soul. It was as though they lifted an invisible dam. Details flooded back, many of them evidence of Mother's love. Time, unnoticed, had healed our rift. I no longer bore her a grudge. By the time you reach thirty, you realise that your parents are like you, fallible people, but not responsible for your failures.

'With my sister gone, the house felt eerily empty. If it had been too big for two of us, it was ridiculously large for one. I kept no more than three or four servants, and I barely saw even them. I now spent my free time searching for Mother's traces, room by room, desperate for the smallest object: a brush with a tangle of her hair, a needle with a length of thread she could have used while embroidering, a bottle of scent which had not completely evaporated. Father had done his best to remove all evidence of her existence.

'Of course, there were still people who remembered her, on both the Oblonsky and the Hartung sides, but I did not wish to talk about Anna to anyone. I wanted my own memories back, physical traces of our shared days. There was one locked chest under my father's bed. "Title Deeds", read the label. When I broke the lock, I saw that it was a box full of yellowing documents confirming ownership of dwellings and pieces of land. There were other things in it too: this portrait you see above us, taken out of its frame and folded carelessly; a handkerchief with her initials embroidered on it; several pieces of jewellery, including a rose-gold necklace with a portrait in enamel of a boy aged no more than four or five. At first I assumed that it was my father, but then I opened the locket and saw a lock of curly hair, my name and birth date inscribed behind it. I stared at the child as though it was an alien. My physical similarity with my father had diminished with age, but as a toddler I was clearly his: the same eyes, the same earnest, humourless expression.

'The resemblance troubled me. I now remembered how I had overheard Mother saying to Nanny that she found it difficult to look into my eyes because they were like his, that she felt I too was judging her. But I was too intimidated by my father then to see our physical similarity. I often strained to hear what she was saying to others about us when he wasn't there, and just as often I misunderstood her words. Wasn't it strange that her husband and her lover were both called Alexei, although the name was far from being that common in Russia? That she would leave one Alexei for another?

'I found a book inside that chest, bound in red morocco, my mother's book for children. She wrote it in Russian, although her written French was better, but the cover bore a French title. *La Crinière sauvage: The Wild Mane*. She wrote the story because she was desperate for something, anything, to do. It was like those carvings people make in prison, out of soap, or bones, out of bread when there is nothing else, depriving themselves of precious rations. I did not remember ever reading or even seeing her book before. The chest must have held the only copy, and God alone knows why my father had kept it.

'I spent that evening reading *The Wild Mane*, and then another evening reading it again, trying to hear my mother's voice from its lines. It was a story of a young man who owned a mare called Joujou, an animal he loved more than anything else in the world. The man came from a wealthy, aristocratic family. Their stables were legendary, filled with dozens of thoroughbreds. Yet he loved Joujou best and only she was brave enough to follow his every bidding. Eventually, he asked too much of her: he spurred her over an impossible jump and broke her back.

'You'd expect the man to have the poor creature put down. Instead, he nursed her for days and weeks. Although he had many grooms at his disposal, he fed Joujou and watered her himself. He spoke to her and brushed her coat. Slowly, she regained her strength. One morning, he went to the stables and heard a neigh from the box where the mare usually rested. There she was, standing, ready for the next race.

'Sentimental? Yes, of course. And how ... This was a woman who needed to believe in the healing power of love.

'My mother's story was the stuff of miracles and redemption, all too obvious and technically impossible. Yet it was also very well written. Her Russian was simple and unaffected, her eye for detail impeccable, and the effect was moving and poetic. Forgive her son his presumption, but I don't think I am biased. Had she been able to write and publish, she might have become as great as Anna Akhmatova.

'I was determined to have her narrative preserved for the future and I knew no one better than my printer by the Tsarskoye Selo station. I took the manuscript to him. I wanted a hundred numbered copies, and I wanted them as beautiful as they deserved to be. Angevin was as taken by my mother's writing as I was. We planned every detail together. He saw that this project was as important to me as – no, more important than – any medieval chronicle.

'There were ink drawings in my mother's copy, several simple vignettes drawn by her. Angevin suggested a properly illustrated volume. He mistook my hesitation for worry about the price of such an enterprise.

'"My daughter, Aimée Antoinette – everyone calls her Tonya – would be delighted to produce some sketches," Angevin said. "You don't have to respond before you see them. Gustave Doré, *Little Red Riding Hood* – we have a copy here – that is the kind of thing I have in mind. And I hope you will hear me out. Tonya is very young, and has little publishing experience, but she is talented. I hesitate to say this, even as talented in the art of drawing as your mother was in her writing. And her contribution won't add to the cost of this project."'

'And this young woman, this Aimée Antoinette Angevin, became your wife?' I asked.

'Yes,' he said, happy that I had guessed so quickly, although it took so little effort. 'Countess Hartung officially, known by everyone as Countess Karenin, now resting in a Chiswick cemetery as Tonya Carr.

'My dear Albertine, I spent most of my youth thinking that I would never marry, but that if I did, I would not choose a Russian woman,' he continued. 'Finally I married one who was nominally French, but who was, in her religion and her love of Russia, almost more Russian than I was. Tonya was sixteen years younger than me, although she mothered me and looked after me like someone much older than her years: it was her nature. And she had only sixteen years in England. She was killed in 1940, at the very beginning of the Blitz, painting one of those baroque corners of London that reminded her of St Petersburg. I feel guilty about that, for I brought her to England, and I encouraged her to start depicting something other than flowers. But the bombs were falling everywhere, and she was adamant about preserving with her paintbrush the memory of that which the Germans were destroying around us. It could have been this house, and it could have been both of us, and that would have been much better. At least she did not live to see Alexei sent to the Holy Land, to worry whether he would come back.'

'But you have not told me about your first meeting?' I worried about the chronology of my still-secret project.

'I leaped ahead again,' he said. 'Why is death so much easier to talk about than love? You are right to remind me. Our first meeting – if you could call it that – pre-dated even my early dealings with Angevin. When I first met Tonya, she was a girl of fifteen or sixteen and I had no idea who she was.

'Whenever Russian winter bit hard, I swapped my walks along the canals with visits to museums and galleries. One day at the Hermitage, one particularly grey, snowy day, when there was hardly anyone else in its galleries, I noticed a girl in a blue pinafore painstakingly copying Raphael's Madonna.

'She was concentrating so hard that she did not notice anyone around her, or anything beyond the canvas. The painting's golden frame makes its scale deceptive. The image is tiny. I stood behind the girl for some minutes, watching her work. Her copy was perfect, and she made it without hesitation, in a series of steady lines. There were uncanny parallels between her and the woman in the painting. Her pinafore was precisely the colour of the Madonna's robes. Her brown hair was parted in the middle, with the same severe, precise parting as the Madonna's, but made into a thick plait pinned up above her nape, like a shiny crown which had slipped down the back of her head. I wondered if the girl knew the likeness, if these touches were deliberate, but she seemed too unaffected for such premeditated action. She wasn't beautiful, but there was nobility in her smooth skin and in her gaze, a kind of grace in her movements. Her hands were beautiful. I couldn't take my eyes off them.

'I did not see the girl again, not until the morning when her father introduced her to me, yet I remembered her very well because I sometimes went back to stare at Raphael's picture. I kept finding details in the canvas that I hadn't noticed before – mysterious figures in the landscape, snow-capped mountains in the distance, a translucent ribbon on the Madonna's chest. Each time I looked at the Madonna's face, I saw the girl.

'And before you draw any conclusions, dear Albertine, don't jump to the obvious ones. No, I did not care for the virginal contrast with my own mother. What fascinated me was Tonya's immersion in the task at hand, her single-minded concentration on her work. This tells you of my own innocence, my ignorance, but I had up to that point considered such dedication unfeminine, possibly even impossible in a woman. Women chatter with one another, I thought. Only a man could be so dedicated to his work. How foolish of me.

'Then I saw Tonya's sketches for my mother's book. Her father was right: she was a formidable talent. His reference to Gustave Doré was not misplaced. The sketches were glorious to behold, and, just as importantly, there was depth in them, there was darkness and longing, enough to add to the thrill of reading my mother's book if you were an adult, yet not so much darkness as to deter a nine-year-old boy. Tonya's sketches did not take anything away from the story; on the contrary, they made you want to read and reread it until you understood the miracle at its heart.'

'I would love to see those illustrations,' I said. 'Your wife's work – there are so many examples of it in this house – seems to me so beautiful. She was clearly an astonishing talent. Yet her subject is always dead – *nature morte*, the French say.'

'Still life, in English,' he said. 'Still, life: that is how I think of it now. It was not so much about death – she was different from me in that – as about stillness and silence, I believe. She became so anxious about change that she suffered sleepless nights over decisions as insignificant as buying a new toothbrush.

'She had once possessed the rarest of skills in depicting horses and people in movement: the arching of a foot or lifting of a hoof, the tensing of the smallest muscle. She painted compulsively in later life, but you are right, Albertine, her subjects ceased to move. She had lost the gumption that had once been her defining trait. Her youthful self-confidence had all drained away. When she illustrated my mother's book, Tonya was an inexperienced young woman; her youth made her art exceptional.

'I was happy to commission the book with Tonya's illustrations, happy to pay the asking price. Now that I knew the extent of her skill, and that the cost of her contribution was thrown in, the amount appeared modest in the extreme. Angevin called his daughter to meet the patron. He spoke to her in French while she was still only the sound of approaching footsteps.

'"Do come to meet the Count, Tonya," he said, and she emerged into the room. The recognition struck me like a bolt of lightning, and it made sense of the sketches.

'"The Conestabile Madonna," I almost shouted in Russian. "Of course."

'She looked at me, puzzled. She was a bit older than when I had last saw her, but instantly recognisable. Her plait now fell over her shoulder and down the front of the same blue pinafore, which was stained with dark paint. I assumed, as she wiped her right hand against it, that she was about to shake mine, about to apologise for her untidiness. Instead, she curtsied, twice. There were smudges of paint, like fingerprints, on her forehead and on her blushing cheeks, as though she had tried to smooth her hair before she met me.

'"Dr Hartung," I corrected her father in Russian, then smiled at her. I was still officially Hartung.

'"I prefer Doctor," I explained. I now blush at my pomposity, but I was driven by the silly idea that as a doctor I would be closer to her than as a count, as though I could ever be her equal.

'She was silent, clearly too shy to speak. I could not have helped.

'"And no need for a curtsy. Your drawings are beautiful. My mother would have been thrilled."'

'"Your mother was a great writer," Tonya finally said. "Her story made me cry each time I read it, and I read it many times while deciding which scenes to draw."'

'"No more talented as a writer than you are as a painter ..."'

'She blushed and offered a simple thank-you in return.

'"I am proud of Tonya's talent," Angevin said. "However, I wish she were more ladylike. Long hair, short mind, we Russians say, but that is not true of my daughter. Tonya's mind is a boy's mind. My daughter is too clever for a girl. And she behaves like a boy."

'The thought that he was speaking to Tonya's future husband would never have crossed old Angevin's mind. My title might have been tarnished long ago, and my working life might not have been suggestive of immense wealth, but I was a count and Tonya was a printer's daughter. In the eyes of St Petersburg, our marriage, when it happened, was the final nail in my father's coffin, one last, devastating consequence of my mother's act. We had slipped from dining with princes to marrying printers within a generation, the evil tongues wagged. The next generation would be marrying coachmen and market traders, they said. They were not far wrong, dear Albertine, even if it mattered so little in the end.

'And Tonya refused me, twice. She was an only child. Her mother had died in childbirth, and she believed that her duty was to look after her father and help him run his business. The father seemed not so much happy at the thought of her dedication as resigned to it. Angevin had no more power to resist Tonya's will than I ever had subsequently.

'As was the custom in the last century, even in its last decade, I approached the father to ask for his permission to marry the daughter. He was stunned but he gave it without hesitation, and yet he immediately added:

'"My dear Count, you know as well as I do that my consent is only a small step. You must now ask Tonya and I fear that you will be rejected even before you complete your question. Do not take it personally. Do not let it ruin our friendship and our business together."

'He knew his daughter well. When I summoned the courage, she stopped me in mid-sentence, exactly as her father had predicted.

'"Dear sir," she said, "it is impossible. Impossible. Please allow me to ask you not to repeat your proposal and to beg you not to let my response influence your relationship with my father. I am not free to marry – not you, not anyone."

'But I did repeat the offer – how could I not? – a year later, and then again three years on. Her father was dead, she was twenty-two and I had the new century on my side. Still, I expected her to say no. Instead, she accepted.'

He paused. I quickly rearranged the decades in my mind – the 1890s in St Petersburg, the 1920s in London. We were circling around the Great War, the Revolution, but that story would follow too, I was sure.

'What happened with Anna's book?' I asked.

'My mother's book could have sold thousands of copies, had I wanted to sell them. The hundred we printed went out to family and friends. Only one made it over to Britain with us. I sometimes think that it must be, again, the only copy of *The Wild Mane* left. I read it to my grandson. We take it out of tissue paper and open it on the dining-room table. My hands have been shaky since the stroke and I now hardly dare turn its pages.

'We wait for Alexei, my grandson Gigi and I, and sometimes, of a Sunday evening, my son reads his grandmother's story to us. My son looks like Alexei Karenin, all three of us do. Alexei fights his impulsive Oblonsky streak, his grandmother's inheritance, but I feel it when he reads, like something pulsating beyond his knowledge of himself.'

7

The Black Sea

Whenever I returned home from Chiswick, I typed the new sections of Monsieur Carr's memoir on separate sheets of paper. I noted his life's events in the order in which he told them, giving each sheet a heading with the place and the period he described, as close as I could guess them. The following day, I reread the typescript and highlighted the details that remained unclear: the names of people and places, family relationships, social events and concepts. The gaps in chronology were still vast, but many episodes from Monsieur Carr's life were coalescing into the chapters of a future volume.

Albie admired this display of efficiency. My work reminded him of our early days. When I walked out of the study – his study – at the end of an evening, I often found him working on his own papers at the kitchen table because he had not wanted to interrupt my typing. The first question he would ask on seeing me tended to refer not to the there and then, the usual small change of household business, nor to Monsieur Carr, but to some long-unmentioned Egyptian recollection.

'Do you remember that little *kafenio* by the hospital?' he asked, for example, and it was clear that he had been revisiting Alexandria in his memory. 'That Greek place serving the camel kebabs you loved so much? The owner who claimed to have been family friends with the Cavafys.'

'Mutton, definitely, not camel,' I said. 'You were too fond of ouzo to tell the difference, Colonel Whitelaw. The owner noted that you called me Cartier whenever you bossed me around about the menu, trying to order something other than those kebabs, Bertie when any of your friends were with us, and darling at the end of the evening.'

'You were like one of my men, Cartier,' Albie said. 'And I called most of them darling at the end of the evening.'

His eyes lit up and he raised his hand to touch my lips as I was about to respond.

'Behave yourself, Colonel Whitelaw,' I said. 'I hope you were not touching their lips like this.'

'Only when we were too close to the German lines to speak out loud.'

He laughed, like in the old days, but he was tired all the time, more tired than he ever was in Alexandria, and the effort he put into laughing was sometimes visible.

'Is anything wrong, Albie?' I asked when I noticed it.

'What could possibly be wrong?' he said. 'Why do you ask?'

I had no heart to tell him that he looked worn out.

As the bundle of pages grew thicker, and I looked forward to the next instalment, my enthusiasm for the Karenin narrative must have become catching. Monsieur Carr seemed just as keen to resume his story. He had a small notebook, and would produce it out of his pocket and stare at his notes scribbled in Cyrillic. Now he too was preparing for our sessions.

'We were talking about your marriage to Tonya,' I prompted. 'You proposed three times before she finally accepted.'

'Oh, yes, and our honeymoon.' He said this with such an infectious smile that I briefly worried he was going to reveal more than I really wanted to know.

'Tonya and I spent our honeymoon at the Tavrida, the Oblonsky villa on the Black Sea,' he said. 'I was never particularly fond of Uncle Stiva when I was a boy. He seemed guilty of exactly the sort of behaviour that people accused his sister – my mother – of. He was selfishly focused on his own pleasure, and he got away with it because he was a man. No one could be angry with Stiva for long, it seemed. So gregarious, everyone would say, and I came to hate the word. I wanted to be the opposite of gregarious.

'Yet after my mother died, Stiva changed. I would not say that he was any less dedicated to his own hedonistic pursuits, but he became more aware of the ways he made other people suffer, and he went to great lengths to be generous to everyone. It was as though he was bent on perpetual atonement despite the fact that he could not stop sinning. He showered me with gifts, secretly, when my father forbade every contact with the Oblonskys, and, after Father died, he treated me as though I was one of his own children. Everything he owned – although that was forever diminishing because of his inability to manage his affairs – was at my disposal, he kept repeating. I turned down most of his kindnesses, but I could not refuse the offer to take Tonya to the Black Sea, to spend a month at the villa.

'Except for an old gardener and his wife, the house remained empty for months on end in those days. Stiva loved the Crimea in his younger years. It was far from the bankers of St Petersburg and the bureaucrats of Moscow, he used to say, yet the women were just as beautiful, and the wine cellars just as great as at home. Stiva was sixty-two when I married, and the closest relation we had from that older generation. He had declared himself too old for coastal escapades. Aunt Dolly, his wife, had always favoured the countryside, and my cousins preferred to spend their summers in Europe. The younger Oblonskys were so taken by anything Western that even a provincial Austrian resort on the Adriatic was superior to the glories of Yalta. When he offered us the keys, Stiva expressed his hospitality in such terms that it sounded as though Tonya and I were doing the Oblonskys a favour.

'The Tavrida nestled on one of the finest slopes between Oreanda and Yalta, not far from the Tsar's estate at Livadia. Stiva described the villa as a "small affair", and so it was, if you compared it to the mansions which dotted the coast around it, but it was big enough to be fronted by a portico of six Corinthian columns, with a perfect white dome above them.

'"It doesn't seem right," Tonya said when we arrived, pressing her cheek against the white Crimean marble, staring at the palaces which rose above the pine forests around us like mounds of white sugar cubes. The expanse of water sparkled for hundreds of miles ahead. If you looked south, there was no land between us and Turkey.

'"It does not seem right for some people to possess all of this while the peasants starve. It is not right to own acres of forest, miles of coast, mountain peaks even ... and then not even bother to visit. Had I not married you, I would not have dreamed that a place like this existed."

'"But the Oblonskys possess only debts, Tonya. They are not wealthy any more," I protested.

'"I know, Sergei. Don't misunderstand me, please. The Oblonskys are kind people. Your aunt Dolly is a saint. But when the peasants also have debts, much smaller debts, they don't get to hang on to their possessions."

'I loved her indignation, her sense of justice. I thought of it as feminine and compassionate. I did not assume her anger to be even an atomic particle of the swell that was coming together into the wave that would eventually sweep away our world. Unlike Tonya, I was born into privilege. I could see the inequalities of our Russia, but I assumed them to be natural, God knows why, and I hoped that, like nature, Russia would gradually evolve into something more enlightened and just. The way England keeps transforming itself.

'Apart from that uncharacteristic outburst, we never talked politics, Tonya and I, not then, not later, when we were freezing in the single room of our palace that remained ours, listening to the gunfire outside. The Russians divide into those who never talk about politics and those who talk about nothing else. Tonya and I were of the former persuasion.

'That entire month of our honeymoon was cloudless. We swam off the silver beaches, read Pushkin to each other under the pines, and in the evenings, rather than go out to dine in fashionable new hotels, we sat by the water and listened to the waves whistling through the grottos.

'Tonya blushed when I called her my Nereid, but the silly, romantic name was apt, and not just because we were immersed in Pushkin. There was something unexpected about her that summer, something suddenly southern – the way she started combing rosemary oil into her hair, the way her tan steadily darkened under the sun and made her look as though she was part of the Crimean world, with a flash of a new knowledge in her eyes. I recognise that touch of the South in you. Something of Tonya's young self. Your French side, perhaps, although both of you denied it?'

'What do you mean?' I asked.

'Tonya's parents were French by distant ancestry, but she had never visited France. The only place she knew, before she married me, was St Petersburg. Her family had converted to Orthodox Christianity before she was born, but they were not devout. Your family history is the opposite of hers in some ways. You say that your people came from Poland, but Poland is nothing to you. You grew up in France. Your lips are the lips of a French speaker. Even your wrinkles, when you grow older, will be the wrinkles of a Frenchwoman: that repeated pout etches itself into the skin eventually.

'Here's what Tonya used to say: I am what I am. *Je suis ce que je suis.*' He tried to gather his lopsided lips into an exaggerated French pout in order to demonstrate the sound, but he produced an involuntary whistle instead.

'Yet she was no longer what she was.' I pursued the meaning instead of the sound. There was always something childish, something evasive in his wordplay. 'You said that Tonya had changed in the South. In the Crimea, I mean.'

'And so she had,' Monsieur Carr said. 'Just as we were beginning to think of our return journey, Tonya started sketching flowers. I remember the first drawing well. She looked at a cluster of flowering lilies in the Nikitsky Gardens, and asked if we could pause for a moment. She took a sketch pad out of her canvas bag, and while I held her parasol, she drew the curves of orange flowers, the dark spots and the heavy golden stamens around which the petals gathered. Her drawing was beautiful – more striking than her work before – for there was now something feminine and erotic about her lines. I asked her if she knew. She continued to draw, without raising her eyes from her work, her hands mapping the curved lines on the white surface.

'"I think I am pregnant, Sergei," she said.

'If I had been happy beyond measure during that entire month by the sea with her, I was now euphoric. The thought of seeing her child turned me into the most eager father you could imagine. That is how much in love I was.

'When we returned to St Petersburg, my euphoria persisted. Even the old house seemed to be rid of its ghosts. It was still too big for the two of us, but there was now a line of rooms on the first floor, whitewashed and empty, waiting to be turned into nurseries. It was as though the space itself was pregnant, awaiting the first screams of a newborn child. The Russians are superstitious. Nothing can be prepared until the child is actually there. My mother's salon, with its milky northern light, became Tonya's studio. She painted, unconcerned about the purpose of her paintings, for the sake of colour and motion.

'Then, just as her pregnancy moved into the fourth month, she lost the child. There was no warning. She bled for days, growing paler and unhappier. I worried that I would lose her. She had barely recovered when she became pregnant again, and lost another child, at the same stage and in the same way, this time in a wintry St Petersburg. I left for the library one morning and came back to find her bleeding and washing the rags in a freezing bathroom. She had dismissed the servants and suffered alone all day. She did not even summon a doctor. She did not want anyone to know, as though she was going through something shameful and humiliating, as though the servants would not have reached their own conclusions anyway. This time, as before, she blamed herself.

'"There is nothing wrong with you, Sergei," she repeated. Whatever I said, made her sob.

'In the days which followed the second miscarriage, she began to despair. Parenthood meant so much more to her than to me. I would have been happy without a child. And through all the tribulations, she painted these amazing, engorged flowers, crowns opening out towards the viewer, still beautiful, still disturbing.

'The third pregnancy did not happen until two years later. Tonya was so thin and so pale that I never believed it would end differently from the previous two. When it became visible, she refused to go out, fearing that people would pity her when she lost another child. Only when seven months had passed did we begin to hope.

'There was a flicker, then finally a glow in her eyes, something of that flame I remembered from Yalta. She got up before me and went to my mother's room to work. I can still see her, heavily pregnant, her shape outlined against the high windows and the naked branches outside. She was sketching and painting, dozens and dozens of flowers, pistils and anthers, sometimes from expensive bouquets I ordered from the glasshouses in Tsarskoye Selo, more commonly from images in her head. She exaggerated the filaments and the petals in a way which made the blooms look three-dimensional, reaching out of flat surfaces. Her work seemed more and more abstract and, in its way, more worrying for me. I did not know enough about art to see that Tonya was reaching for abstraction, decades ahead of her time.

'Before her due date, she cut up and burned all of her paintings. I watched her swollen fingers stuck in the handles of the scissors, her pregnant belly moving with effort and urgency, and I did not know how to reconcile her jollity with such wanton destruction. She seemed to rejoice in the act – folding and cutting the thick paper and seeing its edges blacken and curl moments before the flames burst through her lines.

'"These are the petals I was trying to draw," she would say, looking into the fire, her voice sing-song and joyous. "The bright colours I could not achieve."

'I am ashamed of my cooperation in her act. It is a strange thing, women's art. Our social position prevented Tonya from selling her pieces, but what do you do with the work in the end? There were folders and portfolios of it, so many that there was a kind of relief in its destruction. I am ashamed to admit that I felt it.

'I felt a similar sort of relief, mixed with other emotions, to be sure, but as distinct as a solo voice rising above a choir, at the surge of maternal love so obviously unlocked by my son's birth. There he was, a tiny wrinkled creature just released from the darkness of the womb, his head still caked with bits of Tonya's congealed blood, his cry as thin as that of a kitten, lying in my wife's arms, trying to latch on as she held his head against her breast with more tenderness than I could imagine possible. They seemed equally vulnerable. I knew that I would give my life for theirs in that moment, but I also thought: *enfin*. The French word was so startling when it came to me, so similar to the sound I expected to make, that I said it out loud.

'"Finally."

'My wife misunderstood. She assumed, mistakenly but reasonably, that I meant finally a son and heir, finally a child. She took it to be an unspoken rebuke to her for the long wait. I did not fully know my own sense in that first moment, but what I thought was this. Finally, Tonya's life will have a purpose. She will feel it has a purpose, and I won't have to worry about turning our world into something that seems worth fighting for. Finally. Because I could not do this. Because no one could. I am not sure why I worried about her despair more than I worried about mine. It might well be that some part of me took that lesson from my mother's death. That this world is a much harder place for women than it is for men.

'Russia was in turmoil, but the two of us were so deeply wrapped up in our own small family that we did not notice, or were unwilling to notice the signs. There was unrest, whispers of pogroms, endless arguments in the zemstvos; there were strikes, general strikes, mutinies and assassinations. Our son was learning to walk to the beat of marching crowds, learning to speak against the sound of street protests. Many of these processions unfolded below our windows, but their noise felt as distant as Manchuria.

'The best way to live in Russia is to close your eyes and keep them closed. Even when the city had no electricity and no newspapers, and even when we witnessed, on St Stephen's Day, thousands of people moving towards the Winter Palace, we pretended not to see. When the sailors mutinied on the *Potemkin*, my son was teething. The country teetered on the brink of a military dictatorship. The Tsar gave in. Things improved for a while.

'There would be havoc again. There would be chaos. We did not think that there would be another revolution, a much bigger revolution. The Russians were too deferential, we thought, despite all evidence to the contrary. I had witnessed the explosion of the anarchist bomb which killed the Tsar's grandfather, old Tsar Alexander, when I was seventeen. I was two and in the Summer Gardens with a nanny when they first tried to kill him. I believe that some of my earliest memories, now memories of memories, are linked to that attempted assassination: noises, panic, the crunching footfall on the gravel, an amorphous fear that if I fell I would be lost in the crowd, abandoned, unclaimed. Yet, even after all of that, I still managed to believe that Russia was improving, that it would soon be a great economic power the like of which the world had not seen. We ignore what we want to ignore, we forget what we want to forget.

'Our son's first word, after mama and papa, was *svet*: light. It took a while to understand that he really meant light, because so often there was none. He was our *svet*, our clever boy. He had an artistic sensibility, like his mother, but he was much better with numbers, and numbers interested him more. Although we made him study music and art, Alexei was never going to be an artist; that much was clear very early on.'

'Oh, thank you, Father, thank you kindly,' Alex Carr said as he stepped into the room.

'If you spy on us, Alexei, you deserve to hear whatever you hear. You mustn't make a habit of it. In fact, Albertine and I were just discussing Russian history. You are only an infinitesimal part of it, dearest boy.'

'Oh, I see. You two are now thick as thieves,' said Alex Carr.

'I promise you, Mr Carr, your father was telling me about the revolution in 1905.'

I lifted the notepad and pointed at a few lines scribbled as my aide-memoire, as though they proved something. Monsieur Carr took his tiny notebook out of his pocket and searched for something on its pages: 1905 perhaps.

'Yes, yes, I see,' Alex Carr said, raising his hand in the air like someone dismissing a tedious tradesman in a Middle

Eastern bazaar. 'Of course, dear Albertine. I trust you as much as I trust my own father.'

He unwound a scarf from around his neck, took his hat, gloves and coat off, laid them over the back of a chair, and sat next to the old man. Shoulder to shoulder, the two looked similar enough: one white-, one dark-haired, both thin-lipped, one with a slightly crooked smile, one with an incipient smirk. There was the smell of snow about the son, the smell of it melting against the wool. He had walked from his riverside office. He said something in Russian to his father.

'I am afraid that Albertine and I have been drinking tea all afternoon, dear boy. How about something stronger?' the old man responded in English. 'Some aqua vitae? None of your beer business.'

'You know you mustn't, Father,' said the son.

'I'll worry about what I mustn't when I am in my grave.'

Alex Carr disappeared and promptly returned with two thimbles and a frozen bottle of clear liquid. When his father frowned, he took another thimble from the pocket of his jacket.

'We keep our vodka buried in the back garden,' he said, noticing that I was staring at the thick crust of ice on the bottle. 'Along with a load of old Russian skeletons.'

He poured a measure for each of us.

'Let's drink *po-russki*, *à la russe*,' he said. 'Down in one.'

He tilted his head backwards, opened his mouth and upturned his thimble above it, to show me how it was to be done. There was something endearing about the gesture, the staged wilfulness of it; he was a shy, reserved man.

'To our friendship!' said the old man. Alex Carr refilled his own glass. We clinked the three thimbles and the men downed their drink. I couldn't. It tasted like acetone. They looked at me, then at each other. I drank rarely and I was no drinker of spirits, not beyond an occasional whisky which I barely sipped alongside Albie after his work. Monsieur Carr shook his head in disapproval. I wasn't drinking and I wasn't taking part in the toast.

'Let's try again,' said Alex Carr and refilled their glasses.

'To Russia,' he said.

'To Russia,' we responded.

I threw the liquid to the back of my throat. If Albie's peaty Scottish whisky tasted of ancient rains and smoky bonfires, this vodka was like an invisible fire. Burning was its only aftertaste.

'And again,' said Alex Carr, and he meant it.

'No, no,' I protested. The room was swimming around me, as though we were on a houseboat on the Thames.

He refilled our thimbles nonetheless.

'Your turn to offer a toast, Albertine,' said Monsieur Carr.

They stood up again, facing me, the old man propping himself with a stick in his right hand, holding the thimble up with his left, unsteady. The younger was so tall that looking into his eyes required a deliberate twist of the head upwards, in a way which often made me blush. I couldn't think of anything to drink to, anything to say. They stared at me, waiting.

'*À la silence*,' I finally said and downed my drink in one, ahead of them.

'To silence,' they repeated solemnly in English and drank up, then looked at me.

'What kind of toast is that?' said Monsieur Carr.

'You make us sound like some secret society,' said Alex.

'We are like one, now,' I said.

The armchair swam upwards to meet me.

'We must not, absolutely must not, do this again,' I almost screamed as Alex Carr affected another move to refill our glasses.

He refrained, sat down, took a pipe out of his pocket, fumbled with the tobacco, then lit it. The room filled with a sweet, malty smell. The book spines flickered gold and ochre in the reflected light of the fire. Through the open door I saw Mrs Jenkins as she laid the big table for dinner in the dining room. I heard the clinking of the silver and the china. On the walls behind her there were Tonya's flowers.

The old man dozed off. The son smoked, staring at nothing in particular. I looked at the painting above him, observing the similarity between him and his grandfather, yet also a definite difference: the full head of hair, the deep lines around Alex's mouth, a certain warmth that was surely his grandmother's.

I returned from Chiswick to find Albie writing in his study. He had put my typescript to one side of his enormous desk, pushed the typewriter further towards the window and was jotting something down in longhand. The house was so quiet that I heard the scraping of his pen against paper as I tiptoed in. His shoulders were covered with a tartan blanket.

'You startled me,' Albie said. I kissed the back of his head. His hair smelled of almond oil.

'Are you drunk, Cartier?' he asked.

'Not at all, Colonel,' I responded. 'Two small vodkas. My first two ever, I believe.'

I went to the kitchen to make his supper, but saw that he had already eaten and tidied up. The dishes were drying on the rack and the plates and saucers were arranged as neatly as table placements at the Ritz. When Albert made our bed it took some effort to get into it; everything was folded so tightly, straightened and tucked in. It was unusual, then, but we never wanted any hired help. Marrying a soldier had its advantages in housekeeping matters.

'This is beginning to look like an excellent book,' Albert called from the study. 'A fine biography. I hope you don't mind, but I read your Count's story. You left it on my desk. I noted down a few corrections in the margins. The sequence of tenses, Shepperton with two p's, that sort of thing.'

'Oh no, not at all,' I called back. 'I am so glad you like it. They are sweet, kind people.'

'And you've yet to meet the son's wife? Is she English?'

'English, yes. And no, I haven't met her. He takes events chronologically and tells them in detail, but then suddenly skips decades. You will have noticed my annotations. I will consult the son before I finally put it together. And I will have to read about Russia. I know so little of Russian history.'

I heard Albie moving around the room – several steps, then silence, then the sound of speech again. A fire engine wailed in the street outside; it was impossible to hear what he was saying. I went back to the study to find him standing by the bookshelves with a thick volume.

'I was just about to show you this. *A Concise History of Russia and the Soviet Union*,' he said.

That was Albie too. The moment you identified a problem, he found the most logical solution and took appropriate steps to find a remedy. All I had to do now was to read the book. The concise history.

'Thank you. I'll give it a go,' I said. I flicked through the final pages. I could not get used to the English habit of putting the contents of the book at the beginning. This ended with the index. Even just skimming it, I picked up a few of the names Monsieur Carr had mentioned: the Oblonskys were there, the Sheremetevs, the Vronskys, the Yusupovs. It was daunting, the history of Russia, running to hundreds of pages, even in this so-called concise form. I put the volume down on Albie's desk, next to my slim ghostwriting endeavour.

'It's the last day before their Lenten fast,' I said, continuing the conversation from where we had left it. 'This Sunday. The fast leading up to the Orthodox Easter. They start fasting on Monday. Clean Monday they call it. We are invited to a party in Chiswick: a kind of Dimanche Gras. There will be blinis, sweet and savoury, and more blinis. And a profusion of vodka, I suspect. Would you like to come?'

Albie walked up to me and pressed my body to his against the doorframe.

'Delightful Mrs Whitelaw,' he said, 'forgive me, but I can't think of anything I'd like less. A party in Chiswick with my wife's employer and his son's family: a suburban soirée, only with princes. Would you hold it against me if I said no? I'll happily stay at home and read.'

He noticed my disappointment.

'You must like them a lot to want to see them at the weekend – unpaid overtime. Either them or ... the blinis, is that what you said you'd be eating?'

'Blinis, yes, Russian pancakes. It's customary.'

'Blinis and vodka. I see you'll soon be a Russian expert, sweet Albertine. Even without reading my history book. Are you picking up the language too?'

'*Da, Al'bie, konechno*. Yes, Albie, of course,' I said, imitating the Russian words I heard from Mrs Jenkins, with their softness around the L and the N, feeling the weight of his body against mine, every button, every seam.

I pushed him away gently and walked up to the window. There was a garden square below, enclosed by a black iron railing, like a guard of spears – one of the few that had survived the gleaning of metal in the war. In the square, there were naked trees and skeletal bushes, with park benches and the grilles of litter bins by the pathways. During my first summer in London I had watched the square from this same window, and had often heard the voices of people who were invisible under the lush crowns. I imagined lovers sitting on the benches, speaking softly to each other: what terms of endearment do the English use when they exchange sweet nothings? Then the leafy crowns turned gold, and thinned. The rains came, and after the rains snow. Everything fell silent. I wondered why I had raised my glass of vodka to silence this afternoon. There was too much silence already.

A car waited in the street below, and in it sat a couple, staring ahead, not looking at each other as they talked. The headlights were off. The snow accumulated on the windscreen wipers: a dusting first, then two soft white eyebrows on a worried face. What were they talking about?

Albie stood behind me and pulled at the pin which held up my hair. He caught the coil before it dropped onto my shoulders, wrapped it around his wrist, lifted it and kissed the nape of my neck, then held the pin between his lips. He separated the hair into three strands, and plaited it, very slowly. He coiled my hair back again, took the pin out of his mouth and fastened the coil to the back of my head, exactly where it had been, but now tightly plaited where before there had been an untidy bun.

'There you are, Princess, as demure as you always are, but now Russian.'

'You confuse me, Albie. How do you know how to do this?' I touched the back of my head, the hard, intricate coil of the plait.

'The usages of the army in peacetime – you'd be surprised. Prewar cavalry: I learned the skill on horses. I am good with my hands like that.' He smiled. 'The male and the female are closer than you think.'

He pulled the pin out again, let my hair fall on my shoulders and then slowly uncoil itself under its own weight. The car turned its lights on and made a wide U-turn in the street below, bathing us for a moment in its yellow light, leaving serrated cuts in the virgin snow. I picked up the *Concise History of Russia and the Soviet Union* from the desk and opened it. There was Albie's signature in the top right corner of the inside front cover, his handwriting more childish than the age suggested by the subject matter. Below it was a year, a class number that said little to me, and a school crest stamped on the bottom of the page in black ink, its motto too blurred to read in the semi-darkness.

Albie dragged his index finger over it.

'"*Manners makyth man*,"' he read to me. 'William of Wykeham, the founder of my old school down in Winchester. You would not believe it, Ber. How alone I was, and in how many places, before I met you.'

'And now ...' I started but had no will to finish the sentence.

I have never been so alone, never so alone so often, as since I met you, I was going to say. Is it England, perhaps? I had dozens of friends in Paris, in Bucharest, even in Alexandria. Always someone at the other end of the table, at the other end of the telephone line. Now, most of the time, no one but you. And you are so often away. Or distant, even when you are here.

'*Toska* is one of those Russian words,' Monsieur Carr had said, 'which have no English equivalents. It means "a dull ache of the soul".'

I am becoming a bit of a connoisseur of *toska*, I was going to say. But then you plait my hair like this and you confuse me.

8

Forgiveness Sunday

'Do stay as long as you like, Ber,' Albie said. 'I promise you that I'll be happy. That might not be the right word. I assure you that I'll be napping. At least until four.'

It was the Sunday we were invited to Monsieur Carr's pancake party. I had felt disappointed that Albie was unwilling to join me, but the sight of him was disarming, still in his pyjamas so late in the morning, a newspaper under his arm and a bottle of milk in his hand, as he prepared to return to bed when I left. He needed rest.

'What happens at four?' I asked.

'A couple of colleagues will drop by in the afternoon,' he said. 'Stanford and Abercrombie. I don't know if you remember them from Alexandria. The Europe working party we are called now. We wrote a report last month and now we've had our responses, we are to write responses on our responses.'

'It never ends, does it?' I said.

'No, it doesn't. Never,' he agreed. 'You know how much I love administration. I was born to be a man of inaction. Have as much fun as you can have with your Russians, Ber. For my sake too.'

He saw me off to the door. When I was in the street, I turned back and I saw him looking at me through the tall front window. He took a waggish swig from his milk bottle and waved.

There was a chain of paper ribbons between the gate and the front door of Monsieur Carr's house – a sequence of simple hoops in different colours, made by a child. Lanterns hung from bare branches. I knocked and the front door gave; it was not locked. The house smelled of cinnamon and baked apples. I heard voices from the back garden. Five people. Monsieur Carr, Alex Carr, Mrs Jenkins. With them was a striking blonde woman in a white fur hat, and a boy of eight or nine. They were putting finishing touches to a snowman, a perfect specimen made of three large snowballs, with coal buttons, a carrot nose and a small green apple which the housekeeper had preserved into the depths of winter and which was now halved for his eyes, wide open to match a wide coal smile. A big tin saucepan hat gave him the look of a Byzantine dignitary.

'Mrs Whitelaw,' said Alex Carr when he saw me, 'meet Mr Snowy.'

I curtsied and shook a twig hand. The boy laughed. He had his grandfather's and father's eyes and his mother's hair, with a hint of something darker in the composition, a suggestion that the blondness wouldn't last, that he might revert to the Carr type.

'I am Gigi, Mrs Whitelaw. My real name is Sergei, like my grandfather's, but everyone calls me Gigi,' the boy said and he shook my hand with the exquisite manners of someone much older. He wore a pair of huge sheepskin mittens.

'And I am Diana,' said the woman. 'I have heard so much about you.'

She surprised me by embracing me so firmly that her white fur hat fell off her head. Her eyes were green – an improbable green, like those of the snowman, the bright green of Granny Smith apples.

'Albertine,' I said. 'Delighted to meet you finally.'

'What is such a beautiful woman doing married to someone like me?' Alex Carr said, guessing my thoughts. 'I am afraid I have no answer to that, dear Albertine. And where is your husband? I was so looking forward to meeting him.'

'Work,' I said. 'Work, unfortunately.'

'He should be careful,' said Diana Carr. Her voice was sweet and dark, like heather honey. My ear was not sufficiently attuned to the nuances of English pronunciation, but I thought that she had a trace of London in her accent. Gigi sounded like his father: neutral, educated, unplaceable.

The afternoon was enchanted, bathed in the almost horizontal light of the winter sun. At dusk, we set out for Tonya Carr's grave. It was customary to visit your dead on the day and ask for forgiveness, Monsieur Carr said.

'We have so many, but Tonya is alone in English soil. You start belonging to the land when you bury someone you love in it. We would have taken the sledges in the old country,' he added as we squeezed into the car which had taken us to Shepperton earlier. It was now driven by Alex Carr.

Monsieur Carr was helped by his son into the front seat. Behind them, Diana and I sat with the boy between us. Mrs Jenkins had given him a bunch of holly, tied it with a red silk ribbon. He now held it upright like a torch.

'Be careful with that, Gigi,' Diana Carr said, touching a spine with her index finger.

'Do you have children, Albertine?' She turned to me.

'No. Not yet,' I said.

'Oh, I am sorry,' she said.

I caught Alex Carr's glance in the rear-view mirror. I tried to respond with something meaningful: I am not sure I want children, or, There is still time. Neither seemed right in front of the boy.

'We had them late too, in our family, and we all seem to stop at one,' said Monsieur Carr. 'One boy. It makes for a masculine world.'

Diana Carr blushed, said nothing.

'Not Grandmother,' Alex Carr said. 'She was in her late teens when she had you.'

'Was she, Grandpa?' Gigi asked eagerly, then turned to me. 'I am doing some research for my film role,' he said. 'I am nine in the film, just as I am in life, just as my grandfather was when his mummy fell ill and died. But Miss Leigh, who plays my mother in the film – I don't mean my actual mother, I mean my grandpa's mother ...' Here he paused and looked at Diana. 'Miss Leigh must be much older than Grandpa's mummy was. She is *very* old.'

'Gigi thinks that anyone over twenty is ancient,' Diana Carr laughed.

'We are not fully convinced about the film yet, Gigi,' Alex Carr intervened. 'Let's see what your school says about it first, shall we?'

'And how old are you, Mrs Whitelaw?' the boy asked.

'Gigi!' his mother admonished him. 'That is very rude.'

'Thirty-three,' I said. 'Just like Miss Leigh.'

'Just like Mummy when she had me. And just like Jesus when he was crucified. We learned that at school,' the boy said.

'Gigi!' Diana Carr put her gloved finger on her son's lips. 'This is shocking. Apologies, Mrs Whitelaw.'

'Well, he wasn't very old – Jesus, I mean – was he?' I said. 'I feel sorry for his mummy.'

We drove past the tall brick wall of a stately home. Through heavy iron gates I glimpsed an Italianate villa with dark cedars of Lebanon behind it. One of its wings had been shattered by a bomb and boarded off. There was a scattering of walkers in the park. An Irish setter, red and silky like a fire torch, ran across the snow.

'Chiswick House,' said Diana Carr. 'When this winter ends – if it ever does – you and Papa ought to come here for a walk. Have you been?'

'No, I haven't even heard of it,' I said. 'Before I met Monsieur Carr, I had barely even heard of Chiswick.'

'The grounds are glorious. There is a lake, and a temple hidden in the park. Gigi and I come to feed the ducks,' she said.

A few hundred yards further on was the cemetery. It stretched like a theatrical auditorium. The gate was wide open, but there was no one inside, except for the hundreds of metropolitan dead beneath their tombstones.

Diana and Gigi leaped out and walked in the direction of the river. Alex helped his father out and then opened my door. He took my hand: his was warm, gloveless. His hat sat low on his ears. The tip of his nose was red from the cold. He paused awkwardly, as if expecting me to guide him.

'It won't take long, Mrs Whitelaw,' he said. 'It won't take long and then I'll drive you home.'

Gigi was rushing ahead to his grandmother's grave. Diana had waited for us to catch up and was now holding her father-in-law's arm as they followed the boy.

'I am not in a rush. It has been such a lovely afternoon. To be with a family ... in a family. I haven't experienced that in thirteen years,' I said to Alex Carr.

'It must be strange, your London life,' he said. 'But then, whose isn't nowadays? We are refugees too. Even Diana, fully English though she is, had grandparents who longed for Russia. It's all so complicated.'

'So complicated. My husband always says it is simple.'

The gravestone in the shape of a Russian cross bore an inscription in Latin on one side and in Cyrillic on the other, with Tonya's name and dates. Gigi read out the Cyrillic for me.

'Granny died when I was two,' he said. 'She was almost sixty: that is very old. I don't remember her at all.'

He planted his bunch of holly into the virgin snow under the cross. We stood around the grave like visitors around a hospital bed. Crows shuttled along cemetery paths, leaving cuneiform trails and cawing at each other in intermittent bursts. Monsieur Carr broke the human silence.

'The space next to ours is untouched still, thank God. I wonder if we should purchase it, Alexei. And I might inscribe my name next to Tonya's so that you only have to add the year of death later.'

'An excellent idea, Father,' Alex Carr said. 'London will grow again now, and so will its cemeteries in due course. I was wondering about a space for Diana and me. It would be so much better to keep the family together.'

Matter-of-fact arrangements for an unavoidable event, like booking a hotel room ahead of arrival. Diana and the boy were not listening. Gigi kept straightening his bunch of holly. The original position had left an imprint in the snow, so he started patting the surface around it into a circular medallion.

'Leave it, Gigi,' Diana said. 'Leave it, darling.'

'I want everything to be perfect for Grandma,' he protested, but obeyed. Diana kissed the top of the boy's head.

'Forgive us, Tonya,' said Monsieur Carr. 'Nothing is ever perfect, Seryozha, my boy. That is why there are holidays like this Forgiveness Sunday.'

Alex Carr took a candle and a box of matches out of his pocket, stabbed the candle into the snow at the foot of the cross and lit the wick. He crossed himself. The flame flickered in the dying light. Beeswax melted into oily teardrops.

Diana reminded her son how to make a sign of the cross in the Orthodox manner, the thumb, index and middle finger forming the Trinity. The lines of footprints leading to Tonya's grave seemed reason enough for Tonya to forgive anything that needed forgiving.

We took a different route back. The car stopped next to an imposing villa by the river. The house was large and ugly – yellow Victorian bricks darkened by smog, a profusion of roof finials, spires and pointed arches, a fuzz of ivy tendrils on the walls. There was something vaguely Germanic about it on the outside, like a forbidding home from a Grimm fairy tale. Judging by the view through its high windows, the inside seemed to be the opposite. The rooms on the ground floor were lit, and there was gold and red on the walls, books, a grand piano, lattice windows on the side facing the river, dark velvet curtains and the sight of the Thames flowing between them. It was a house of comfortably off, intelligent people, not a house of immensely rich people.

'This is our house,' said the boy proudly. 'You must come and visit us sometime, Mrs Whitelaw.'

'You must, with your husband,' echoed the mother. 'We have a lovely garden. It descends right down to the edge of the Thames. I could throw a small party when the weather improves, make some Pimm's and lemonade, or punch. Yes, you must.'

'Thank you. That would be lovely. In the spring, perhaps,' I said as we bade our farewells and watched them disappear along the path to the front door. It looked massive and solid, the door of a castle.

Alex Carr insisted on taking me home after we dropped his father off into the care of Mrs Jenkins. We drove in silence along Bath Road. I was still in the back, as though he was my chauffeur. It had seemed awkward to change places for that last leg, and it would have been even more awkward to sit next to him. The streets around us grew poorer, darker, more congested. The slush churned and crunched under the wheels.

'I do apologise if you found Gigi too exuberant this afternoon,' Alex said.

'He is an only child,' I said. 'It must be difficult to know when you can and can't be childish. He is a lovely boy.'

'And while we are on the subject of childishness, I hope you are not finding my father too taxing,' Alex said. 'It's been a month now, roughly a month into your job. He tells me that you've gone through *Madame Bovary*, and quite a chunk of family history, that you are taking notes. He says that you are more interested in Russia than any of us.'

'No, not taxing at all. It has been my best month in London so far. And, in fact, I am writing down your father's story. I would like to create a gift for him, for the family. I'd like to think of myself as his ghostwriter – that is what my husband calls it. A scribe, if you like. An inefficient one: I am sure I have all the names down wrong.'

'You have my sympathy. All that nineteenth-century Russian stuff. If you'd like me to read it, do not hesitate to ask. Any time.'

'I am reading *A Concise History of Russia and the Soviet Union*, very slowly. I reached the revolution of 1905 last week and have just heard about your family's story up to the same point. You are taking your first steps and the Tsar is making his concessions. I am trying to keep up with your father, as you can tell.'

'Survival followed by breakdowns, that's our family story in a nutshell. It has its colour. I was so keen to become English as fast as possible that it took years before I became interested in our Russian past. You will soon know more about us than I do, I am sure.'

'I don't think so,' I said. 'But I would be delighted if my notes were to be of some use. To Gigi, perhaps, if not to you.'

'And Father will love it,' he said. 'I would not be surprised to hear that he already knows what you are up to. He and Mrs Jenkins are like the KGB. Nothing passes them by.'

The roads became wider and brighter again. We crossed over a multitude of bridges and past a striking exhibition centre. It looked ghostly in the thickening yellow fog, like a piece of Art Deco furniture under dust covers.

'I drive into central London so rarely nowadays,' said Alex, 'that I forget what it looks like. We are like a village over in Chiswick. Self-contained; fully suburban.'

Our house was in darkness when the car pulled up in front of it.

'Is this the right number? It's such a lovely house. I did not imagine ...' Alex said. I assumed he imagined that we were poor, that I had to work.

'My husband bought it ten years ago. This is the smart end of Earl's Court, he says. Which is not saying much, apparently. The neighbours call it the Danzig Corridor, because there are so many Polish exiles here. Not that I know any neighbours. The house on the left is occupied by a pianist who is never there; the one on the right is empty. I sometimes feel I am the only resident in the square. The resident alien.'

He laughed.

'Are you going to be all right?'

'Of course,' I said. 'Of course I am going to be all right.'

He accompanied me to the entrance. Our square was too insignificant to be cleared regularly. There was ice under the layer of untrodden snow. He slipped and I steadied him.

'Thank you. It was meant to be the other way round,' he said.

Albie was sleeping in the chair by the fire when I entered the drawing room. The newspaper had slipped onto the floor by his feet. The room was lit by the street lamps and the whiteness outside. When I switched the main light on, I heard the car pull away.

'I needed that,' said Albie, stretching his arms towards me. 'I travel too much, and sleep too little. I slept until two after you left, and then again after I saw Ian and Peter off. I hope you've had a nice day, Ber.'

He offered his hand and, when I took it, he pulled me down to his lap, still in my coat and gloves, took my hat off, flung it to the opposite chair and kissed me.

'My little family, that's what you are, Ber,' he said. He had guessed what needed to be said.

I told him about the party, the visit to the cemetery, Forgiveness Sunday. I was driven back by my employer's son, I said.

'Oh, I'm jealous,' Albie said. 'When I go to work, I don't get lifts home from glamorous young women.'

'He is not young and he is certainly not glamorous,' I said.

'We are a modern couple, you and I, aren't we, Ber? You look happier when you come back from work and that makes me happy too. My female colleagues are expected to resign when they marry. That seems so unnecessary. I'm sure things will be different, soon. Even in your homeland, France, women now have the vote. Men and women will be equal soon. You and I are the forerunners, aren't we, the harbingers.'

I did not see us as equal. He carried the world on his shoulders.

'Work, Albie?' I asked. 'I can't imagine anyone would call listening to Monsieur Carr, or reading to him, work.'

'I saw your notes, pages of your Russian story,' Albie said. 'I hope you don't mind. You may well have something there that will be remembered. Most of what I write is unsigned, or signed by others. Not that it matters, so long as it works.'

'So we are both ghosts ...' I said.

I tucked a hand under his jumper and followed the bony ridge of his shoulder, then moved it down along the blade and left it where the white cotton of his shirt covered the scar tissue, his baby wing.

'I know what your gesture means to imply,' Albie said, took my hand out from under his jumper and kissed the tips of my fingers. 'I'm fine, Ber, no need to worry about me.'

'We haven't spoken about the war,' I said to Monsieur Carr when we next met. 'Your war, I mean. I told you about mine.'

'This last war was Alexei's war, if that's the war you mean,' he said. 'I was old already and I was useless. I am not sure I deserved to survive it after Tonya died. But I was old and useless in 1914 too. I am a nineteenth-century man, Albertine. A relic.'

'So tell me about 1914,' I said. 'My own father fought in France and Macedonia. I don't remember him when he left for the front. I was a baby. I remember him coming back in the winter following the Armistice, seeing my sister Arlette for the first time, although she was three and a half.'

'Alexei was ten when the Great War started and I was fifty,' Monsieur Carr said, 'the son too young to fight, the father too old, and that may have been our salvation. There was euphoria on the streets of St Petersburg when war was declared. We had to defend our Serbian brothers, and we had to defeat Germany and Austria.

'That August the city was renamed Petrograd. My cousins fought, and died, in places dotted all along the Eastern Front – from the Baltic to the eastern reaches of the Black Sea – and I felt guilty and unmanned staying in the city. By the time Alexei was twelve, he was desperate to join the fight. There were boys his age, boys from the countryside, he claimed, who fought, who pretended they were sixteen. General Brusilov was part of our rich cousinage. Alexei kept his picture by his bedside, wanted to be a soldier when he grew up. Don't all boys? He dreamed of serving in Galicia, with Brusilov and Wrangel. He cut a four-pointed star and a cross out of cardboard, made his own Order of St George, and wore it pinned on his left shoulder when he played.'

'So difficult to imagine your son as a soldier,' I said. 'He is one of the most peaceable men I know.'

'Dry, you wanted to say. He was a funny boy, Alexei was, not sweet exactly, but endearing. Neither my father nor I were army types. When I was a child, I played with trains, felt destined to be a new Isambard Kingdom Brunel, to head the Department of Railways, but my mother's fate changed everything. Tonya hoped to see Alexei grow up to become an artist. Yet in 1914 he joined the First Cadet Corps, a military gymnasium – just like my mother's lover. Had the history of Russia been different my son would have been happy there, happy as a Russian officer, just as he was happy in Palestine as a British officer. He works in the brewery, he doesn't complain, but I know that the ledgers don't nourish his soul.

'Alexei was thirteen in 1917. We had been prepared for the events of that year, in the sense of expecting the Revolution, not in the sense of knowing what to do. The Germans got ever closer to Petrograd. The Tsar abdicated in March. After October we went through hell. I can't even speak about those months now. We moved to the country after months of suffering, then to the Crimea. In the dying days of the Civil War Alexei was just old and tall enough to claim to be eighteen and enlist with Wrangel. We were evacuated to Istanbul with Wrangel too, all three of us. We lived in a pension in Pera for almost a year, the most miserable year in lives that included no shortage of miserable years.

'We continued to believe that we would soon be back in Russia, that communism would not last, throughout those dire months of screeching seagulls and icy rain followed by baking heat, without work for any of us. Tonya painted her flowers and sold them to antique dealers and galleries – nowhere near enough for us to live on, but just enough to slow down the erosion of funds. I call them galleries, but they were wretched little junk shops. There were no tourists on the Bosphorus, and the Turks were hungry and disoriented themselves, another empire collapsing under our feet, though I was not sorry to see that one go. The Ottomans had caused more misery in the world than you can begin to imagine.

'There were Russians in Yugoslavia and Czechoslovakia, White Russians, people who could help, we were told, Russians who still had their wealth because they had taken it out of the country long before 1917. They loved Russia, those wise patriots, like a husband loves a faithless wife: spending on her for the moments they shared, never investing in her future.

'We hoped for help from those wise Russians when we took the Orient Express northwards out of Istanbul. When I stepped out of the railway station at Belgrade and saw Orthodox crosses on the churches above the Danube, it felt like a second birth. Vronsky had died for Serbia. I felt that we might be at home in what had been a tiny Orthodox kingdom, no more foreigners than we were in Peter or in the Crimea. But there were thousands of White Russians there already, looking for new livelihoods in the new Kingdom of Serbs, Croats and Slovenes, and where Orthodoxy was diluted by Catholicism and even Islam. Although the country was much bigger than Serbia had been in Vronsky's time, there was no room in it for us.

'We knew we had to press on further north, following our instinct like flocks of cranes on their return migration. Prague,

Paris, Berlin: they were all full of homeless Russians, once princes and generals, now taxi drivers and doormen in fashionable hotels, or worse, receptionists of brothels for French and German shopkeepers.

'London, Tonya said. London it must be.

'We had that address in Kingston, belonging to Hannah Wilson. In 1924, we turned up on her doorstep, unannounced, hungry. There had been the boat to Dover, the *Ville de Liège* I have told you about, then a boat train, and finally this big, unending city, swallowing us as it was to swallow you in 1945.'

'I remember that,' I said. 'Our train from Southampton, full of suntanned young men and women who had won the war. We are in London, Albie said, finally. And then it took almost another hour to get to the terminus. Albie's friends chanted "Waterloo, Waterloo," and glanced at me furtively. It took a minute to realise why.'

'Ours was Victoria Station,' Monsieur Carr said. 'And although I came to love London, although it looks in so many places more like St Petersburg than any other European city, it seemed strange and depressing from the train. The garlands of miserable houses backing onto the railway, with outdoor lavatories, and forlorn rows of bamboo sticks marking vegetable patches in the backyards, the washing lines with greying underwear dangling in the sulphurous smog: I can see them all as clearly as on that first afternoon. We were used to poverty, used to the fact that it appears so much more depressing in the north than in the south, but this was worse. Perhaps the Protestants did little to hide their poverty, were not ashamed of it. We were at the very heart of an empire on which the sun never sets, they said. It seemed to me, then and for a while later, that it was the heart of an empire in which the sun never rose.

'I remember how Tonya held my hand on the train, her face blank, poised between growing fear and vanishing hope. Alexei was almost twenty. He had become a man in the worst times imaginable and he knew how to hide his feelings. You did not even know that he had any. His expression was even more inscrutable than Tonya's. Yet I knew that his adolescence had been stolen, that he was both much older and much younger than his age.

'At the end of our journey, the final local train full of clerks returning to their dormitory suburb was like a phantasmagoria of some kind. We felt like travellers from a different planet. This could not be, it wasn't supposed to exist any more: ordinary life. There it was, finally, a world of ordinary people returning from their office work in a country with a king and a palace in the centre of its capital. We walked across the market square in Kingston, while people stared at us, at our unseasonal clothes. I understood why. We wore thick winter coats and fur, and the day was not particularly cold, just wet, with endless drizzle. I was sixty already, an old, white-haired man. What was I expecting to find in this city? How does one start again at that age? Were it not for Alexei and Tonya, I might have followed my mother long ago, in Istanbul, in Crimea, in St Petersburg even.

'Were it not for Alexei, I should say more truthfully, for Tonya often held my hand late at night, when we lay on our bed staring upwards like those medieval effigies in English cathedrals, and, when she thought that I was asleep, that I could not hear, she would say: "Why don't we just go, Seryozha, why don't we just go, quietly, together?"'

'Oh dear,' I said. I was feeling tearful. I could not think of anything to say that did not sound trite. 'What happened when you finally reached Hannah Wilson's house?'

'I have no idea whom and what we were expecting to see when we knocked at the door of her house in Grove Park Road. In retrospect, I hardly believe the journey we dared undertake, on such a flimsy premise, a hope that was less substantial than a drop of water. There was a sound of footsteps and a vague sense of an eye looking through the peephole for what seemed like an eternity and finally a scream coming from behind the black door with its brass dolphin knocker. I remember it now as though it were yesterday, the sound of that scream, that strange dolphin with an ungainly, stubby nose which I studied as we waited. You could not believe, Albertine, how odd everything seemed, the lion's paws and the dolphins people had on their front doors instead of bells, the suburban streets, the front gardens so small as to make you wonder why they were there, just for that step which divided the house from the street, just for that single step which said this is mine, do not trespass, the single step which in Russia no longer meant anything.

'And, coming from a Europe criss-crossed with the still-vivid scar lines of conflict, everything seemed so remote from any war, so blissful in its smallness, in its tidiness. We stood at the bottom of the steps in that little garden, scared, like trespassers, between two box trees trimmed into a strange spiral shape, under a hanging wall lamp, before a sign which read Orchard Villa although there was no sign of an orchard anywhere, waiting to hear that scream which would have been frightening but for its suggestion that we were recognised, that we were at the right address, that in some strange cosmic balance my mother's charity was about to be returned to us. I don't think that the world repays its charity in this way, but it did, just that once, to us.

'It was Hannah – my mother's ward, our Diana's grand-mother – who opened the door, sixty and white-haired and as old as I was, and with a different surname, although we continued to think of her as Wilson. She was agile and somehow much more youthful than I expected her to be, in that Englishwoman's way. They grow into old age as though they have been just waiting to become old all their lives, Englishwomen do, as though they know all along that their seventies and eighties must be their best years.

'She looked at our son for a long moment and then rushed towards him and screamed again, more quietly this time. "Alexei," she screamed, before she looked at me and whispered "Dear Count" in Russian, "Dear Count," and fell on her knees and started kissing my hands, both my hands. "Dear Count, dear Sergei Alexeievich, am I dreaming? Am I dreaming? I have thought of you every day, of you and your family, and of our Russia, of our Russia," she said, "of its tragedy, every single day." She was still on her knees in that small front garden between those box trees, and she hugged my calves, although she was, now, incomparably wealthier than us.

'A man came by, on his way back from work, I remember well, with a briefcase, in a pair of striped trousers, a black jacket, a waistcoat and a bowler hat, and he slowed down to take a good look. He looked so strange to us, but how much stranger must we have seemed to him, our little scene on the black and white tiles of Hannah Wilson's minuscule front garden, a white-haired Englishwoman kneeling, kissing an old man's hand, a young man looking at them, three battered suitcases lying between him and a woman standing back, dressed *à la française*, a woman in her forties, still striking, still young, but worn out by the hardships she had lived through, a woman who was the mother of my son.

We were all crying now, and speaking that strange soft language I now know Russian is to the English, the way it sounds like falling snow.

'"Please, please come in, dear Count, dear Countess." Hannah was now kissing Tonya's hand, still on her knees, and Tonya was crying too and begging her to stand up. The door of the house opened wide and inside, half hiding, was a young woman, no more than seventeen or eighteen, Hannah's grand-daughter, blonde like an angel, her green eyes so unreal and so beautiful. It was Diana, my daughter-in-law, appropriately named, although the Wilsons might not have known it, after Diana the huntress, the goddess of the moon.

'During those first two months in London, everything was still uncertain and yet it felt to us like coming up for air. We went for a walk in the park soon after that first day, a long walk up the hill to Richmond Park, and suddenly, London seemed exactly like our Russia, except like the Russia that no longer was. There were dried grasses and bracken, and deer – herds of deer moving through the morning mist. We reached the top of the hill. There was a mound where the trees were trimmed to preserve a view, like a canyon cut through foliage. The Thames was curling behind us, winding its way into central London through the water meadows, and, before us, a hazy, shimmering view of St Paul's Cathedral ... It was some distance from us but it seemed to flicker ever closer as we stood, like a mirage, the ark of some new covenant.

'"Like the Isaakiyevsky Sobor," Alexei said. It is perhaps the loveliest of churches in St Petersburg. It pleased me that he still remembered it.

'"Like it, but more majestic," said Tonya, and then, as if she had had a premonition, she added, "I will die in this city. I do not want to travel any further."

'"But we will go back to Russia," I said. "Give it a year, two at the most."

'"No, we won't," Tonya said. "And stop saying it, Sergei. It's no use pretending. Alexei perhaps, he is young, but not you and I. We will never see Russia again. We will die here. I am happy to die here."

'"Alexei is young," I said, "but you are young too, there is only one old person here."

'Secretly, however, I was relieved that she was content. I too was happy to die in London.'

9

Borzoi

'They don't feel guilty,' Albie said of the Germans. It had been two years, almost, since Hitler died in his bunker, and there were still days when Albie spoke of the war as though it was not over. We had just walked from the Wigmore Hall to Baker Street and caught the Underground home after a Schubert recital. My head was full of music as we sat down to one last cup of tea before bed. I listened to Albie, but I resented his mood. It was unfair of me; he burdened me with his worries less and less.

'Rather, they do,' he continued, 'but it is the wrong ones who feel the guilt. Those who have suffered themselves; the children who are not children any more. The fathers and grandfathers don't. They say, "We were defeated" the way you might say fair cop. They understand the need for punishment. The defeated have to take their punishment. But their regret, Ber, is about the defeat, not about the vision which took them to war. Many continue to say that the English work for the Americans and the Americans work for the Jews. They see their own towns in ruins, their own suffering, and they call it defeat, not just deserts. It is insidious, that vision. I see the ruins and I feel guilty. The rubble makes me feel that our victory wasn't clean. As though there are clean victories, victories without rubble.

'Or they go on about the Russians. We did not fight you, they say, we fought the Russians. Every German man I meet fought on the Eastern Front. As though there were millions in the East and only a handful in the West, just a few enlightened souls in SS uniforms, walking through Paris of a Sunday afternoon with a Baedeker guide. So civilised, the group promenade in tailored uniforms on the Champs-Élysées. It gets to you. You are not supposed to hate the millions of frostbitten kids who suffered on the Eastern Front, are you?

'The Americans employ them. A spot of manufacturing, that's all, a bit of scientific expertise. Of no consequence, everyone says, nothing political. They have the know-how, those Germans. We have to forgive or we'll never get the workers we need, the place won't function. One has to be pragmatic. Send them food and clothing. A loan or two. You can't punish an entire nation. I am confused, Ber. I sit in wood-panelled rooms and I feel I no longer know right from wrong. I see small men with spectacles on both sides of the bar, bookkeepers in uniform. I wonder if I am one of them. How do I know that what I serve is not evil? That it won't come to look evil even if it does not seem so now?'

I walked up to Albie and massaged his temples, slowly, barely pressing in. I was struck, for the umpteenth time, by the unreality of his blond hair as it passed through my fingers, smelling of almond oil. The strangeness of the gesture – the sense of power women have when a man surrenders like that.

'You don't wear spectacles, Albie. You no longer wear a uniform. Though I can see it on you even when you've got no clothes on. I read an article in *Le Monde* about Stanislavsky, who was, they say, a famous theatre director in Russia. It was written by a Frenchman who went to see him at work in Moscow in the 1930s. Stanislavsky described how he prepared for some grand Shakespearean role, Othello perhaps, by wearing a turban all day, onstage and off, to adjust the posture, to acquire the comportment of someone in a heavy turban, so that even when he took it off, he stood and walked as though there was that heavy, bejewelled burden on his head. Perhaps I am dreaming this, dreaming this article, only to say that I see your uniform even when you are naked in our bed, Albie, and I don't understand why it has to be so. I see your muscles tense for the fight even when I hold your head in my hands. I feel that tension too, as though someone is about to knock on my door with dreadful news. We can't live like this, Albie. We have to relax somehow or we will be lost, and I am no help, am I?'

The shadows of branches played on the ceiling, throwing dappled light into the room. I massaged his temples and I felt him frowning. It was easier to talk to him when I was not looking into his eyes. When we faced each other he slapped the surface of the table the way old men slap their knees. He got up and walked away.

'Cheer up, old girl,' he said, 'cheer up.'

Easier to talk to him when we both looked straight ahead, in the dappled light of the room.

Whenever we made love, Albie kept his eyes closed. I kept mine open. If he opened his, I closed mine. It was as though we couldn't go on doing it, making love, if we both acknowledged what we were doing. Our marriage stood beneath a dam of unacknowledged matter. A levee of sand-bags against the flood; we seemed unsure what we feared, what more could have burst in. I wondered what other lovers did.

I had only had one lover before I met Albie: an engineer from Perpignan. Fresh-faced, dark-haired, moustachioed, he was as young and as inexperienced as I was. We stared at each other as though neither of us could quite believe the situation we had found ourselves in. Without guilt. As though we were having breakfast together; we were eating because we were hungry, because it was time for breakfast. Our lovemaking was more beautiful in retrospect than while it was going on. The engineer proposed. A young woman, living with her aunt, I might have looked like someone who might be longing to become an engineer's wife. I escaped to Bucharest to avoid hurting him.

In Alexandria, I lied to Albie. I told him I had had three lovers before him. For some strange reason I thought he wouldn't want me if I owned up to just that one, that he would stay away from the responsibility for someone who did not take lovers lightly. I invented three men. Or, rather, two. The engineer from Perpignan was still there, but there were two imaginary Parisians on either side of him, like bookends. The first was much older and a professor. He took my virginity. The third was a publisher and a Communist who must have vanished into the maquis the moment the Germans marched into Paris. The third was the love of my life, before I realised that Albie was.

I told these lies because I thought that Albie was going to leave Alexandria without me sooner or later, and I did not want him to feel guilty. I must have understood something of his unbearable decency even in those earliest days. But I invented these men so thoroughly that I almost fooled myself into believing they had existed. There were times in Alexandria when Albie was on leave, when he kept wanting to know everything about my past life, when he kept asking questions. I relayed the professor's imaginary obituary from *La Croix*. A small lie led to a bigger one until I forbade him to ask about my past lovers. We never spoke about any of these men again. The lovers were buried from that boat to Southampton, given a sea burial. I sometimes wonder why Albie's largesse in accepting an experienced Parisienne was less scary, less of a burden than taking on a fearful near virgin in her thirties. My shame at not coming clean from the word go: buried too. Innocent lies, perhaps, but how do you undo them years later, how do you come clean? How do you say: I lied to you, Albie? I invented those two lovers because I was too old when you met me to have had just the boy from Perpignan. Because I did not think you would last, I did not think these stories would commit me to a version of myself. A less virginal version of myself. The war had robbed me of something too. So many people were raped and butchered, how could I even consider an absence of love a loss?

I massaged Albie's temples and felt him frowning. He was too young to carry the guilt of Germany on his naked uniformed shoulders, on his thin-boy's epaulettes. I looked at his feet in lambskin slippers and that felt wrong too. I knew his feet in polished leather and I knew them in blood-spattered desert boots. Blood from an exploding anti-tank grenade. Albie's blood. O positive: a universal donor. I knew that from my index card before I knew how right it was.

He held my hands and pressed my fingers into his temples and he knew that these fingers which were touching him had touched three lovers – one so old that he had died, one a man in the prime of his middle age, a political man, one practically a boy from Perpignan. That last, the only real one, was an inexperienced provincial boy who nonetheless knew enough to grab a linen towel, to come cleanly he said, to come out clean.

'We never come out clean, never come clean out of such things,' I told Albie. 'The Germans know it. They must know that they are unclean. Does it matter what they say?'

'What on earth are you talking about, Ber?' Albie said, pressing my fingers deeper into the sides of his face.

'About that which you know when you are alone, when there is no need to step into a version of yourself that is like a concrete bunker surrounded by sandbags. They, those book-keepers in uniform you are talking about, they know it when it's two a.m. and the dead millions come out and march past them, they know that it wasn't just the Eastern Front that counts, but the home business too.'

'You are wrong there,' Albie said. 'The guards wake them up at six. The guards wake them up to prepare for the courts. They sleep like lambs. The guards get less sleep than these men do. You are wrong, Ber. They do not torture themselves. They think we will torture them enough. But to torture them would diminish our victory.'

I watch his feet in lambskin slippers, his thick woollen socks, and I feel like kissing those feet, because seeing those feet is like seeing Albie naked.

For Monsieur Carr the Second World War barely existed. The only war that counted had happened thirty years ago. I mentioned the last one, but he said: 'We will come to that.' He waved his hand in the air as though he was chasing away an inconsequential thought.

'I signed on, dear Albertine. Early in 1925, I signed on. There was an employment bureau just to the north of the National Gallery, a short way off Trafalgar Square, where they registered unemployed aliens like me, for work in the hotel industry. So many of us had the languages and the manners to go with the doorman's uniform. Like *Nutcracker* soldiers; I had the face for one too. Times were hard, but when weren't they in this wretched century? The bureaucrat who took my details just shook his head in sorrow rather than disbelief. He had seen dozens like me already, that day alone. A count, you said? Polish? Lithuanian? No, Russian. What a pity, he said. Languages? French, German, Russian obviously, all at mother-tongue level. Other? Church Slavonic, Latin, Greek, Aramaic. He looked up, smiled a thin, reproachful smile. I had been a curator of ancient manuscripts, once, in St Petersburg, I explained. You won't need those languages, Count, don't count on them. He paused to give me the time to register the pun. There are no vacancies in manuscripts that come through my offices. He lifted his notes again and read – Count Karenin – then looked at me in such a way that I decided to change that too, as soon as possible. You won't need that title of yours either, Count Karenin. He did not say that but I could hear it. We will be in touch, he said. My name, at least, I could change. At sixty-one, I could see, there were few jobs anyone would rush to offer me.

'Tonya cried herself to sleep that night, as she had many nights before. I had brought her nothing but sorrow. But we had to believe, had to go on, for our son's sake. I never thought that we would come to depend on charity. Those formidable English ladies who make cakes and jam and organise balls and raffle sales in their churches, they took us on. You've never had to depend on them, Albertine, I am sure. The Karenins did, for several years. And we cried ourselves to sleep, Tonya and I, in secret even from each other, in Hannah Wilson's guest bedroom in Kingston. We slept in twin beds in that room. We held cold hands over a chasm, too timid to move the stand with a porcelain jug out of the way, too shy to push the beds together at our age.

'"Whatever happens, Sergei, you must remember that I love you," Tonya would say, worrying me with that "whatever" of hers. What could happen that was worse than what had already happened? And back in Russia she never told me she loved me, nor had she pleaded that I must remember it: both were implied in everything we did for each other.

'But the employment bureau did find something for me after all: the Splendid in Mayfair. My uncle Stiva, my mother's brother, used to frequent the hotel on his many visits to London. His champagne bills from the 1880s alone would have amounted to more than the total sum I earned over all those years during which, in one of its many back rooms facing the similar back room of a gentlemen's club, I dealt with customer correspondence and complaints. *Thank you for looking after us so well* arrived on my desk much less often than *Our room was woefully small, Our mattress not as soft as we have come to expect, the breakfast delivered by room service not as hot*. I responded with polite, handwritten expressions of delight or regret – mostly regret. I wrote hundreds of those in English, French and German, even in Russian, yes, sometimes in Russian too. My boss, a boy of thirty-five, praised my reliability, my unerring sense of good measure. Well done, Count, he would say, and pat me on the shoulder, this boy from Penge who was progressing fast in the hotel business. I saved the management hundreds of pounds over the years, he said. It was as though I was born to deal with customer complaints. And, it shames me to admit this, I was not unhappy in that office. I had a gift, honed to perfection in my teenage years, for escaping my own misery; such a gift, indeed, that the miseries of the Splendid's guests often seemed to me greater than my own.

'At least Alexei was young enough to change his life. He won a scholarship to Cambridge from one of those charitable bodies established by the good ladies of Barnes, Richmond and Kingston. He was not as academic as me, yet he did not wish to be a soldier any more, not in England, not after everything that we had witnessed. He was a good, hard-working student and he did not disappoint those excellent ladies who helped him with their charity. After three years at Cambridge he was almost English: an industrious, steady, uncomplaining young man, Protestant almost, practically without a trace of an accent, almost a secret to me and his mother.

'Little by little, as Alexei studied, Tonya and I rebuilt our world. We moved out of Hannah Wilson's house in Kingston, and into this house in Chiswick. It had once belonged to Princess Trubetskoy. The Princess was my age, but she was, in her own words, old, old and dying. That was charity too, Russian charity. Chiswick was the centre of Russian London and Tonya was the Princess's final companion: just as you are for me, Albertine. Mrs Jenkins was close to the Wilsons – the families had known each other back in Russia – and she had engineered our move.

'She herself had been one of the many English people in St Petersburg. There had long been an English church in the city, an English club, even an English shop, from which my mother used to get regular deliveries of shortbread and proper marmalade. We Russians had always loved England much more than England loved us. The good ladies who helped us were an exception.

'This house too, indirectly, was the work of our guardian angels, the ladies' circle in South-West London, a network into which Hannah Wilson had miraculously tapped. I am not sure if I should be proud or ashamed to have been put back on my two feet by so many women.

'She had no children, Princess Trubetskoy, no one to look after her, and she loved Tonya and loved Alexei as though he were her own son. Much of what you see in this house, if you exclude Tonya's art, is hers. The Trubetskoy coat of arms is imprinted on most things. We brought over so little from Russia that we were grateful for everything that could remind us of our world. The Princess even had recordings of old Russian operas here. But the house is not ours in perpetuity. It will revert to the Trubetskoy clan when I die. The heir is an actor in Hollywood. Of all the strange things my compatriots have ended up doing in the West, Hollywood is perhaps the least strange.

'Alexei worries that Gigi will become an actor, but how much stranger is that for a Russian count than working in a brewery, or than dealing with customer complaints in a Mayfair hotel? How much stranger than being half Karenin and half Wilson? Than seeing his English blood as the blood to be prouder of, as, I am afraid, Gigi does? That is the way children are. They don't want to differ from their friends. Gigi's friends are bourgeois, and his mother and his father are trying to be. Alexei is so determined to be invisible, he has effectively turned himself into a philistine. Have you noticed?'

I nodded, then quickly shook my head. There was no correct answer to that question. The old man understood my predicament and laughed. I blushed at his laughter. His son was not invisible to me.

'But you are not a bourgeoise, dear Albertine,' Monsieur Carr said. 'You are a bohemian who has not found a way to live like one, like my Tonya. She would have been so much happier as the wife of a painter or a poet, not the wife of a librarian, let alone an office boy.'

'I am sure you are wrong, Monsieur Carr. Painters and poets perished in Russia in huge numbers, whereas your library kept Tonya safe,' I responded, but I did not like the sound of 'safe'. I knew that 'safe' rarely sufficed. Did he perhaps sense that when he called me a bohemian?

'Why did I say that you were a bohemian, Albertine? Is that what you are wondering? I will explain it, but you must promise not to be angry with me. Not to be angry and not to try to change. Those green stockings you are wearing: everything black, head to toe, then those green stockings. Your hair: the moment you take your hat off it starts running away from you. Your hands: there's always a piece of plaster on them somewhere, as though you are always burning yourself or cutting yourself doing housework. Did I guess right? Tell me, did I guess right? And, please, forgive me. It is not polite of me to comment on your appearance, even to show that I, an old man, notice those things.'

I crossed my legs in their bright green stockings. It was the only pair I could get with our coupons a month or so ago, but I loved the hue. I tried to smooth my hair.

'Please don't do it, Albertine. Korda said you look like Vivien Leigh, but you are prettier and this is why.'

'If Miss Leigh had my hair she would need a hairdresser in attendance twice a day,' I said. My hair was Jewish hair, I thought, but did not say. 'And I am indeed hopeless with housework. We always had housemaids in Paris, not because we were wealthy but because both my mother and my aunt toiled hard in the workshop. Then in Romania I lived alone and had no need to learn more than the most basic elements of housekeeping. I now try to please Albie, although he has no expectations of me, to show off even, but these English machines and utensils follow their own logic. You have to light the gas, and it's always in some strange place; you turn the tap on and forget that there are two, that the hot water is scalding and the cold is freezing, for some unfathomable English reason, that you have to wait for the water to fill the basin. It is as though I am a left-handed person in a right-handed world.'

'I do know,' said Monsieur Carr. 'But how do they wash their faces with these low taps, and two at that? Tonya used to wonder when we arrived; how do they wash their hair? It comes from being first in everything, even modern plumbing. Pioneers: you have to live with the imperfection of the proto-type while others reap the benefits and move on. But you are modest, Albertine. I am sure you are better with your hands than you admit. And your clothes, Albertine. So unusual and so beautiful in these drab times. Severe, one might say, at first sight, but then there is always a detail that surprises, that runs away, excites the senses: a knitted collar, an unexpected knot. I am sure you don't need an old man to tell you this.'

It was my turn to laugh.

'I make my own. I have a sewing machine and so much time on my hands. And it is in my blood, dressmaking. I come from a long line of tailors. You would never ever have called me a bourgeoise in Paris. "You can't leave well alone, Albertine," that's what my mother used to say, "even at the price of ruining things." *Le mieux est l'ennemi du bien,*" she would say. *Perfect is the enemy of good.'*

'Oh, how my Tonya needed to hear that,' Monsieur Carr said. 'I wish she had had a mother to tell her that. *Le mieux est l'ennemi du bien.* I will remember this.'

Gradually, the bitter winter began to weaken. I read the *Concise History of Russia* through to the end and continued drafting Monsieur Carr's memoir. I called it *Karenin's Story* at first, then changed this to *Karenin's Winter*. Most of the episodes he had narrated were accompanied, in my mind, by a soft, whispering sound in the background, much softer than the pattering of rain.

'What sound does the snow make when it falls?' I asked Monsieur Carr. 'You are Russian, you should know everything about snowfall. What do we call it?'

He thought about my question for a moment.

'Susurration,' he said. 'The same as in French.'

That March I started studying Russian with an old woman in a basement flat in Queen's Gate. She was called Elizaveta Furst. She was the only daughter of General Baron Furst, as she never tired of saying, and she was as White a Russian as you were likely to meet in those times, and a crushing snob. She seemed to know and despise everyone. I did not tell my teacher about my work, about the Carrs. In order to read your lovely literature in its original language, I said when she asked why I wanted to know Russian, and that seemed good enough. Russian writing was so beautiful, clearly, that such an effort made sense.

Twice a week I sat with her, one-to-one, deciphering simple phrases written in the Cyrillic alphabet. I usually went on to Chiswick straight from these sessions: my days with the Russians, I called them.

One evening, at the end of a Russian day, I decided to visit the grounds of Chiswick House. It was a good twenty-minute walk from Bedford Park, but Albie was away and the air felt almost warm after weeks of sub-zero temperatures. The streets became steadily quieter as I neared the river. Here and there I noticed wives or maids opening the front door to greet the men returning from work. As they took their hats off or wiped their shoes on the doormat, I heard sounds from inside the houses: children's voices, music from the radio, dogs barking, the sounds of suburbia.

I envied these men and their wives. I wondered if Albie's life with me would eventually shape itself into something like this. These were beautiful, spacious houses, away from the grime and the smog of Earl's Court, with their ornate fences and their carefully maintained front gardens. They offered lives of warmth and comfort for those who had survived the war, lives destined to get even better and more plentiful; English lives.

I am not sure why, but I could not imagine Albie and me in a house like this, in a suburb like this, yet neither could I imagine any other story, any other scenario. You make a life, step by step, each one taking you further into a territory that is always half familiar, half new. Gradually, your life shapes up into something barely recognisable. A lover in Alexandria becomes a husband in London. You can no longer call yourself 'displaced', living in a nice house in Earl's Court, but you don't feel at home either.

Perfect is the enemy of good: isn't it just, Mother? I was thinking of her and reciting Russian declensions, sotto voce – *mother, of mother, to mother* – as I walked through the iron gates and towards the Palladian villa I had glimpsed on the day of our pilgrimage to Tonya's grave. I walked along an avenue of lime trees trimmed into enormous box shapes, almost French. There was the hint of fresh buds, something less than the harbingers of spring and more like the long exhalation of winter. I almost walked into Alex Carr. He emerged out of nowhere, from a side alley obscured by trailing wisteria branches.

'"To mother," Mrs Whitelaw?' he asked, raising his hat, raising his voice.

'Oh dear, Mr Carr, good evening. I am afraid I don't know what I was saying.'

'But you do know you were saying it in Russian, I hope. You never mentioned you knew Russian. That is sinister, almost. I am beginning to worry about you, Mrs Whitelaw.'

'Yes,' I said. 'I mean no. I am learning. Just beginning. It was supposed to be a secret, a surprise for your father.'

'It certainly is a surprise.'

'When you say that you are beginning to worry about me, do you mean that I am—'

'A KGB spy.'

'A what?'

'A Soviet spy. Sent over from Moscow.'

'You sound like my husband,' I said. 'He sees spies everywhere. He thinks I am a spy too.'

Alex Carr started to say something but changed his mind. A dog ran up and circled us. I have never seen such a dog: tall, slender, with a long white silk coat, a frill on its elegant neck, its narrow muzzle like a Roman profile, with almond-shaped eyes set close together.

'Amur, I almost forgot about you.' Alex Carr took a leash out of his pocket and hooked it to the dog's collar. The animal buried its muzzle into its master's hand.

'What an amazing creature ... and Amour is such a wonderful name ... What kind of dog is it?'

'Amur ... A-m-u-r ... not French for love but the Siberian river.'

'Of course,' I said. I had never heard of this river.

'It's a borzoi, a Russian wolfhound. Amur is four.'

The dog wagged its long, feathered tail like a white sabre in the air.

'I am so glad we met,' I said.

164

'Isn't it just beautiful here?' he asked. 'Have you noticed that chameleon quality in London, how it turns itself into any European city you'd like it to be? Suddenly you are in Rome, or in Paris, or in Vienna, or, God forbid, even in Berlin. Suddenly you are at home.'

We followed the amazing creature through the grounds for a little while. There were patches of snow like scattered white kilims. The Palladian house glinted behind the trees. The boarded-up section to one side was like the sad stump of a severed limb: how could anyone want to drop a bomb on a building as beautiful as moonshine? The branches of the cedars drooped low, as though they were defying gravity for a moment, before an already predestined fall.

10

When the English Speak of Russia

When I next saw him, I was about to tell Monsieur Carr about my walk in the grounds of Chiswick House and my meeting with his son, but he started talking while I was still unbuttoning my raincoat in the hall.

'I did not sleep last night,' he said, and held the door of the library for me, then shuffled behind me. 'There was a wireless programme about famines in the Soviet Union. Almost two years since the war and still so much hunger everywhere in Europe. Even here, in London, we queue and make do and pretend we like Spam. But at least we have that. In St Petersburg, after the Revolution, we threw a party when one of our *muzhiks* smuggled half a sack of millet into the city, a gruel party, we called it. Russia now seems no better off than Russia then.'

'In the places Germany occupied, people ate cats and dogs, with grass and tree bark instead of vegetables,' I said.

'I know,' he went on. 'Millions of Russian lives were sacrificed to put an end to that. Yet there seemed to be glee in the voice of the BBC's presenter. The Soviets may have won the war but they can't eat the party books, can they? They may love our music and our novels, but they don't like us. There is always a hint of that when the English speak of Russia. Have you noticed it, Albertine?'

'I couldn't say I have,' I admitted. 'The French are the same. They think the Russians are barbarians and the

Germans cultured, in spite of everything that has happened in the last ten years.'

'Exactly so. Less pity for the Russian ally than for the German enemy,' Monsieur Carr agreed. 'That's what I see in England. We sit on our respective edges of the continent, the Russians and the English, heirs to the two great powers that dominated the nineteenth century, believing that we can run the world better than all those in between. But I don't want to sound as though I dislike the English, who have been our hosts, our saviours even. They are unassuming, frugal, hard-working. They have their own ways, but I have never thought of them as perfidious in spite of the prevailing stereotype.

'Gigi is half English. It is likely that his children will be more English than Russian, that they won't speak a word of Russian. Your children will be like that too. That is the story of Europe. We think we are different from the Americans, with their melting pot, but it has been going on for centuries, the churning of peoples. There was a Russian melting pot too. My ancestors were German, and God knows what else, yet we became Russian, more Russian than most. My son married an Englishwoman, a wonderful woman, not of our class, but I now think about class differently anyway. Diana is the best of the best of the English.'

He produced his little notebook and examined his notes for a moment, then put it back inside the breast pocket of his knitted gilet. It sat there like a starched cotton square.

'Let me cheer you up,' he said. 'Let me tell you about Alexei's gallanting.'

The term was so unsuited to his son's character, so unlikely, that I giggled.

'I knew you would find it amusing, Albertine. Even as I could not sleep last night, I thought of ways to make you smile. Gallanting is not right, I know. We are like wolves or swans, we Karenin men, we mate for life.'

The notion of Monsieur Carr and his son as wolves, or indeed swans, made me laugh even more. He could just as easily have said otters or white mink.

'And ho ho, dearest lady, what's so funny about swans?' He had regained his childish mirth.

'I know that Alexei liked Diana the moment he first saw her, staring at us in confusion from behind her grandmother's back on the doorstep of their Kingston home,' he said. 'She was just out of school. He was young too, not quite twenty, though we tended to forget it. He had seen such hardship in his teenage years, and those experiences made him behave like a middle-aged man. By the time he returned from Cambridge, Diana was a young woman, a secretary at the brewery for which he now works. Alexei rushed to settle down, to lead a respectable, English life. Diana was his way into it.

'It was the smallest of weddings. They were married in the old Russian Embassy chapel in Welbeck Street. There was Diana's family, the three of us, Princess Trubetskoy with her three walking sticks, only a couple of years away from death. I don't think we were ever as happy in London as we were on that day when we watched them, Diana and Alexei, under their wedding crowns. She was as beautiful as the Snow Queen, my daughter-in-law, so foreign and exotic was her beauty to our Russian eyes. The English are so insulated by the sea that they underestimate the mystique they arouse in the minds of others. That blonde hair and those green eyes seemed to belong to some Viking archipelago more than to the London smog.

'After the ceremony we walked to the Langham Hotel. It was the most modest of all Karenin nuptials, the most discreet. They went to the Isle of Wight for their four-day honeymoon. That was modest too, so like Alexei. You seem so sombre and self-contained with your stiff upper lips, you young people, this new English generation. When I was young, men used to fight duels over matters of the heart. No more. What about your wedding, Albertine?'

'If you call that wedding modest,' I responded, 'you should have seen ours. Albie and I said to each other that it was just to procure the documents, to satisfy officialdom, so that I could follow him to England. We pretended that the real thing would follow when we gathered our families, but I had no family to gather and he must have known even then that there would not be any other festivities, that it was just me and him, till death do us part, as they say. The voyage to England felt much more celebratory than the wedding.

'In Alexandria, the boat was full of men and women learning to be young again. We took one last look at the Corniche, and shouted hooray. But there was sadness too. The family I was lodging with were preparing to leave. The Ashkenazic Europe had vanished, now the Sephardic Levant was about to disappear. That is what we spoke about during those last evenings while the suitcases stacked up in the corners of our rooms and walls revealed pale patches behind paintings that had been undisturbed for centuries. My landlady had cried every day for weeks. They were moving to Palestine, a short distance away, but Alexandria was the only home she had ever known.

'The British were in a different mood. They were going home. And of all the British soldiers, Albie was the handsomest. In the ports where we stopped to replenish supplies – in Malta and in Gibraltar – people came down to the docks to greet the British with flowers, with cakes and oranges. Young women stared at my husband. I felt almost drunk with my own future. Of the many hours the British are wont to call their finest, this one certainly deserved the adjective.

'In Gibraltar, Albert and I went ashore. We left the others and spent the night at the Rock Hotel. We had our breakfast on the balcony overlooking the Alameda Gardens: fresh orange juice, real coffee, toast with butter and marmalade. I had never experienced such luxury. Albie and I will travel the world together, we will have days and days like this, I thought. In the morning – the Sabbath morning, as it happened – he took me to the synagogue in Irish Town. The temple was empty.

'"Here, Albertine, in front of your God, I promise to cherish and to obey," he said and lowered himself on bended knee, then pinched me, just to offset the solemnity of his words.

'That was our only religious ceremony, without witnesses, on the edge of Europe. I knew that I was happy then. We ascended through the Old Town to the top of the Rock and just stood there watching the two continents, the mountains of Morocco pale in the morning light. Europe and Africa seemed to be parting to let me through. It was perhaps the last time, on my journey from Alexandria to Southampton, that I thought I knew where I was going, that I did not feel lost.'

The Count stirred in his seat.

'I know it won't help, Albertine, but allow me to say it, for you are becoming like a daughter to me, more than Diana in a way. She and I never have these kinds of conversations. Those are the luxuries of the West, those kinds of sentiments. You feel lost because you have a home. You feel that a safe home is not enough. You remind me of my mother when you say things like that. She was Western too, I now know. Be careful what you wish for, dear girl.'

He leaned over and patted my hand.

When we had started these sessions, it would take ten minutes to walk from the Underground station to his front door because I worried about slipping on an unseen patch of ice. The dying winter bade us farewell with snowstorms in the first week of March, one last howl to remember it by. Now the rain fell softly and green buds appeared on the branches. At night, when everything was quiet, there was birdsong.

I returned home that evening to find Albie with a couple of colleagues. Army men, I could see it immediately from the way they sat, from the way they combed their moustaches. The smell of cigarette smoke hit me as I opened the front door, and, as I got closer, the smell of alcohol, but they were neither tipsy nor jolly. This was work, whatever their work was. Their faces were serious and the conversation carried on in a half whisper, falling dead as I approached. The taller man, in a dinner jacket, clearly on the way to somewhere more glamorous, stood up and kissed my hand. It was not something that British men did often. They were confused by the new notions of equality.

'Mrs Whitelaw, so delighted to see you, finally,' the tall man said. 'I haven't seen you since I was brought off that hospital ship in Alexandria. You wouldn't remember, I am sure. You carried a pot with a palm tree into our hospital room, left it by the window, next to this young man's bed.'

He nodded towards Albie.

'"With fronds like these, who needs anemones?" Albert said when he saw you. It was one of those things we repeated for days. Seems silly now, but it made us laugh then. I don't think you understood. It was the palm in the pot, but it was also the scarf you were wearing after work. No one in that hospital was quite as memorable as you. The French girl. We envied Albert his conquest.'

'All those jokes about the failures of the French Resistance,' Albie said. 'I had to listen to no end of them.'

Albie's colleague was tall and imposing, verging on stout, with a booming voice that he tried unsuccessfully to keep in check. On his left hand, he wore a signet ring with the crest carved deep into a green stone. His suntan seemed strange amid the London pallor. Everyone looked like that in Alexandria. In London, most people's faces were chalky white, and women, when they went out, accentuated the whiteness with dark eyeliner and bright red lipstick. Their faces resembled Venetian masks.

I did not remember the man, but I assumed that three or four years can change a face, emphasise the difference between war and peace. I did remember the scarf. I had knitted it myself – a semi-successful experiment in stocking stitch – on a garden bench in Alexandria, in the deep shadow of a fig tree, improvising a pattern of fern and spruce, the dream of snowlines, northern Europe. It was a dark green thing with huge holes, useless against the cold, even more useless against the Mediterranean sun. Perhaps Monsieur Carr was right. I was more eccentric than I thought.

'Ian Abercrombie,' the man said bowing his head a little. 'My friends, while I had them, called me Cutter.'

'Peter Stanford,' said the other man, and stood up to shake my hand.

'Colonel Stanford and Brigadier Abercrombie,' Albie explained. 'They were here the other weekend, while you were with your Russians.'

'I do hope that London is being kind to you,' Abercrombie said. 'The times are still difficult, but things are getting better.'

'Very kind,' I replied. 'And I know.'

Albie offered to pour me a glass of the brandy they were drinking.

'A present from Ian here, who is just back from the Cape. Klipdrift. Boer name, French taste, we were just saying. You'll like it.'

'Just a little sip, please, Albie.'

I made my apologies. The three of them stood up as I walked away with my tumbler. A moment later I heard them resume their conversation.

'Lucky man,' Abercrombie said in his booming voice.

'Oh, yes,' Stanford said. Then the whispers continued.

On Albie's writing desk – I did not have and had not wanted one of my own, although I now worried that I was usurping his space – the pile of paper that represented Monsieur Carr's memoir was growing. Each time I returned from Chiswick, I added a few pages. I reread the story and added explanations of places and names as they became clearer to me – explanations for Gigi and his future English children, I thought. I was writing in English because the chances that they would speak French, or indeed Russian, these future generations, seemed increasingly remote. I hoped Monsieur Carr would not object to my choice of language. I did not aspire to Tolstoyan power, but I discovered that I could be faithful to his words, convey something of his voice.

Next to the side of the typewriter, there were Albie's folders and envelopes. There were two new novels among his papers

– one English, the other a translation from Russian: *Brideshead Revisited* and *Days and Nights*. I did not recognise their authors' names. I looked at the blurbs inside the dust jackets: the former was a narrative of English decline, the latter an account of the Battle of Stalingrad. Albie was a keen reader, but not a reader of fiction, of made-up stories. The books were gifts, I assumed, for someone in Germany.

The sound of the conversation went up and down next door, like waves, then Albie knocked and announced our guests' departure.

'We apologise for stealing your husband, Mrs Whitelaw,' Abercrombie said. 'We appreciate that you have a right to him in the evening.'

'No, not at all,' I said, and wondered if that sounded right. Had I just said that I had no right to my husband's company in the evening? Or that I did not care?

'He's indispensable, your husband,' Stanford added. 'I'm sure he's too modest to make you realise that.'

He said this in perfect French and took everyone by surprise.

'Most impressive, my dear man, most impressive. The accent too,' Albie said and patted him on the shoulder.

'Ah well, all those summers in the South of France with my mother and her lover,' Stanford said, 'while Father looked after the colonies.'

They treated everything, themselves included, as a joke. I liked that about Englishmen. Even when I couldn't speak to Albie because of his urge to tease the humour out of every situation, I found it comforting. But once the front door was closed, Albie slumped into the armchair, refilled his glass of Klipdrift to the brim and crumpled, as though he had been keeping up appearances only for his comrades' sake. He smiled but I could see that he was unhappy. Unhappy and tired beyond endurance.

'Come here, Cartier. It's an order,' he said and patted his thigh. There was no warmth in his voice, only exhaustion. I did as I was told and hugged him. I realised that he had asked me to sit on his lap only to press his face against my back and hide from me whatever expression he wore.

'I am so tired, Ber,' he said. His voice was muffled by my clothing. 'I am exhausted and Berlin is a tragedy, no point pretending otherwise. We'll soon be surrounded inside the city and cut off. What do we do with Germany? You tell me.'

That night, he sighed in his sleep and said things in German and in the morning looked as though he hadn't slept at all.

We had porridge for breakfast and he drank his tea in one gulp, then left for work early, too early. It was still dark outside.

'There is no point in sitting here, Ber. I might as well get on with it,' he said.

And I did too; got on with my day.

My Russian teacher's basement in Queen's Gate was a dark place, an Orthodox catacomb full of icons and flickering oil lamps. The air smelled of cats and mouldy books. The windows were protected by thick grilles outside, and by heavy net curtains inside, yellowing lace which sagged under its own weight. Two Siamese cats stalked behind sofas and armchairs like miniature pumas, staring at mouse holes. There were mousetraps here and there along the skirting boards, primed with bits of desiccated cheese. I noticed a smudge of blood and gut on the wall.

While I recited the Russian alphabet, Elizaveta Furst walked around, straightening her icons or adjusting the shawl that was pinned to her bosom by a large brooch. A firebird, she explained. Her arthritic fingers stood almost at right angles to her palms. They grew strange bone spurs, like ginger roots, above and below an array of rings.

When she wasn't speaking Russian, she talked in a mixture of English and French, with a Russian accent so thick that you couldn't tell where English ended and French began. She was, she boasted, a baroness, an alumna of the Smolny Institute.

She let out little yelps whenever I answered the question or did the exercise correctly, short squeals that sounded like yelps of a puppy in pain, and which made the cats jump out of their hiding places. This happened regularly enough: I worked hard.

'Dear Albertina Abramovna ...' She had asked me for my father's name and insisted on using my first name and my patronymic, Russian style, just as she insisted that I must call her (we are very informal here, she had explained) Elizaveta Maximilianovna, a patronymic I found impossible to pronounce at the beginning of my halting Russian sentences.

'Dear Albertina Abramovna, you are the best student I have, and I have seven at the moment. All handsome young Englishmen, all clever, but not nearly as clever as you. I should introduce you. Perhaps you would like to practise together?'

She had a mischievous smile on her face.

'But I am married, Elizaveta Maximilianovna.' It came out as Maxilovna.

'How very bourgeoise of you, Albertina Abramovna, to need to point that out,' Elizaveta Maximilianovna said. 'Both the aristocrats and the Bolsheviks have stood up against prudish adherence to the patriarchal order.' Or at least that's what I think she said.

'But you are right, perhaps, to turn my offer down so politely. You already have an English husband. Why ask for more of the same? You should take a Russian lover. An old-style Russian gentleman, not these Soviet *muzhiki* who have milled about London since this last war, and can't tell one end of a spoon from the other. I see them sometimes, in Kensington Gardens, going to their wretched embassy. Have you ever met a Russian man?'

'No,' I lied. 'No. Never. Only in books.'

'To deny three times, like Peter, in one breath,' Elizaveta Maximilianovna wheezed with laughter. 'And so fast ... you are a dark horse, Albertina Abramovna.'

That same day, early afternoon, I was sitting at the kitchen table, with a slice of toast, a cup of chicory coffee and my Russian primer before me, when the telephone rang. The black Bakelite was cold against my ear.

'Oh, my dear Mrs Whitelaw, I am so glad I found you at home,' Mrs Jenkins said. 'You are supposed to come to us this evening, but I am afraid Sergei Alexeievich is in hospital. He had a fall. They will keep him in for a couple of days.'

'What happened? How is he? Where is he? Can I visit him?'

'I found him in the back garden this morning and called an ambulance. He had fallen and he was concussed and confused. But he is better than we feared he might be. He is in Acton Hospital, on Gunnersbury Lane. But it is quite a journey for you; do not feel obliged to make it.'

I insisted. She relented. The visiting hours were between five and seven.

I left a note for Albie and set out for Acton. After endless winter stoppages, the journey seemed easy. The buses were moving again. Snowdrifts were reduced to dirty scraps here and there. There were floods beyond London, people said, as if to say there was no end to misery, but in West London, for the moment, the weather offered a promise of something better.

The upper deck of the bus was full of people speaking in languages which I now recognised as Slavonic. I picked up words here and there, sometimes whole sentences. No one threw me a second glance as I leafed through my Russian notebook trying to memorise a few lines with which to surprise Monsieur Carr. Even my features fitted. In this corner of a London filling with survivors, I looked less foreign than most.

He was asleep when I arrived, tucked in like a child under a grey blanket, his left arm bandaged but not in a sling, luckily unbroken. That side of his face which was always sad now carried a large bruise on the cheek and forehead, a dark, beetroot colour. His eyes were bloodshot when he opened them.

'Oh, my dear Albertine, I wish you hadn't bothered,' he gurgled hoarsely. 'I must be a spectacle.'

The asymmetry of his face was emphasised by his injuries.

I took his outstretched right hand and said, in Russian: 'You look fine.'

I wanted to say you look much better than I had feared, but my vocabulary did not stretch that far yet. My accent was too hard, too unyielding.

'You make me laugh, Albertine, and that hurts. I am impressed. Have you been studying Russian in secret all along? And where, if I may ask?' he responded in French, realising that I had already reached my linguistic limits in his native tongue.

'Yes. With a woman called Elizaveta Maximilianovna Furst, in Queen's Gate,' I said.

'Baroness Furst? I am amazed that old biddy is still going. At least she is teaching you Russian, not Georgian or Armenian. She offers those too. Her father, General Baron Furst, Furst von und zu Something or Other, I think he was styled, had a peripatetic life. Her first two husbands were Russian. Husband number three was Georgian. Number four Armenian. Number five Georgian again, but this time of the Atlantan variety.'

He laughed so hard that his laughter turned into a cough and the pain made him clutch his ribs.

'And has she submitted you to one of her anti-Semitic tirades yet? The only people she hates more than the Jews are the Armenians. Once when we met in Piccadilly – what, ten years ago, I think – she was just divorced from number four. He was the honorary consul of El Salvador to the Court of St James, her Armenian of cosmopolitan upbringing. She said that there were no Jews in Armenia because the Armenians were the only people who got the better of them.'

'We pretend that I am French but not Jewish,' I said.

'And she pretends she is echt Russian, the old hag. A great beauty in her time. You should have seen her in the 1890s.'

He was in a room shared with two Polish men, a Slavonic gathering. The Poles were younger and apparently in more serious conditions. One had a bandaged head, the other a leg in plaster, suspended from a pulley. They smiled painfully at my initial Russian efforts and returned to their own conversation when Monsieur Carr and I switched to French. We sat together for an hour, me holding his bandaged hand. A matron popped in from time to time to check on us all. The sky grew darker above the roofs.

'We were planning a party for Easter,' Monsieur Carr said, speaking as though in his sleep. 'For the crew. To mark the start of filming. Orthodox Easter. Leigh and Olivier promised to come, as did Korda. I hope my ribs will have mended by then. I hope you will finally introduce us to your Vronsky. Everyone will be there.'

'Vronsky?' I repeated, confused by the analogy.

'Your beau. Your pretty boy. I imagine him thus. An officer, a gentleman, a heartbreaker. And all the Egyptians worshipping him like Amun-Ra. I have the imagination of a Tolstoy, you see.' He attempted another chuckle and winced again.

'My son was in Palestine, but he always makes it sound as though his war was no different from his current job. Administration.'

Alex Carr materialised out of thin air again. His black Crombie was sparkling with rain and far too heavy for the promise of spring.

'Whenever I step into any room, Father, you and this young lady seem to be talking about me, and it's always the same. In the least flattering terms possible.'

'And where is my grandson?' The old man ignored his son's comments.

'At school, I am afraid. They have a founder's day service this evening. Diana is going to bring him over tomorrow if you are not out by then. You are nothing but an inconvenience, Sergei Alexeievich,' he said. 'What were you up to when you fell?'

'Feeding birds, I have to admit, and talking to them, like St Francis of Assisi.'

The son touched his father's cheek with the back of his hand.

'Don't surprise me like this, Father, ever again. Mrs Whitelaw is too kind to you. I am not sure, if I were her, I would follow you to the four corners of London to find you bruised like this.'

'Don't worry about me,' I said, 'I spent four years in a hospital, seeing injuries much worse than these.'

'I envy my father,' Alex Carr said. 'You tell him your war stories and he refuses to share them with us, yet he shares mine *à volonté*, or so it would appear.'

We watched Monsieur Carr take his painkillers from the matron and drift to sleep. Alex Carr took a book out of his coat pocket and left it on his father's bedside cabinet.

'*Ottsy i deti*,' he said to me. 'Now that you speak the language. *Fathers and Sons*. Turgenev. He asked me to bring him something to read, though I don't suppose he will. He said to make sure that, whatever book I brought, it had a nice binding. It's just for the nurses, the old flirt.'

'*Poydem*,' I said, and then, not trusting myself with even a single word, I translated it into French. '*On s'en va*.'

He smiled, and offered his hand.

'*Da, poydem*. Let's go.'

The air in the hospital was thick with the smell of disinfectant and soup. There were marble tablets with a roll call of names on the walls along the corridor, the Great War memorials. British names, almost to the last, in a rapidly changing city. I looked for the Whitelaws. There was always one, on any list of those who died for the homeland.

Nurses walked past us carrying kidney-shaped bowls, thermometers, blood pressure monitors. A nun in a brown habit and a black veil hurried by, her rubber soles drumming on the stone floor, a long stretch of black and white terrazzo, her Franciscan rope belt keeping the beat of her footsteps.

'I miss all this,' I said as we walked down the flights of stairs to the hospital entrance. Suddenly and without quite knowing why, I burst into tears. They streamed down my face unstoppably – but noiselessly at first, so that Alex Carr did not notice them. Then he did.

'What is the matter, Mrs Whitelaw?' He froze on the step next to me. I could not answer. I did not know.

'What is the matter, Albertine? Do tell me,' he said, producing an enormous silk handkerchief from deep under his winter coat. I just stood there. People walked past, visitors, taking no notice. Perhaps we were not an uncommon hospital sight: a crying woman, a confused man. We could have lost someone, seen someone die.

'All this,' I replied. It made little sense but I couldn't say anything more. It was as though some inner membrane had burst. A relief, and yet a kind of shame, came with the tears.

If Alex Carr was embarrassed, he did nothing to show it. He pressed his handkerchief against my eyes and face, as gently as he had pressed his hand against his father's bruised cheek only moments ago.

'Now, now,' he said. 'It will stop. Don't worry. It will stop. Things will get better. Things always do.'

He sounded like someone who was used to promising that things would get better.

'It was so awful, me breaking down like that,' I said as we stepped out into the London evening. 'I am so sorry.'

I collected myself, took his handkerchief and rubbed my eyes with it. Just then, he took the final step down and turned to face me again. His eyes were almost level with mine when he embraced me so firmly that I could feel his ribcage under the layers of clothing. A moment passed like that, then he released me and said nothing more.

11

The Russian Party

We were sitting in our back garden for the first time that year, Albie and I, surrounded by empty flower pots, inhaling the smell of drying soil in the afternoon sunshine. It was a Saturday, the day before the Carrs' Easter party. The winter had seemed endless; then March brought nothing but rain, as though the year was trying to provide an example of the worst of British weather. Finally the sun burst through the clouds, timidly, like the first rumour of a distant summer. Albie had returned from work early – we lunched indoors, and then took the newspapers out.

'Let's just read,' he said. 'Let's just stay here and read.'

He never said 'at home', always *here*. I was the same. Home seemed too far-fetched. There was nothing like *chez nous* in English. We did not read. *Le Monde*, *The Times*: the large sheets rustled on the table, teacups as paperweights. The kitchen window was open. From inside, the radio played Duke Ellington. No one was saying anything: not the two of us, not the continuity announcer – as though he too had abandoned the studio after a few introductory remarks, gone out somewhere and let the music play.

Earlier I had asked Albie if he would come with me to the party. There was the promise of a Russian Easter with its as yet unknown delicacies; the promise of film stars in a suburban garden; an evening walk by the river after the party was over.

Only the last seemed to tempt him. Albie was weary. There were so many gatherings, he complained, for which he dressed up only to spend hours listening to speeches or, worse, indulging in small talk. Men more senior than him brought wives along, he said, they had to. He would not make me suffer the tedium.

'Not that there's anything to be jealous of, Ber, you should never envy those women. Anyway, I'm thinking of changing my line of work,' he said. 'I'm thinking of donning the uniform again, joining a different regiment if need be, though I'd rather not. The Far East, perhaps. There are things brewing over there. The same fissures. The Chinese as well as and instead of the Russians. I'd like to look at the world through the cross hairs again, for clarity's sake.'

'And me,' I asked. 'What about me?'

'Oh, Ber,' he said, 'there are married postings. And even if there weren't, you might well be happier without me here. You don't know ...'

'You must promise me not to talk like that, Albie. Anyway, promise not to leave me alone here.'

A magpie landed on the flat roof of the neighbouring house and emitted a short call that sounded suspiciously like an echo of my plea. Albie noticed it. He looked at the magpie, then at me.

'I was just playing with the idea, Ber. Nothing concrete in the offing. You don't know ...'

He repeated the half-sentence but did not explain what I did not know. The world settled back into jazz. The sound of choir practice from the church in the square behind us floated over, like the top note of a musky scent.

Whether it was the almost forgotten warmth of the day, or the murmurs of the city beyond our small garden, Albie suddenly relented and said yes, why not, to the Russian party. Our conversations were often like that, sentences fading in and out, sometimes percolating through, nothing quite forgotten.

'You've been working for these Carrs – for, what, almost three months now? – and I haven't met them. It's high time. Why not?'

A line of smart vehicles were parked on Alex Carr's riverside drive when we arrived. Monsieur Carr's house in Bedford Park, Diana had apparently decided, had too small a garden for a party. Her own, by the water, was more appropriate. We were ushered in and then immediately back out through the tiled hall. The lawn was cut in half by the high tide, yet even so it was more than big enough for the twenty or thirty guests who were already dotted around in clusters, glasses and plates in their hands.

Several men wore light grey pinstripe demob suits, not quite the right size in one or two cases: they looked as though they could be Alex Carr's colleagues from the brewery. A few others were in bold checks that could not have come with any clothing coupons.

'Transatlantic plaids,' Albie said. 'Those must be your film people.' He had a set idea of the kind of cloth from which a gentleman's suit should be cut.

The women's dresses, light coats and hats came in many hues. They were bright and exuberantly patterned, as if yearning to say goodbye to the years of austerity. They looked like flowers strewn across the lawn and you could hear, even in the echo of conversations as we approached, that the women knew it and loved the effect they were creating.

The Thames rippled over the border of translucent grass. A lone swan floated under a willow tree, next to a half-submerged cast-iron bench. The conversation rose and fell against the lapping of the water and the sound of oars from the rowing boats midstream, the two clusters of sounds independent of each other, as though the party and the real world were separated by a thick pane of glass.

'Heigh-ho,' Albie said as he readied himself to shake unknown hands. He might have disliked such engagements, but he was obviously used to them.

I saw the tall figure of Alexander Korda speaking to Diana Carr, leaning towards her, spectacles in hand, as though he was trying to see her better without them. His black and white houndstooth suit produced the effect of an optical illusion, like a myriad of atoms in perpetual motion. With a white fur stole thrown over her shoulders, Diana looked more like a film star than any of her guests. She was wearing an emerald dress with a most unusual skirt. It was pinched at the waist and then as full as a crinoline, like the dresses shown in Paris by Dior only a month or two before. I had seen pictures in magazines, but I had not seen the cut on anyone before. The effect was both stunning and profligate – so much fabric for one dress. It made the narrow-skirted peplum dresses worn by most of the other women look mean; like a flowering camellia on a branch of tight, unopened buds.

I muttered the names of people I recognised to Albie while he was already stepping ahead, walking to greet Monsieur Carr. The old man was not difficult to spot: white-haired and unsteady, with a yellowing bruise on his face, propping himself against the back of a garden chair. He looked up at Albie, then past him, at me, realising immediately who he must be.

He raised both hands and took Albie into his embrace, startling him into submission. I could not believe that my husband was hugging someone he was meeting for the first time.

Alex Carr appeared by my side.

'Your husband is so young,' he said. 'So young, and so obviously an officer.'

I blushed. Albie was not much younger than Alex Carr but he was better turned out, effortlessly so. And there was no trace of visible unease about his socialising. Alex Carr, on the other hand, almost exuded unease. Not shyness so much as a desire to be anywhere but in this place; a discomfort that vanished when he was surrounded by his family. Before he materialised next to me, he had seemed to lurk in the shadows, under the trellises, pretending to busy himself, speaking to no one.

'I avoid social occasions if I can help it,' he said, as though he needed to account for his behaviour. 'The how-do-you-dos, the what-do-you-dos. If I say that I work in a brewery people say how fascinating and they mean the exact opposite. Then they ask about Russia and say, again, how fascinating. But I don't like to talk about Russia any more than I like to talk about my job. Sooner or later someone says how terrible. It tempts me to pretend I am a Communist. You don't have much small talk either, do you, Albertine?'

'Happy Easter, Mr Carr. Lovely day. Aren't you, in fact, a Communist?'

He relaxed. We hadn't spoken since the hospital.

'We went to church this morning, as all good Communists do. Would you like a tour of the estate, while my father entertains your husband? They seem to have hit it off. You've more or less exhausted the grounds, but there is the castle behind you.'

He gestured over the sloping green apron and then towards the house. Gigi was showing Amur off to Elizabeth Montagu, who, alone among the women, wore a suit, a grey three-piece with wide trousers and a lilac pocket handkerchief. The dog stood on its back feet and placed its white front paws against Elizabeth's thighs. Its muzzle and its long hair made it look like a Hollywood leading lady, a match for his mistress. I am sure Elizabeth was aware as she kept glancing towards Diana Carr. I turned to face Alex, to say yes, I'll come with you, and nearly bumped into his wide chalk-striped lapels.

'*Me voilà*,' he said. 'Let's go.'

The door into the dining room was wide open. A long table was covered in rows of glasses. A maid had just brought in a tray of blinis and savouries and was arranging them on the table. There was a basket full of painted eggs, and around it bowls with salt, pickles, salad and red and white radishes. It was a pleasing enough display in the face of austerity and rationing, but there was nothing extravagant about the feast.

'The produce comes from my workers' allotments, a few hundred yards upstream,' Alex said. 'I don't mean the salmon, of course, and I don't mean my workers in any Russian, land-owning sense. We had a party at the brewery last week. Between two Easters, they called it, in my honour. A charity sale; no one does that sort of thing as well as the English, but you probably know that already.'

'And you bought everything, by the look of it?'

'Yes, as a matter of fact. There wasn't much competition for the radishes. I know my father promised you some caviar. He told me. There will be a bit of that later. From Petrossian in Paris, courtesy of my grandmother.'

He noticed my confusion.

'I mean Miss Leigh. Another gift. She is too kind to us. Her husband's secretary, a Russian woman as it happens, delivered two tins this morning when she stopped by on her way to Richmond. How excited Gigi and Diana were. I wish I could say the same about myself.'

We continued into the reception room next door. It was furnished with the same good taste: simple, measured and much more anonymous than Monsieur Carr's rooms. The grand piano stood out, with its sheets of Russian music.

'I am the pianist, I am afraid,' Alex said. 'My one extravagance. And I am not very good at it. I started learning as a child in St Petersburg, but always with the knowledge that I was not going to be a musician. It is a kind of meditation, when you play music without any ambition. It requires just enough concentration to take you out of yourself. And this is not an unfair replica of the piano we had.'

'I wish someone had told me that twenty years ago,' I said.

'About the replica?' He looked at me, puzzled.

'No. About meditation. Playing music without ambition. The relaxing effect.'

He was still not sure what I was trying to say. He did not know about Arlette, her music, my refusal to play. It did not matter.

'Mr Carr, Alex.' I seized our moment alone and spoke to him in French for the first time that day. 'I must apologise for my breakdown at the hospital. Seeing your father, perhaps; thinking that he might die.'

Alex Carr gave his shy little laugh, *ha ha*, like reading a script again, not really laughing at all.

'Please don't mention it. If I could help, if you'd like to talk, I am always here.'

'I have forgotten how,' I said. I imitated his laughter, involuntarily, but he seemed not to notice.

'Forgotten how to what?' Albie stepped into the room and echoed my final words, his French deliberately exaggerated so that he sounded like a joke Englishman at the reception of a French hotel.

'We were talking about music,' Alex Carr said. 'My first piano lessons in St Petersburg.'

'Ah, I see. You Europeans. That makes me feel wretchedly philistine. The only instrument I ever played was a recorder. And I found even that impossible.'

The red glow of the setting sun illuminated the lawn when Vivien Leigh and Laurence Olivier arrived with Julien Duvivier. They stepped out on the back terrace, as though the moment was directed. There was a buzz around them, a movement of air, even here, in this small, private circle. He was in a slate-grey suit not that dissimilar to Elizabeth Montagu's. His was cut with the kind of precision that takes years of training, and adorned with expensive detail: a golden watch chain, a pocket handkerchief and a tie of grey silk so rich that it shone across the lawn.

She was wearing the kind of dress that the cut of Diana Carr's emulated, but hers was an item of clothing that subtly but indubitably declared itself to be worth more than most people earned in a year. It came in a brilliant shade of white that set off her blue eyes and her dark hair, and signalled cars and drivers, red carpets and teams of servants.

The sleeves were short and the shoulders soft and strangely girlish after the years of square, masculine padding. Her waist was even narrower and her skirt fuller than Diana's. It was lushly, obscenely full – yards and yards of expensive fabric – as if meaning to say to all of us: 'We are fine. We can afford garments like this. We shall never go hungry again.'

We all smiled at her, beguiled by the promise. If Scarlett O'Hara could walk into the late 1940s, I thought, she would be wearing this dress.

'Here's Vivien. Here's my Anna,' said Korda and walked over to greet her. 'I will take her to her sons. Her two sons, so to speak: Prince Karenin and our little Gigi here.'

He held Gigi by the hand and walked towards Monsieur Carr. The three men stood together as the two stars approached them. They were radiant in their luxurious familiarity, Leigh and Olivier, yet smaller, both slighter than one had imagined. We all watched them, bewitched, as they talked to the boy and the old man, the aim of the afternoon accomplished.

Diana Carr rejoined Korda and spoke to Vivien Leigh with an air of ease, the blonde towering over the brunette, looking at Alex Carr, who made no move to join them even though he obviously featured in their conversation. Vivien Leigh followed Diana's glance in our direction, looked at me for a moment, and smiled. Our physical similarity, on which everyone had commented, did not seem to register with her.

'Well, I never,' Albie jibed, looking at no one in particular. 'I hope no one can read my lips, but you are so much prettier, Ber.'

Olivier threw us a flicker of a smile, as though he had registered Albie's words.

'We must introduce you,' Alex Carr said, but made no move to follow the suggestion up. He would have heard Albie well.

'That would be lovely,' Albie said, not moving from the spot either.

Alex Carr touched my arm above the elbow for a moment and gave it a barely noticeable squeeze, like a teacher urging his best pupil to come forward. He laughed his awkward laugh but all three of us stayed rooted to the spot.

'Well, that was fascinating and tedious in equal measure, Ber,' Albie said as we walked along the river. 'I had guessed that much in advance. But I enjoyed meeting the old Count so I can't quite say that I regret coming along.'

Trains rattled the railway bridge, the stars were out and the tide had receded so much that you could see mud-caked objects on the riverbed. An oar, plastered in brown clay, glimmered in the moonlight. You could almost wade across to the other side.

'Mortlake,' Albie said, pointing over to the other side, and the name sounded like something from a Romantic poem. There was a warm, brackish smell about the water now, and the Thames looked like a village stream far too insubstantial for its wide riverbed. It was difficult to believe it was the same river that, only a few miles further east, flowed by Parliament and carried boats full of people.

'She is nothing like my mother, the Count told me as we parted,' Albie went on. 'Not a trace of Russia about her, he said. But he thought she was just right for Scarlett O'Hara. Who would have believed that the old man had seen *Gone with the Wind*?'

'I know,' I laughed. 'Monsieur Carr told me that Greta Garbo was nothing like his mother either. They seemed so much in love with each other, Olivier and Leigh. They were married to other people, and left their spouses and their children to be with each other. She must know what it feels like to be Anna.'

'Or not at all,' Albie said, 'not at all. But how could I know? I haven't read *Anna Karenina*. You know I don't read novels, Ber.'

He walked ahead, along the edge of the embankment, his arms spread into a T to keep his balance.

'Then who is reading those two novels on your desk?'

'You little snoop,' Albie said. 'Is nothing private? One has to do something to pass the time in those wretched hotels. I recommend *Days and Nights*, since you've noticed it. I respect the Russians, these new Russians, perhaps even more than your Karenins and their Easter blinis and kuliches – is that what you called them? – nice people though they all are, particularly the old man. The society these new Russians are trying to build is much more important. They are clearing the path for all of us, Ber. In the twenty-first century we shall all live in socialism. In a shared Europe, and in socialism, for good or ill, whether we like it or not.

'I know I am making a speech here,' he continued, his arms still spread into a T on the edge of the embankment, 'but it is inevitable. Your Alex Carr agrees. Just don't let his father hear it.'

'Why do you call him mine?' I asked.

Albie kicked a pebble towards the water. He liked to think that everyone was in love with his wife.

'He seems quite smitten with you, even though you affect not to notice. But I like him, Ber. He's a decent chap.'

We walked downriver, in silence, thinking of the party. The city gathered its streets and houses in, as though the moon was pulling it upwards by invisible strings.

'How I love London,' Albie said as we passed under Hammersmith Bridge. 'To me it is synonymous with freedom.'

'London was kind to us in the twenties, much kinder than it was to the Tsar, who was left high and dry although his mother was evacuated by sea,' said Monsieur Carr two days later, as if continuing Albie's train of thought. 'It fed us, clothed us and allowed us to extend our foreign roots in its soil, to survive without losing our soul. And that is something in itself. Just look at us when we arrived and look at us now. Look at us and don't feel afraid, Albertine; in twenty years' time you will say the same.'

In Shepperton, the filming of *Anna Karenina* was about to begin. The magazines and newspapers were full of Leigh's photographs by Cecil Beaton, interviews with Korda, articles about the cast, costumes and sets. The Carrs stayed out of the limelight, in spite of Korda's best efforts to get them to speak to the press.

'I can't imagine giving interviews, responding to questions about Anna,' Monsieur Carr said. 'Tolstoy's story speaks for itself. It is like one of those reconstructions of homes made for the great museums: more telling and more perfect than us. The sooner the prototype is forgotten, the better for everyone.'

We were sitting in the house in Bedford Park, Monsieur Carr and I, rereading *The Wild Mane* for the third or fourth time. Since I had owned up to taking Russian lessons, he often volunteered to read Anna's book with me. He would read a line or two, I would repeat it, and we then translated her words into French and discussed the simple lines and the allusions only he recognised. We compared his mother's sentences and his wife's drawings, and we turned the pages with care.

There was a bookmark at the last page, a ribbon of red leather. Monsieur Carr handed it over to me, put it on my palm. There was, almost, nothing to see: a few tooled lines, a segment of an image etched on leather. It was impossible to say what it represented, perhaps a section of a bird's wing. He stretched his hand out to take the piece back, then held it for a moment in mid-air. He was looking away from me.

'What is this, Monsieur Carr?' I asked. 'Tell me, please.'

The red bookmark now rested on a checked blanket on his lap. His head was bent over it, his side parting straight, a rosy glimpse of scalp under the white hair. The final page contained one of Tonya's drawings – a horse inside a stable, an open door, a glimpse of a snowy landscape outside, a naked birch tree with the moon caught in its branches.

'That chest I found after my father's death, there was my mother's book in it, her locket with my picture, their portrait, as I told you, and then this, this scrap of red that I could never make sense of, these strange frayed edges. I understood, when I finally read *Anna Karenina*. That specific small detail, which seemed like the wildest leap of Tolstoy's imagination, was perhaps the truest to life. I can't begin to understand how he knew it.

'She was at the railway station. All the railway stations were new then. She carried a red bag. She threw it aside before she jumped. When they pulled her up, when they lifted her body off the rails, someone must have taken her bag and brought it to my father. Empedocles took his sandals off before he jumped into the volcano, left them by the crater, like someone taking a swim in the municipal pool, intending to come out at the same spot. My mother's dive must have been different. I imagine it as a plunge taken by someone escaping a house fire in a panic, finally getting away.'

He touched the strip of leather. We were at the mouth of a tunnel that connected this quiet room in Chiswick with a small station outside Moscow in pre-revolutionary Russia. On the other side, I now saw, there were people like us, a woman like me.

'Obiralovka,' Monsieur Carr said. 'Not an elegant name. A place of fleecing. It is as though she threw herself to death in Slough. No more elegant than the Steel Road Town, the name the Soviets came up with. Poor, poor *Maman*.'

He held my hand.

'Did you enjoy the party, Albertine?' he changed the topic. 'Your husband is a remarkable man. Olivier and Leigh shone, but they competed against each other, although he pretended otherwise. His suit may have been grey, but it was so flashy, and there was so much silk on him. Albert and you were like the male and the female of some noble avian species, you in your funny little purple jacket with that blue scarf, prettier than Miss Leigh. His charcoal worsted was understated, all matt you could say, letting you shine.'

'Thank you. You notice everything. What a glamorous party. And it felt so good to be there with Albie, a privilege to have been invited.'

'Duvivier asked me about you,' he added, 'asked what you were doing, if you wanted a job. Speak to her directly, I urged him. Find out. He promised he would. Would you like that, Albertine?'

I contemplated an answer.

'Don't allow yourself to become consumed by unhappiness, my dear. Do something,' he said. 'Just tell yourself you mustn't give in to sadness, as your husband must do. I can feel that in him, self-restraint in the most literal sense of the term, although we spoke of nothing personal.'

'Consumed by unhappiness? You mean like your mother?'

He was puzzled.

'My mother was different. She had allowed herself to be consumed by happiness.'

Although the weather had improved, when I returned the rooms of our house were as cold as ever. It would take weeks to soak up the warmth outside. I spent an hour waiting for

196

the fire to make a difference, while trying to read Albie's copy of *Days and Nights*. There were two notes tucked inside its pages, between the last lines of the novel and an unenticing afterword written by an American academic. One had several scribbled sets of numbers, the departure times of a train or a flight, most likely, no words, no explanation. Another, on the notepaper of a Berlin hotel, contained the beginning of a letter. Several beginnings of a letter, crossed out, restarted. A letter to me.

Dear Albertine. Dear A. Darling Bertie. Darling. I cannot. Dearest love. I hope you will understand that

Only the last few words were not crossed out, but there was nothing more. I folded the paper as I found it and tucked it back into the book. Albie had never sent me a letter, never even a postcard. Something had happened, the letter suggested, but, whatever it was, it was obviously over. I could not decide whether to tell him that I had found the note, or to wait until he mentioned it, if and when he saw me reading his book. I could not imagine Albie with a mistress, in Berlin or anywhere else. Yet there was this paper, this note.

Was he thinking of leaving me? I changed my mind. I took the note out again, felt the thinness of the writing paper, its texture between my fingers. I tucked it inside the folder with my Russian exercises. I would wait to see whether Albie noticed that the note had gone from his book. I would wait until he raised the question of its absence.

The house was getting warmer. The water on the stove was slowly coming to the boil. I needed a distraction. There were bones in the refrigerator, big, beefy bones I had queued for at the butcher's on Gloucester Road, carrots and parsnips I had purchased from the greengrocer in Chiswick on my way back from Monsieur Carr's. I had queued for them too, worrying that they would run out by the time I came to the head of the queue. Parsley was an afterthought. They had plenty; no one had wanted it. I carried the large green bunch on the Tube like a wedding bouquet. It was unlike any parsley I had known before I came to England, curly, dark green, black almost. I also had a branch of laurel from Monsieur Carr's garden. Mrs Jenkins had snapped it off a bush by the front door when I told her that I was on my way to the greengrocer.

I halved some onions and roasted them along the cut, until their burning caramel smell rose up from the stove. There was time enough to make the stock, concentrated and sweet, to keep it simmering, then cool it off overnight until it jellified. I would heat it up again tomorrow, add a dash of that South African brandy, keep it simmering again, wait for it to get darker and darker. I was willing myself to stop thinking. Notice the perfection in the ordinary, hang on to it, I kept telling myself. Tell yourself that you mustn't give in to sadness. I wondered if that's what Tonya Carr was doing with her flower paintings; a route to salvation can seem disconcertingly similar to a descent into madness. Monsieur Carr told me that people in solitary confinement start speaking to themselves, out loud, sooner or later. How did he know?

Albie was in Bristol. Some meeting with the Royal Artillery, he said, as though it made a difference. Back on Wednesday, he had added, this one is close by. Bristol: every French city seemed to have a posh hotel of that name. I found Bristol on the map of England, in an atlas in Albie's study. It was close by, just as he said, but also on the other side of England, next to a body of water that looked like an immense fjord on the map, a deep cut, an axe fallen on the land mass.

*

That night I fell asleep almost immediately. I had a strange dream. I rarely remember my dreams, and never when Albie wakes up first. The images vanish the moment he flicks on the light switch. This one stayed with me. I woke up alone, noticed a thin white line of light between the curtains, the pillowcase wet under my face.

In the dream, our kitchen was empty. It was raining outside. I could hear rain drumming on the window. There was a large pot on the stove and in it bones, carrots and parsnips and a bouquet garni in a muslin bag. The water was simmering and the bones moved slowly, clinking faintly against each other, and against the heavy walls of the copper pot. The actions mirrored exactly what I had done earlier in the day, but everything else felt alien. I was in London and Paris at the same time. I was me, and I was my own mother. The stove was mine but the copper pans and the wooden ladles were all hers.

I had forgotten how to do this, I thought. I was preparing the mirepoix in my dream, throwing handfuls of diced vegetables and chopped parsley into the simmering pot, although I had never done it before, although my mother had never taught me how. Thirteen years since her death, thirteen and a half almost; I rarely thought about her. I did not need to, I thought now. I knew somehow that this was a dream even as I dreamed it. The liquid slowly thickened, the bones got hotter and hotter. Marrow fell out of them and melted, glistening slicks of it appeared on the surface.

'What a lovely smell,' said Arlette. I turned and she was sitting at my kitchen table with an empty bowl before her, an enamel bowl, white with a dark blue rim. She was pale and unbearably thin. Her hands, holding the bowl, were like pigeon's feet, red, dry, raw and twig-like.

'I am cold,' Arlette said. 'I am always cold these days. You would not believe it, Albertine.'

I went over to hug her, and her frayed padded jacket gave way. Her body was not there. It felt like hugging a clothes hanger, a worm-eaten wooden yoke instead of shoulders.

I tried to say something to her but I could only speak English. She looked at me in panic.

'What are you saying, Albertine, what are you saying? I can't understand you. Say it again, *ma mignonne*, say it in French, please.'

I tried to repeat my words, in French, but again, only English came.

'Albie! Albert,' I shouted. I called for help, although I knew, even asleep, that Albie was in Bristol, that he would not be able to respond, that he would not be there to help translate my words. Then Alex Carr came into the kitchen.

'You called,' he said.

He carried his father's checked blanket and he wrapped it over my sister's shoulders.

'So soft,' he said to Arlette. 'So soft. You will be fine.'

And she smiled.

'Why are you crying, Albertine?' he asked. I did not know, in that dream, which language he was speaking, just as I did not know it seconds ago, when he addressed Arlette, but I understood him. Both of us did.

'Why are you crying, Albertine?'

I tried to respond, and I thought I was speaking English, but he just looked at me.

'You see,' Arlette told him, addressing him with an informal 'you', as though they had known each other for a long time, 'I cannot understand her either. I can't understand

Albertine any more. She now speaks like the rain falls, just pitter-patter.'

She pushed her bowl away. The rings under her eyes were the colour of dark indigo. Alex Carr looked at me and tried to ask again.

'Why are you crying, Albertine? I have the right to know.'

12

The Meaning of Cowardice

It was a bewildering dream but I knew, when I woke up from it, something that I had not known before. Had Alex Carr not been so self-effacing, I might have realised it before he became my third lover. My fifth, depending on how you calculated it. Albie was not going to enumerate because he was not going to know. No one was going to know.

Had Alex Carr not been so set on playing the dependable, ordinary Englishman that he wasn't, I might have realised it long beforehand. I might have felt a sense of relief when Albie said that he was coming with me to the party, the Easter film party, because some part of me had already known that I was not to be trusted. That in fact I could not be trusted from day one, that first evening when I kissed Alex Carr in the milky light of the approaching train. At least he did not try to pretend that he was unhappy. At least he did not fake anything.

'I am a devoted husband,' he said that early afternoon when we had lunch together. We were sitting side by side in a bistro in Hogarth Place, almost opposite Earl's Court Underground station, a cold place in those rationed days, not a place you would choose for an adulterous assignation, if you had thought of it as such. If Earl's Court was the Danzig Corridor, that corner of it genuinely felt as bleak as Danzig.

'I am a faithful husband, Albertine, an uxorious man. You might find that distasteful. The fact that I am saying it, I mean, the fact that I need to say it just now and did not need to say it to you before.'

His spectacles were resting on the table, his long thin arms raised not towards me – I was by his side – but towards an invisible Diana who was sitting opposite and to whom just then he was, still, faithful in deed. He stooped a little, I noticed for the first time. All that desk work, I thought. His spectacles had a strange shape. The lenses were circular but the thin gold wire which framed them was straight on top. The spectacles looked as though they were made in the last century. I stared at them, on the table, because I was sitting too close to him to turn and look him in the eye.

'They were my grandfather's,' he explained later.

Just then he said: 'And I know you are too. A faithful wife. I am not sure what the female equivalent of uxorious is; a good wife, I guess.'

I tried, unsuccessfully, to think of a way to improve the adjective.

'I am not uxorious,' I said. 'I am not even a good wife. I fear that I never was. There is something unanchored about me. I look at everything as though I am floating two feet above the world. And I don't blame Albie or the war. I was like that already when I left Paris.'

If there was one single thing that led to everything that followed, it was perhaps that I had mentioned my dream to Alex Carr when he had telephoned the day before. He was intrigued, amused even, but arrived at the restaurant looking like someone who had given the conversation too much thought, who had prepared an unnecessary, redundant speech.

I am responsible for it. There are things that you don't share, and if you do, things that, when you are as old as I am, you have to take responsibility for. I was not to blame, but I am responsible. If there is, indeed, a difference between blame and responsibility in this case.

He had telephoned about his father. The usual call; we had had at least one a week since January, brief, necessary conversations, leavened by courtesy. Then, after Acton, the calls changed, became more cautious, more deliberate, but they did not stop. It was as though there were now stony, unmentionable islands around which our conversation continued to flow as before, but more tentatively, more carefully, and I noticed a change. The awareness of it made me scrutinise our exchanges, think about the things I had said, worry about the things I would say. I would have forgiven him if the calls had stopped altogether, if Diana or Mrs Jenkins had taken over the arrangements. Instead, he continued to telephone, but still, those islands ...

'We' he said, always, but so that it often wasn't clear whether he was speaking about himself and Diana or himself and his father. 'We were thinking ...' 'We were planning ...' 'We wanted to check, if it's OK ...'

I responded in the same way. We will, of course, I would say, we knew, we saw, we were delighted. In my case, it was always clear that I meant Albie and I. I had no one else. But every now and then I had to say I. I will come. That's all right. Albie is away. I am alone. And if I said 'I am alone', I could now sense that he was grappling with a meaning that had not been there before. He ceased to drop by his father's as he had so often in those early days, knowing the timing of our sessions, five or ten minutes before the end. Not after that evening at the hospital.

Then, on a Sunday evening, he had telephoned, as usual, to talk through the coming week, to agree the times. I mentioned that I was about to complete Monsieur Carr's biography. A memoir, I called it; I was the ghostwriter.

'I think I am almost done. And I believe I have succeeded in catching the charm of your father's voice,' I said. 'It feels, almost, as you read it, as if he had written it himself. Except, there must be a hundred mistakes. It is meant to be a surprise for your father. I would like to check all those Russian names with you. I would really love him to be the first to read the text in full, so I have prepared a list of questions, a set of cards ...'

I said all this without any suggestion that I was arranging a tryst, without any premonition that a tryst was what it would become.

'I will, of course. I'd love to. Shall we meet?' It felt as though he had said it before he knew what he was saying.

I thought for a moment then named the place. A bistro opposite Earl's Court, practically outside the Underground station. I had had a cup of coffee there alone once or twice before. It was run by the Free French during the war, they said, and it remained unchanged, a French provincial islet in the British sea, with smoky posters advertising events from the 1930s, the smell of garlic, butter and tarragon fighting against boiled potatoes and stale tobacco, a long bar with sticky bottles of mint liqueur no one ever ordered, and candles which had once burned in glass holders but were never lit again. They served slightly sour wine in small carafes. Monday lunchtime. It could fit into his lunch break, almost. I was not going to see Monsieur Carr until Wednesday.

'Oh, don't worry about my lunch break, Albertine,' he said. 'We can take our time to do what needs to be done. I am not proposing to rush back.'

To do what needs to be done. It was drizzly outside, and the place was almost empty, except for a couple of old men sitting under a poster for the Monaco Grand Prix, smoking and sipping coffee from tiny cups, speaking a language not unlike Russian to each other. Ukrainians perhaps? We were not going to have a secret language here, Alex Carr and I, I thought as I walked across the grimy linoleum. There were no secret languages in London any more. It did not matter; what would we need a secret language for?

He was already seated, his raincoat hanging off a hook to the left of him, his briefcase on the chair – the chair which, for the first quarter of an hour at least, was to be occupied by the ghost of his wife. The green-eyed ghost. He stood up to help with my coat, to move his bag. There was for a moment just the click-clack of metal – Blakey's, Albie called the half-moons men had nailed beneath the toes of their shoes to make the soles last – and I worried that he was fussing too much.

'Don't worry, Alexei, please sit down and leave your briefcase where it is, I will sit next to you. That way we can look at my questions together. We won't have to read anything upside down,' I said.

Although his father – and often Alex Carr as well – had been calling me Albertine for weeks, I had tried to persist with formality: Monsieur Carr for the father, Mr Carr for the son. Or I avoided the name altogether. I am not sure why I felt that the intimacy of the first name – and the particular close-ness of its Russian version used by his father alone – was suddenly more appropriate.

The coat hooks were nailed too high, well above head height. The waiter rustled away with my raincoat. It took three attempts to hang it. Water dripped off its suspended fabric, like blood off a fresh kill, creating a dark puddle between us and the Ukrainians. I remember everything.

It was not a good idea. Sitting side by side, like couples in Impressionist paintings of absinthe addicts, we were – it turns out – intoxicated before we had the first drop of wine. We spoke as we would not have spoken had we been facing each other.

There were preliminaries: worries about Monsieur Carr, the good work I was doing, my Russian lessons. We ate the lunch – a salad of grated carrots, a bourguignon stew, dark, shiny and a little bitter.

'English mustard,' I said. 'Bourguignon does not call for mustard, but – if you felt you had to add some – Dijon would have been better.'

The meat tasted like soggy paper – but most meat did in those days. With mashed potatoes and a glass of red wine, the meal was OK, even not bad at all. The French did their best with what they had.

And then the table was cleared and I opened the book, typescript pages in a spring folder. I had prepared cards with page references and names I was going to ask about, and I spread them before me like a fairground psychic casting her cards for a reading. Instead of looking at them he started reading the pages in the folder. I could not bear to remind him that I had wanted his father to be my first reader. But Albie had read most of the manuscript, I thought, Monsieur Carr would not be the first anyway.

I stared at Alex Carr, feeling so nervous about his judgement of my work that I was tempted to walk out and come back only when he had finished with it. But I stayed. I saw that his hair had much more grey in it than I had thought. I looked at his profile as he read, his sensible profile which Monsieur Carr said reminded him of his own father, and I felt a tenderness for him that was still nowhere close, not for another hour at least, to an irresistible attraction.

'Oh dear, did my father really say that?'

'You have done well, Albertine. You have done so well. He will love it.'

He repeated such remarks intermittently in French and English.

He paused from time to time to correct a name or explain a detail with the patience of an elementary-school teacher. I jotted things down on my cards. It took almost two hours to reach the last page. The waiter was reading a paper and smoking at the bar. My coat had dried. The Ukrainians had long gone. I collected the cards and held them together with an elastic band. I heard a soft snap as the band fell into place. I thanked Alex Carr for his help and apologised for the time it had taken. He turned to face me and, at that same moment, I turned too. I could see that his father's story – his own story – had had a deeper effect on him than his detailed, uncomplaining explanations had suggested. He looked at me as though he was expecting, desiring even, another question. I had none.

'I had a strange dream, about you and my sister, the other night,' I said. I had mentioned it on the phone but now I tried to describe it. The moment I started, the details came to seem so embarrassing to me that all of a sudden I regretted having mentioned it again. There had been small steps before, small steps leading to where we were now heading, I thought, but I have now taken an irrevocable one.

He knew it. My hand was already so close to his that I could feel the warmth of his flesh. The warmth now grew to a current which could be stemmed only with a touch. He took my hand. For that, perhaps, I am to blame. It was then that he said: 'I am a faithful husband, Albertine, an uxorious man. And I know you are a faithful wife.'

No one would know.

So the world changed and no one knew. Afterwards I locked the front door and listened to the sound of footsteps fading away with their metallic echo. I sat in the kitchen for the best part of an hour before I picked up my raincoat from the floor in the hall. It was dark outside and the rain had stopped.

I went to the cinema. *The Years Between*: that was the film I saw, a war story. The plot was preposterously English in its chain of resisted temptations. A colonel returned from the dead just as his wife was about to remarry. His voice could have been my husband's. I closed my eyes, and felt so warm that I thought my body must be glowing in the dark.

When the film finished, I walked, as fast as I could, along the King's Road, through Eaton Square and further and further east, past terraces and churches and pubs and shops, until I ceased to recognise the street names and felt only my aching feet. On the near edge of the City there was a pub not far from the Thames, like no pub I had ever seen before, a slim wedge of a building. It was all marble and alabaster inside, and a riot of reliefs: plump monks carrying water, boiling eggs, singing, making music surrounded by satyrs and gargoyles. *A good thing is soon snatched up*, said a motto on a banner above an empty booth. Devils played accordions on each side of it.

The place was practically empty. It was quarter of an hour before closing time, the publican said, puzzled by the sight of a woman alone, and so late; by my accent too, perhaps, and by my ignorance of what was on offer. He suggested a small dark sherry.

'Yes, why not,' I said.

I sat with the tiny tulip glass in the alcove until the closing bell. The only sip I took tasted warm. There was something a bit salty in the sweetness, like lovemaking and oblivion. I walked back out into the street. Cold air did little to clear my head. In the underpass by the Underground station a beggar asked for a shilling to get home. I saw through his lie but gave the coin nonetheless.

On Wednesday I went to see Monsieur Carr as usual. I had spent the whole of Tuesday typing his story again, simultaneously trying to forget the previous day and relive every detail of it. The work helped pass the time. The memoir was now in my bag, a red folder with neatly arranged pages, the names and places all corrected. But first I wanted to ask about Tonya, the question I had not dared ask before.

'Was Tonya happy, Monsieur Carr?'

'You see those pictures, Albertine,' he answered, raising his hand towards the closed door and the dining room with its flower paintings behind it. 'Do you think they were painted by a happy woman?'

'Yes,' I said, then quickly: 'No.'

'Tonya was as silent as those flowers,' he said. 'She was happy when we first married, happy when Alexei was born ... but I don't think, although I loved her, that I was a good husband. I am a weak man.'

'A weak man, Monsieur Carr?' I said. 'I don't think so.'

'Let me tell you something I have never told anyone before,' he said.

'We were in Istanbul, and Tonya went out to sell her pictures, as she often did in those months in Turkey. I stayed at home, writing letters of supplication, useless letters which got nothing but empty courtesies in reply. I spent most of my days writing begging letters. It was early evening when Tonya returned with an empty folder. The sky over the city echoed with calls to prayer and that awful cry of hungry seagulls. She put the folder on the table and said, "I've sold them all. We can move on now." She took a wad of bank-notes from her pocket and put them on the table. Francs and marks and liras: rolls of paper unfolded on the bare wooden surface.

'There was just too much of it. "How come, Tonya?" was the first thing I asked. She had never sold more than a couple of her little pictures on any one of her expeditions before, and now several dozen in a single day. Antiques shops in Pera offered a lot of Russian frippery in those days, knick-knacks by Fabergé, pocket watches, cigarette cases and medals, more medals than anything else perhaps. Tonya knocked on those shop doors, left a painting or two to sell on commission. A few days later she would knock again, usually to find that nothing at all had sold. Or that a picture had gone, for not much more money than would buy lunch.

She would replace it with a new one, if the dealer felt charitable. Often, they just said: no more. Even in charity they took their cut, those old Armenians and Jews whose families had been in Istanbul since Hagia Sophia was built, and who were now suffering and hungry themselves. They took their deserved cut, usually leaving so little that the sum would not get us to Edirne, let alone to Prague or Paris. And now there was this.

'"How come, Tonya?" I asked.

'"Hush," she said, "hush, Sergei, my love. I was lucky today. There was someone who loved my art. I will tell you about it when I have rested."

'Our son walked into the room, saw the money and yelped, like a happy young puppy. He was still a teenager, and he was too old for his age in many ways, but in that split second he could have been seven or eight.

'"Did you place a bet, Father? Did you place a bet on a winning horse?"

'"Yes, Father did, Alexei," Tonya responded before I could say a word. She took a box of Turkish delight out of her purse and opened it. There was the smell of rose essence, mounds of powdered sugar inside. She took one piece out, pushed the box towards us, then ate her piece slowly, her eyes wide, bewildered, looking at me as if to say I dare you to ask another question.

'"We can leave this horrible city now," Alexei said. "We can go back north again."

'Even at that age he knew better than to say go back to Russia. Although some people did. Go back. Thought it better to die in Russia than to live like dogs elsewhere.

'That night, in our rooms off Istiklal Avenue, Tonya extinguished the lamp and drew the curtains before she undressed.

She usually did one or the other. She was not shameless, my Tonya, but neither was she shy. She knew that I enjoyed looking at her body, and I don't mean her nakedness – forgive these details, Albertine, they are important – for there were always layers of camisoles and petticoats in those cold days, layers of undergarments which revealed at best a flash of a shoulder or a breast, a hint of a calf. That evening, I was not allowed to see anything, not an inch of her skin. But I did glimpse deep bruises on her arms – four bruises like four fingerprints above her elbow, deeper on her milky skin than the darkness around us – and I did see dark stains on her underskirt. And God will never forgive me for it, I was so angry with her when I saw this that I thought if I asked her one more question I would strangle her. She was too brave, you see, Albertine, too ready to suffer alone, and in her courage, she had shown me up as the lowest of the low, the weakest of the weak.

'But I only knew that many years later. That evening I had my own version of events, a husband's idea of what might have happened before she returned with her wad of money, a husband's insight into why she had insisted all along on knocking on those doors alone. It did not occur to me that she was trying to protect me, a count, from the humiliation of salesmanship, or the disgrace and pain of the violence she had suffered, just as it did not occur to me that night that she did not sell what should never be on sale. I thought her, that evening, so much worse than my mother, but I turned my back and feigned sleep.

'I feigned sleep in order to avoid becoming anything even more terrible than the coward that I was. People did that too – things much worse than male cowardice. Men murdered their wives and killed themselves. The option did not seem untempting when the dawn call to prayer came and I was still awake, still feigning sleep. It seemed rational, the only right thing to do, but for Alexei, Albertine. A boy alone. I could not leave my son alone in this world, and although some men did that too, I could not murder my own child.

'It was only years later that I knew the truth, when it was too late, when Tonya had almost stopped speaking, here in London, when she painted and painted yet never once wanted to sell a painting again. She hardly spoke to anyone except Princess Trubetskoy, but even then she mostly listened, rarely said a word. The Princess was happy to have a mute companion. The old woman was so full of stories that she never noticed another person's silence. Much later, when it was too late, when Tonya had practically ceased to speak to me too, I realised that a part of me had known it all along.

'Tonya was not going to say a thing to me and Alexei about the horrors she had been through because she did not want to make our lives harder than they already were. We know too much about men at war, but women's wars, dear Albertine, women's wars are what damn us all to hell. We don't want to know how women suffer because we realise that we cannot fulfil our duty to protect them.

'When Alexei was old enough, when he was making his own living, Tonya and I would sometimes lie in our bed, side by side, and if she thought that I was asleep, Tonya would talk to me again. She had always used a Russian *vy*, a *vous* form, to address me, as Russian women were wont to do in aristocratic marriages, as my mother had always addressed my father. Yet late at night, in those whisperings of hers, she always used *tu – ty*, Sergei – and she used the close, informal conjugations of the verbs.

'"I hope you can hear me, Sergei, my love," she would whisper. "You don't have to respond, but I hope you can hear me. It is time to go. Our boy does not need us any more. We should only stay here for as long as is necessary to help our children and not remain to hinder them. It's not just my feeling, it is the logic of Darwinism. And as for religion, I know self-murder is a sin, but God will forgive us, I am sure, as he has forgiven your mother. It is time to go."

'That is what she said, in those late-night soliloquies of hers. I pretended not to hear, and then, at daybreak, we resumed as before. When Alexei told us that he was to marry Diana, Tonya changed for a while, or pretended to have changed, for the sake of her son. At the church in Welbeck Street she almost appeared to be her old self. When Alexei and his bride walked around the nave with the golden crowns on their heads, her face was bright in a way it had only been when she was young and nursing our boy.

'Alexei will be the perfect husband, she said. From this projected perfection I knew how thoroughly I had failed. You asked if Tonya was happy, dear Albertine. Yes, I think she was happy when that bomb fell on her, happy in the hour of her death.'

I heard the front door open, caught the smell of fresh bread. Mrs Jenkins stepped into the house and stood at the door of the library, unbuttoning the single large collar button of her coat. She smiled the wide, jolly smile of a hunter-gatherer who has had a successful day.

'It is like Soviet Russia, this England of ours, nowadays,' Monsieur Carr said. You could not discern, from his tone, that he had just told me a dark, disturbing story. 'Every household has to have one person in a queue somewhere, full-time.'

'I trust you will stay for tea, Albertine. I've made some carrot cake,' Mrs Jenkins said. 'Mr Carr always complains about our English habit of making cakes with vegetables. What next, he asks, a beetroot génoise? But why not, I say. He always eats whatever cake I make. He always polishes it off. However much he complains.'

'Because I am a good boy,' Monsieur Carr responded. 'I am telling Albertine my life story and we had just reached Alexei and Diana's wedding.'

'Oh, what a day that was,' Mrs Jenkins said. 'Diana in white, with her green eyes – you should have seen her. The rite is just not the same in an Anglican church. Sorry, I am not sure I should be saying that. Yours was an Anglican wedding, I assume, Albertine. But it seems much nicer, probably, when you are new to it.'

'Mine was a wartime, civil ceremony,' I said. 'A blue wedding, not a white one. I wore a cobalt blue suit and the Mediterranean obliged with the backdrop: a cloudless sky, the sea. But I wore pink in the evening, at the Cecil Hotel in Alexandria, my only evening gown.'

'I am sure it was just as lovely a day. Weddings always are,' Mrs Jenkins said.

I did not feel I could take the folder out of my bag and present it to Monsieur Carr over carrot cake. I felt inexpressibly sorry for him, and even more so for Tonya. I looked at my watch, made up an excuse, said that I had to dash. Monsieur Carr stood up and walked me to the door.

'I wish I had a daughter like you, Albertine,' he said. 'You are a good woman.'

So I returned to Earl's Court and re-entered the empty house, and put together some leftovers for supper. Why, I did not know, when it seemed likely – when I said what I had been planning to say to my husband since the moment I heard Monsieur Carr regret his cowardice – that we were not going to eat leftover meat or anything else together, Albie and I, not that night, not together, perhaps never again.

The evenings were still cool. I laid the table then lit the fire in the sitting room and sat in its orange glow, waiting to hear Albie's footsteps, thinking of the words I would use, matter-of-fact, unambiguous words. I owed my husband that. I have committed adultery, Albie.

There was the sound of the car, stopping for some moments, then moving on, and I did not get up to look through the window. I sat where I was, in the armchair by the fire, facing the door through which Albie was going to step at any moment, waiting to hear the unlocking, the footsteps, the sound of a suitcase coming to rest on the tiles, the rustling of a raincoat being taken off.

'Albie,' I was about to say, 'Albie, I am afraid something has happened.'

I heard the key and the footsteps, but Albie was not alone. He was urging someone to come in, to close the door quickly, to leave the bags in the hall, to take their coat off, and then Peter Stanford pushed through the door.

'Oh, Mrs Whitelaw, I'm so sorry. Are you all right sitting there? There was no light. We didn't expect to see you here. Albert said you were at work.' He straightened his jacket as if to start again.

'I hope everything's all right, Mrs Whitelaw,' he said, just as Ian Abercrombie and Albie came in, a couple of big folders under Albie's arms, a heavy, square bottle in Abercrombie's. Albie switched the lights on.

'Albertine, my dear, were you napping? Do forgive us,' Albie said and kissed my hand demonstratively, somewhat tipsily I thought. 'What's new? How have you been?'

'Well,' I said. 'Everything is quite all right. I went to the cinema on Monday night.'

'Ah, cinema,' said Abercrombie, not bothering to ask about the film.

Albie had gone into the kitchen and returned with the plate of cold meat I had prepared. He held a radish, a small, perfectly red, perfectly round radish, like a nipple between his teeth.

'We're going to have to do some work here,' Albie said, chewing the radish. 'Don't mind us, Ber.'

'I will be upstairs,' I said, 'listening to the wireless. Do say if it disturbs you.'

'Don't you worry, Mrs Whitelaw,' said Peter Stanford. Of the three men, he alone had a trace of anxiety in his eyes, a sense that the scene had been set for a different conversation.

It was well after midnight when Albie joined me again. The bedroom was lit by the full moon. I watched him undress and hang his clothes in the wardrobe, item by item, then climb into bed.

'Ber, dear, I saw as I came in that you were bursting to talk to me. I'm sorry. I've had a long day, meetings, then an interminable drive back, and I'll have a very early start tomorrow. Whatever it is, unless it's burning, can it wait?'

He was setting the alarm.

'No, nothing's burning, Albie, just you sleep.'

He pulled over the eiderdown and hooked one of his feet around my ankle, as if to say I am here, worry not. I heard the eastward rumbling of the last Underground train.

'I love you, Albertine. That's all that matters. Please don't worry about it, whatever it is, I'll sort it out.'

And with that, he was away.

13

The Wronged Party

Elizaveta Maximilianovna had placed a selection of excerpts from Chekhov on her dining table. They consisted of sheets of paper in a wide fan around a spread of tarot cards she kept turning, even during our Russian lessons, as though she needed the tarot to interpret my stammering responses. She murmured and whispered, clapping her chubby hands with their gnarled fingers when she liked the way the cards fell, screwing her lips into a small pouting circle when she did not.

She had written the passages out in Cyrillic block capitals, wide spaced, to allow me to note the translations down before we discussed them. Chekhov was not ideal for a beginner, but I did what I was asked to do in longhand, in English, with painstaking slowness, consulting a battered Russian–French dictionary. While my trilingual translation went on, Elizaveta glanced from time to time at an array of icons. From inside their golden halos, the long faces of saints with dark eyes that followed you around the room were the very opposite of her own soft, round face, of her blue eyes which hardly ever looked straight into yours, yet saw everything. She never kept the time. The one hour I paid for sometimes extended to three or four, with endless cups of tea and visits to her freezing lavatory, where outlandish hairnets hung from the hooks inside the door like equipment for some surreal butterfly hunt.

Her two cats sat on her lap, purring, one next to the other across her knees, leaving a trail of hairs on her skirt every time they moved. The room was filled with the sound of footsteps. The basement window looked – through the grilles – onto the pavement of a busy road, showing only about twenty inches of space. There was a procession of trousered and stockinged legs, of headless children and pram wheels, and just occasionally a whole dog, a dachshund or a spaniel, looking in, straight at the two of us. Only the passing dogs roused the cats to full alert, ready to jump off their mistress's knees.

'Lev Nikolayevich was a genius,' she said, her French so heavily accented that it always took a minute to realise she was not speaking Russian. 'Anton Pavlovich, however, was more like the son of God. He died so young, he saw everything and his mercy was boundless, whereas Lev Nikolayevich was ...'

That second mention of Tolstoy's name and patronymic was the point at which I realised she was speaking French. Had her outlandish comparison between Tolstoy and Chekhov been delivered in Russian, I would have assumed that I was misunderstanding her completely. She enjoyed seeing me startled by the eccentricity of her claims. She liked my Frenchness, and forgave my Jewishness.

'Like Proust, you see, some of the best Frenchmen – and women – were Jewish,' she once said to me, having assumed that I needed reassurance, although I cared about my status in France no more than she would have cared about hers in Soviet Russia. Having said it, she did not wait for my reaction but reached instead for a silver casket on the shelf behind her and opened it to show me a glass container of soil from Lorraine, several teaspoonfuls, proof perhaps that

221

France meant more to her than it did to me. She was a Francophile, and she despised the English only marginally less than she despised the Germans, in spite of her German-sounding name.

'You think I am exaggerating, I see, Albertina Abramovna,' she continued, pursuing her wild parallels still further. 'Lev Nikolayevich was difficult and vengeful, and too prolific in every way. Thirteen children, like thirteen Apostles.' Here she paused and crossed herself, but I chose not to question the number. 'Whereas Anton Pavlovich had only his readers. Have you read "The Lady with the Little Dog"? Have you done your homework?'

'Yes I have,' I said.

'So you know it then. It is a fraction of *Anna Karenina*'s length, but it achieves so much more. What complexity of feeling, don't you agree? Can you find the quote from the story on the table, Albertina Abramovna? Could you read it to me? Russian first, then your own, French translation.'

And it seemed as though in a little while the solution would be found, and then a new and splendid life would begin; and it was clear to both of them that they had still a long, long road before them, and that the most complicated and difficult part of it was only just beginning.

I read this in stammering, halting Russian, then in my own French translation, as quickly as I could, not giving her the time to think about its quality. I did not want Elizaveta Maximilianovna to focus on my word choices and turn this into a French lesson, as she often tried to do, to prove that her French was superior to mine.

I waited for her question. She sighed and sighed for a good couple of minutes. Her stomach expanded into a large round balloon, then shrank, again and again. The cats made no concession to the movement of her body.

'Even Chekhov's most devoted admirers,' she finally said, still in French, 'hated that ending. They expected Anton Pavlovich to tell them what happens, to spell out the adulterers' fate. They wanted them punished or redeemed. They demanded to know what that most difficult part was. Lev Nikolayevich gave them that. Death on the railway line. Bang. Nothing so simple with Anton Pavlovich.'

One of the cats jumped off Elizaveta Maximilianovna's lap, the other burrowed a sleepy head deeper under the balloon. A cloud of hairs flew into the air.

'What do you think, Albertina Abramovna?'

'I think they – both of them, Tolstoy and Chekhov – load the dice a bit. The husbands are boring in both cases, undeserving of love. It makes the equation simple.'

'But if it were otherwise, why would the wife stray? Any husband who is deceived must ipso facto deserve to be deceived. Don't you agree?'

'No, I don't. Not at all. I am sorry,' I said, uttering my words with more vehemence than I had intended to. Elizaveta Maximilianovna laughed.

'Oh, I see. But we can disagree. This is a Russian lesson, not an ethics class, my dear Albertina Abramovna.' She was delighted by my outburst. '*Au contraire*, I think there's nothing wrong with adultery. It is so very bourgeois of Lev Nikolayevich to get into that judging business.

'My father and mother, for example ...' She reverted to Russian and the now familiar history of being a daughter of an aristocratic general. Her story, with its ever-increasing accumulation of details, was the pivot around which my Russian vocabulary grew.

She sipped sour-cherry vodka and refilled her glass liberally and often, although it was just ten in the morning, and she went on about dances and revolutions in a dizzying way. There were more revolutions in Elizaveta Maximilianovna's tales than in Monsieur Carr's, many more than in any Russian history book. She kept patting her chignon. She looked, in spite of her much emphasised aristocratic background, like a large Russian matryoshka.

I struggled to understand her, anyone would, I thought, yet my Russian progressed nonetheless. Barely two months of classes, and there was already much more Russian than French in her sentences – to the extent that I sometimes feared there would soon be no French left at all, that I would be cast adrift in that soft language which sounded like feathers falling from the sky, like being lost inside a paperweight snowstorm. Yet, by some strange miracle, I managed to understand more and more.

After the language class, I lunched at home and went to Monsieur Carr's. He was nursing a heavy cold and an eye infection. He was wearing a pair of sunglasses behind which tears trickled in a steady stream. He refused to shake my hand and kiss me on arrival.

'I don't want you to catch this,' he said. 'I have come to depend on your visits.'

'I am stronger than you may think,' I said. 'I haven't had a cold in years. And I have a surprise for you.'

I took the folder out of my bag, the manuscript I had intended to give him the previous time. He held it up close against his face and examined the cover.

'"*Karenin's Winter*",' he read. 'My life. Albertine, have you written this?'

'Yes, I have,' I said. I could not tell his reaction from his tone and so I started explaining my reasoning behind the volume. 'I thought it would be something to give to Gigi, and any other grandchildren you may have one day.'

Given Diana's age, the likelihood of another grandchild was relatively small, but I blushed when I said this. I realised that I had betrayed not only my husband, but this woman and her child, and possibly this old man too.

'You are the sweetest person, Albertine,' Monsieur Carr said. 'Would you read the book to me? Would you read *Karenin's Winter*?'

He handed me the folder.

'Of course,' I said. 'It will take a couple of hours. Do tell if you get tired. We can always pause and continue next time.'

'Get tired of my life?' He laughed and I saw more tears streaming down his cheeks. I joined him in his laughter.

'Oh, Albertine, you are the only person to laugh at my jokes. I so love puns and double entendres even when they are trite and childish. It comes from being a linguist, I suppose.'

'Or being a foreigner, in my case,' I said. 'Always on full alert, worrying that you will misunderstand, that you will be caught out.'

I read *Karenin's Winter* to him as he sat in his usual chair, looking, behind his glasses, like a blind man. I could tell from the rhythm of his breathing that he was attentive, listening. He did not interrupt, not even with his usual 'Oh, dear,' but would occasionally sigh a quiet yes, or, at times, a no that sounded like a yes.

When I finally finished, he reached out for the folder and looked at its cover again.

'That is so lovely, Albertine. I can't believe you did all this. The hours the work must have taken,' he said. 'And I can't believe I told you so much. You organised it all so well and the writing is beautiful.'

'And I kept it loose-leaf deliberately, so that you can add photographs and further stories to it,' I said. 'Or I can do it for you.'

'Dearest scribe,' he said, 'you have left yourself out of *Karenin's Winter*, but I demand a colophon at least, a line or two with your name at the end, and a small illumination perhaps, like those ancient books. Would you do that for me?'

'Of course,' I said. 'But please give me some time to think. It is not easy to know what to write. The ending is the most prominent spot.'

'Albertine,' Alex Carr called. 'I had expected you to come by much earlier.'

I was at the bottom of Monsieur Carr's street, next to the green opposite the Underground station. The day was almost over. Men left the station, hurrying home to dinner, to their families. Their clothes were as grey as the dusk, their shoulders relaxing as they walked away from their trains. He was sitting on a bench at the corner of Bath Road, just outside the reach of a cone of street light. He was half hidden by a cluster of budding hollyhocks and crimson peonies, flowers the colour of a deep wound, like something his poor mother might have painted. His thin body fitted the scene: the wooden slats, the high stalks, the flint-coloured dying light of the day. His face was long and wan, like the crescent moon just rising beyond the tile roofs, the circles beneath his eyes darker than the peonies. I sensed the tension. It was radiating from his very bones.

'Albertine,' he repeated. I sat down next to him. There was a pub opposite, its small garden wedged into the corner below the railway line, a space criss-crossed by bunting above a collection of ramshackle tables, like the washing lines with drying bandages in the courtyards of Egyptian hospitals. Towering above the courtyard were the crowns of horse chestnut trees, dark leaves supporting candelabras of buds about to burst open. Alex looked across the road as though he was thinking of inviting me over, then changed his mind.

'How are you, Albertine?' he said finally. 'How have you been?'

There was no easy way to answer the question.

'What shall we do, Albertine?' he asked.

'I have no regrets,' I said.

'That is not what I'm asking, Albertine. Although I'm happy to hear it.'

'But it is very hard, your question. I am confused. I have never been in anything like this situation before. I keep changing my mind. I am not sure there is anything to do. Anything we have to do, I mean.'

'I want to do the right thing. I have been in a similar situation.' He hesitated, noticed my expression. Had he not said that he was a faithful husband?

'Oh, not that similar,' he said. 'I was the one who was expected to forgive. The wronged party, as they say. And I was in Palestine when the question arose. I really can't say any more.'

I liked his unwillingness to share Diana's secrets, his sense of propriety, even as I felt it shaking to the foundations.

'Contrary to what you might expect,' he continued, his voice almost inaudible, 'to forgive is the easiest thing to do in this situation. It does not demand any action beyond itself. The declaration of forgiveness, I mean, that first step, the sign of goodwill. I gave that sign long before I could forgive in reality, but I had all the time in the world to deliver on what was expected of me. Until you arrived, Albertine. That was difficult, but this is so much more so. What do you think, Albertine? Dearest?'

I shivered. I shivered so much that I had to get up and move on. He followed. We walked in silence for half a mile or so. I hoped that he knew where we were, that he was not simply coming after me. The chances that someone could see us and recognise him were considerable, yet he did not seem to care.

'Have you told your husband?'

'I tried. But I did not in the end. Not because I could not. Does Diana know?'

No, no, no. He repeated the word three times, each time after a long interval.

'No one knows then,' he added. 'No one but us.'

'Your father? He often says things which make me feel that he knows everything, sees everything,' I said.

'No,' Alex repeated one more time. 'There is no way he could ... But what does all that matter, Albertine? Does it matter who knows? You mean a lot to me. I want to do the right thing. Except, I have no idea what the right thing is. I will obey your wishes. Whatever you ask me to do, I will do.'

This, the delegation of power, and I could see that it was meant, made me shiver again. It seemed to me that he was paralysed by his need to act honourably and an inability to see what the honourable thing would be. *You mean a lot to me*: the words of someone who did not love. Or the words of someone who was afraid.

'I have no idea, Alexei. Has one afternoon changed so much?' I said one afternoon because I couldn't call it anything else. I was, it turns out, the sort of person who could betray her husband, but who could not say the word sex out loud.

'Of course it has,' he said. 'It has changed everything, don't you see?' He paused. 'Oh, Albertine, your lapels are completely wet from this silent crying of yours.' He had caught up with me.

The survival instinct of a pogrom baby, my mother used to call it. You had to learn how not to make a sound. She was, and I was not, a pogrom baby. Alex Carr took a handkerchief out of his coat pocket, reached out towards my face, as he had once already at the Acton hospital, and now, as then, he embraced me instead. I knew his smell under the rough cloth: tobacco, tar soap, and something clear and bright underneath, like ozone after a spring shower.

'Would you prefer me to sob loudly?' I said.

Someone was coming down the road. An old woman with a dog, I saw as she walked past us, slowly, limping a bit. Her left shoe was stacked by several centimetres.

I stepped away from him.

'We will need to pretend that nothing has changed,' I said. 'See how that feels, at least for a while. Get used to the feeling, both of us. I don't see how anything else could be possible now.'

He took a deep breath, abruptly, as though I had hit him in the solar plexus, and stared at me. He seemed to bend a little, caving in under an invisible force, then straightened up.

'I am used to acting as normal; you can say that about me, Albertine. An accountant in West London: how do you think a dispossessed Russian becomes one? So yes, if you are sure that is what you wish. But, please, dearest, remember that I had wanted to do the right thing by you before I did right by anybody else.'

We had looped back to the Underground station. In his tiredness, his anxious expression resembled his grandfather's face in the portrait in Monsieur Carr's library, yet he now seemed much more handsome, for a handsome, good soul shone out of his eyes. I kissed his cheek, once, quickly, and walked up to the platform alone.

'There was something you wanted to talk about last night, Ber,' Albie said when I returned to Earl's Court. He was in the kitchen, eating. I apologised for my lateness. He waved my apology away.

'I have not forgotten. Is it about your allowance?' he asked.

'Oh? Did I? You may remember but I don't. I have no idea. It certainly isn't my allowance. I don't think I spend a third of it, Albie.'

Here we are. The shape of silences to come. I was saving us both, saving all four, five, six of us, I thought. I wondered how many people could be said to have been deceived on Monday afternoon.

Albie looked relieved.

'But you should, dearest, you should go shopping, please yourself. And I used it, but I hate that word, "allowance". You have your own money from the Carrs. Or is it the job that worries you? You don't have to stick with it, Albertine, if it bores you, just because you thought it was a good idea four months ago. You don't have to prove anything to anyone.'

He put his knife and fork down. He was eating a kipper – a pungent butterflied smoked fish, like something crucified on a plate, with a fried egg on top, burnt and dry around the edges, a supper he had improvised while I was out in the streets of Chiswick talking to Alex Carr, a meal which looked so English and so joyless that it made me want to cry for Albie. He was washing it down with a cup of tea so strong that a drop of milk had turned it the colour of copper. I heard the liquid as it descended Albie's gullet, a roll of waves on a shallow beach. I thought it was going to crush me, just that sound. I stood up to make a cup of black tea for myself, then sat across the table from Albie and watched him eat. He mopped up the last smears of yolk from the plate. The moment passed.

He might well have waited for me, wanted us to eat together, before he gave up on the wait, before it was too late to make anything more elaborate, but he had not asked why I was late. Was the question there, wrapped in another question, drowned by the tea? Was he waiting to see if I would tell him anything? I knew Alex Carr better than I knew Albie, I thought.

'Shouldn't we invite your parents over, Albie? I don't understand their continuing absence. They have been promising to visit us for so long. Is it perhaps because we don't push, because we don't insist, that I haven't met them yet? A weekend, perhaps? Or just a Sunday lunch, if you prefer. East Anglia is hardly the other end of the world. It's almost two years since we arrived, since you brought me here. It doesn't seem normal. Don't you miss them at all?'

'Is that what has been troubling you, Ber? Is that what you wanted to talk about?' He looked relieved. 'Dearest, you should have said it. I don't care if my parents visit or not. I missed them, horribly, for a month or two when I was eight or nine, never since. They made sure I had enough for the tuck shop, enough to blunt my sorrows with sweets when other parents visited. They couldn't just nip over from Darjeeling, could they? Even their letters were written in a kind of code: You're having a wonderful time, boy, we know that. Please don't say anything but yes. But we are on speaking terms. At least I assume so. If it means so much to you, I'll invite them, of course I will. I'll write to them. You're a good person, dearest. You had me worried.'

He was the second man to call me dearest that day, the third to call me good.

A day or two later, I promised Albie that I was going to go to Debenhams for lunch; that I was going to shop, to have my hair done. How can you not love a husband who makes you promise to do whatever you want to do?

The department store was full of women, alone or in twos and threes, walking from floor to floor under artificial light, sniffing scents, fingering fabrics, turning the saucepans upside down to see what they were made of.

'How can I help you, madam? That's lovely, that silk, excellent quality too, and I don't say that often about Indian fabrics. You have an eye,' a sales assistant said.

I was looking for a project, twisting the corner of a bale of silk chiffon, a spray of blood-coloured petals on a khaki background, the fabric so fine, so slippery that it was bound to test my sewing skills to the limit, running away long before the first cut. The assistant spelled out the width of the bale and suggested the lengths I would need for different garments, in inches, all too fast.

'A shirt,' I said. 'A long-sleeved shirt with a ruffle collar.'

Everything seemed absurd, but I tried this new life, like someone trying a new garment for size in front of a mirror. I kept promising myself to give it a decent go. The young man took the bale to the cutting table, turned it over and over to unroll the lengths of silk I wanted, measured it carefully, counting inches out loud through his thin, feathery moustache, stretching the fabric along a measuring stick, drawing a thin line with chalk, cutting then rolling the silk into a thin salami, saying see, it rolls into nothing, wrapping it, tying the parcel with a red string and handing it to me, walking me to the till to pay, like a gentleman walking his lady to a promised dance. The idea that I would be making a ruffle-collared shirt, that I would be wearing it at some point in the near future, seemed the most absurd of all.

At the hairdresser, an hour later, I asked for the most elaborate set, a profusion of curls and twists, and then a chignon. I sat for the best part of three hours in a small salon on Half Moon Street, looking at taxis going past, at a roofless house across the road, leafing through women's magazines, sitting under a dryer in a gaudy floral gown with pads over my ears while curlers got hotter and hotter and my scalp burned. My new hairdo emerged gradually from under the comb and a newfangled spray pump, more spray than I thought it possible to need.

'An updo is always the elegant option,' the young woman said, teasing the odd curl out of the interlocking plaits that formed the complicated chignon. Updo: not a word I had ever heard before.

'Too much control never looks good,' she said. She held up a mirror at the back to show me how elaborate it all was. I saw myself reflected in triplicate. I saw what Albie would see some hours later: an alien woman.

'You have such lovely, lustrous hair, madam, so un-English. You are so lucky. I am sure your husband will love it,' she said, looking furtively at my left hand, noticing my wedding ring, touching her tight blonde bun, which was no bigger than a golf ball. Her own rings sat in an ashtray by the washing basin. She looked at them too, as if to make sure that they were still there. I had a hairdo fit for a wedding ceremony. I wanted it to speak for itself. To speak to Albert of hours wasted, pleasing myself in order to please him, just as he had urged me to do. If I was not happy, he would see it as his own failure, not mine.

Someone gave me a seat on the Underground. I smelled of hairspray and scents from the department store. There was a young man with a wooden leg next to me, a crutch protruding out of his unseasonally heavy winter coat, a field-grey coat with strange buttons. I wondered what made me deserve this seat. I wondered if I looked too ladylike for public transport, or like a woman unhinged in some way. There was no shortage of men with wooden legs, no shortage of unhinged women, in London.

Albert loved it all: the silk, my plans for the shirt, the curls, the lot. He circled me, tugged at one of the curls, took it all as proof that I had had a wonderful day, just as I said. We sat on the sofa in the drawing room, his head in my lap, and I massaged his temples. He stretched one of his legs up and along the top of the sofa, the other rested on the arm. His toes danced inside his black socks, aping the slow rhythm of my fingers, as though I was making his whole body unfurl. He reached up, touched my curls again. There was music on the radio, one of those pieces with long violin solos you always recognise but cannot place. Albert's eyes were closed.

'When I was last in Berlin, just before that Russian party of yours, I went to the opera,' he said. 'A golden, baroque space which by some miracle had survived the war. The audience applauded for fifteen minutes after the last curtain call. I was in the dress circle, first row. Next to me, a German woman of perhaps seventy or seventy-five, mouthed every line, and cried at the end.

'She stayed in her seat through five or six curtain calls, sobbing all the way through. On my other side, an American couple took off in a hurry and left a box of chocolates on the edge of the balcony, an almost empty box, a couple of pieces left behind at the most. I could hear the rattle as I took the box from under the railing and put it on the seat behind me, just so that the box did not fly off into the stalls when someone's coat-tails swept by. I let the German pass in front of me. She looked me straight in the eye, took the box, then hid it behind her programme, like stolen treasure.'

'Oh, Albie, that is heartbreaking,' I said.

'I know. And the way she looked at me as she took that box was not furtive at all. Rather, there was something both proud and accusing in it, as if to say, "See. This humiliation I'm going through. This is your doing."'

'I am sure you are imagining it, Albie. I am sure she was thinking nothing of the sort. The British were their liberators.'

'People survive on four hundred calories a day in Berlin now, less than the inmates had in Belsen,' he went on.

'The concentration camps are full of people – displaced persons – with less to eat than the inmates had in the war. I know I've often said that now it's the Germans' turn to suffer, Ber, but I've changed my mind. I can't take any more suffering. What do you think, Albertine? Don't tell me to give it time. Everyone says that. What is the right thing to do?'

'The question never gets any easier,' I said from under my ridiculous edifice of hair. 'I am not sure, Albie, I am not sure what I think. There are places in London where they collect food aid for the Germans. Many of the people who run these collections are Jewish. Do you want me to take food there?'

I caressed Albie's crown, observed the first silver lines in his hair, wondered if I should encourage him to give it all up. Some of his fellow officers had become farmers. They came to London sometimes, stopped by to see us, their tweed suits smelling of milk and cheese, their faces ruddy and wind-beaten. They seemed happier than us. Albert could do that; he belongs to the *terroir*. He could grow new roots. This is his land.

When I next saw Monsieur Carr, both his cold and his sunglasses had gone. His eyes were still rimmed with red, but he was full of the joys of spring.

'I showed Korda your book,' he said cheerfully. We were sitting in a pair of ancient wicker seats in his back garden. The weather echoed his mood. The air hummed with pollen; the trees in the garden were bursting with new leaves in a dozen shades of green. Then there was the blossom on the fruit trees: when there was a breath of wind, the petals took off, swirled in the air and landed on our shoulders like wedding confetti. Even the left side of Monsieur Carr's face managed an upward smile.

'He loves my life story, Korda does; he sees only glamour and privilege in it, even where there was just hunger and poverty. "I wish we could make your life story into a film, Prince," he says, "I can see Trevor Howard in it, playing you."'

'Trevor Howard, no less,' Monsieur Carr repeated and chuckled. Whenever we talked about the film people, he was improbably enthusiastic and sarcastic at the same time.

'You wrote it all down so well, Albertine, as though we were your own family. Such a sense of measure.'

'It was hardly a huge task,' I said. 'The story typed itself. You told it well. But I wish you had given me more details.'

'Korda mentioned that job for you again. There are cliques in Shepperton,' he said. 'Expressionists fight the realists. Duvivier now insists on speaking French, the Brits insist on pretending they understand. Gigi is there too from time to time, doing his bit, even missing school on occasion: Alexei has relented under our concerted pressure. Diana is chaperoning the boy and they both love it. They are the only ones who seem untouched by divisions. Gigi loves the costumes. In his little sailor suit, he looks uncannily like me at his age. But he seems to have taken against the actor who is playing Vronsky for some reason – fittingly, perhaps.'

'I shall be glad to speak to Mr Korda's secretary,' I said. 'It might be the right job for me, after all. I'll give her a call.'

There was commotion in the hall, the sound of dog paws scratching on the tiles. Amur dashed into the garden, brushing his head against Monsieur Carr's palm.

'A job?' Diana Carr asked. 'You are not about to leave us, Albertine?'

Amur was now rubbing his back against my thigh, his beautiful silky back, his eyes so dark that they looked as though they had no irises.

'No,' I said, blushing. 'I thought Monsieur Carr might like to have an informer amid the film crew when Gigi completes his acting duties. I think I can manage both.'

'I am glad to hear it,' Diana responded. 'We like you so much. You seem to have a magic touch with our men.'

She smiled. There was no obvious malice in her words, no irony. Alex Carr had said that he was the one who had had to forgive Diana something. I did not think I would ever know the truth of it.

14

The Descending Blue

I never did call Korda's secretary. Days after that conversation, mid-morning, after one of my classes with Elizaveta Maximilianovna, everything changed. Albie was away again. In Europe, he said. It had been a merry class, oiled by quantities of cherry vodka on her part, and on mine by a kind of euphoria induced by the fact that I suddenly and miraculously started to understand a great deal more, that I could answer her questions in Russian and in more than a few very basic words.

I would revisit the day, again and again, because I kept returning to those last moments before I had known how it would end, and they seemed impossible. How could I not have sensed anything? There was the whole night, then a good chunk of the morning when I did not know. Seven hours' sleep, bracketed by two meals, a thousand steps under a million raindrops: how could all that be? If the earth slips off its axis, if the road under your feet disappears, how do you not know it and keep walking?

I walked from Elizaveta's basement flat off Gloucester Road, back to Harrington Road in South Kensington, where I bought a copy of *Le Monde* in the same shop in whose window I had first spied the Carrs' job advertisement. That had been barely five months earlier, yet it seemed like decades. The horrible, deep winter had already been transformed by memory into something beautiful, white and silent under the blanket of snow. There were the chilblain scars on my fingers, dark red with dry patches, to remind me of the hardship. Almost everyone had them, yet almost everyone loved that winter in hindsight.

Perhaps I deceive myself, but that morning the city sang to me for the first time. I had come to know the grid of streets between Earl's Court and Hyde Park so well that I could veer off the beaten track, look up, notice a striking building, say Brompton Oratory, its dome dwarfing the mean streets to its east and creating a vision of Italia in Anglia, or the seemingly pointless Queen's Tower alongside Imperial College, or simply see the sun, and realise where I was, the route I needed to take. People asked me for directions, and I gave them confidently.

Even my English seemed fluent. In Alexandria, I got used to calling my husband Albie because he teased me when I uttered the French version of his first name. When I pronounced Albert's name now, I sounded the final t.

When I returned to our square, I saw Brigadier Abercrombie waiting at the top of the steps. He was wearing a mackintosh, a fedora on his head, and he was leaning against the pillar by the entrance with his left shoulder, his back turned to me, looking towards Chelsea as though he had been standing there for a long time, expecting me to appear from that direction. I sensed that something was horribly wrong even without seeing his face, so wrong that I wanted to turn away and run, as though, whatever he had to say, the non-delivery of the news would prevent its happening. Whatever the happening was. It was clear that the news had something to do with Albie. Such was my unspoken dislike of Abercrombie that I was convinced, in the split second before I took the next step, before I decided not to run away, that they had arrested Albie. 'They', for some unfathomable reason, included Abercrombie. 'They' were Albie's own. The army, the intelligence services, the government; I had no idea.

But then Abercrombie saw me and I knew. Albie was not under arrest, he was dead. This man, his comrade, stood there, on the top of the stairs, waiting for me to approach, to unlock the door, to let him in. He expected me to crumple when I heard. He was not going to tell me anything out in the street. Except to confirm what I already knew, that what he had to say was not good.

'I'm afraid I've some bad news, Albertine,' he said. He had never used my first name before.

'Bad news?' I echoed. I already knew that it was bad. 'How bad, Brigadier Abercrombie?' I asked.

'Can we step in?' His voice was breaking. Speaking seemed far from easy for him too, and that meant very bad indeed.

I took a bunch of keys out of my handbag, unlocked the front door. It was suddenly too heavy, this door of ours, and Ian Abercrombie held it for me. I let him close the door behind me, heard the latch click.

We stood in the hall for a moment. He took off his fedora. Unbuttoned the collar button on his mackintosh. I fainted.

I remember trying to hold the coat rack the moment before I fell. I remember the metal under my fingers, the rustle of the coats as they dropped on the ground, the way the cloth cushioned the crash of the rack, as though everything took minutes, and in each one of those minutes I knew and did not know it yet. There was still time to save Albie's life. I remember being held by Brigadier Abercrombie, wanting to fall further. I remember coming back, regaining consciousness, perhaps seconds later, perhaps hours, in the armchair by the fire. Which was unlit. Unlit fire behind a black grate, smelling of old ashes.

'I'm afraid Albert is dead,' Abercrombie said.

I said nothing in return. The soundless crying must have been as disorienting for him as it had been for everyone else before. He did not know about pogrom babies. I could not save Albie by making no noise now, yet I could not sob either.

'How?' I said. 'Where?'

'Berlin.' He answered the second question first. 'May I sit down?'

I nodded. Of course.

Still in his mackintosh, he took a seat opposite me, on the other side of the unlit fire, Albie's seat. He undid another button, took a deep breath, as though the coat had been making it impossible to breathe. One of his shoelaces had come undone after I dropped. He was a big man, a large man, but his ankles were unbearably slim. I hated that.

'Berlin,' he repeated. Then, and this seemed astonishing, he started crying too. He made little gurgling noises, like someone trying half successfully to stop burping. Big wet blotches dissolved on the front of his beige coat, like drops of rain landing on a dusty pavement, in some scorched, dry place.

'I'm so sorry, Albertine. I knew Albert for thirty-six years. We were at school together. We were in the war together. We were never not together. Except from now on. He's ... he was ... the best officer we had. I'd no idea.'

'No idea what?' I asked.

'No idea that things had gone this far.'

'What makes you say that? How did he die?'

'I'll say this to you, and I'll never say it again, because the consequences, if it became known, would be grave. For you and me. Both of us. Not even our own people know that I am telling you this. You could lose everything if people even suspected.'

As though I had not lost everything already.

'I'm afraid we think it was suicide. I'm afraid we know it was,' Abercrombie said.

I wanted to say that suicide was impossible. I could not say that it was impossible if it had happened.

'How did he die?' I asked again.

'A train,' he said. 'Dahlem-Dorf. South-west Berlin.'

As though it mattered. As though the exact station mattered. As though the detail could alter the outcome. My parents, my sister, twenty kilometres east of Paris. Between Pomponne and Lagny-sur-Marne. I remembered that news too, the unwanted precision of it. For fourteen years, I had hated trains.

'How did Albert die?' I repeated the question.

'Late yesterday evening.' Again Abercrombie answered a different one.

So, I had a night without Albie when I believed he was still alive, I had a Russian-language class, I took a walk. There was this morning when I believed London was a happy place, a city singing to me. Had I turned away when I saw Ian Abercrombie, Albert could still be alive. Alive in my head, and is that not more than he was now, is that not life? He had told me once about an Austrian scientist whose thought experiment proved one could be dead and alive at the same time. I had failed to understand then. I knew it now. Albie was both dead and alive last night, this morning. Not now. It was too late.

'I should not have come here,' I said.

Abercrombie misunderstood.

'We'll help,' he said. 'We'll need to agree on a story about the cause of death. We'll sort it all out for you, Albertine. We'll bring him back.'

'Can you do that?' I asked.

'Oh, yes, the army can do everything. It is not our usual practice, but we'll have to, this time. I mean, you won't have to go to Berlin. Not now. We'll fly the body back.'

'Oh, the body,' I said and shrugged, as though the body did not matter, as though I had only just realised that there was a body too.

'Please don't regret coming here.' Abercrombie misunderstood again. He meant London. 'We will look after you. You won't suffer.'

'I will, I promise you,' I said.

'We'll provide,' he said. 'We look after our widows.'

'A widow.' Not an English word I'd ever used before.

'How exactly did Albie die?' I asked again.

'The station was empty. There were no eyewitnesses except for the train driver,' Abercrombie said. 'A former soldier. A German one, I mean. The Eastern Front. Released early because of his skills, lucky bugger. He gave a statement. Albert was in uniform, he said. That was odd. There was no requirement. In fact, rather the opposite. But do you need these details?'

'I can take them, Brigadier Abercrombie. I have already heard the worst.'

'Albert was waiting for the train, the man said. He had noticed him from some distance, alone on the platform. There are sculptures at Dahlem, Dahlem-Dorf I mean, wooden carvings, human forms, like small huddles of people waiting for the train, like wooden families almost, but they are in fact benches. You only realise when you get very close.

Albert was leaning against one, sitting in its lap almost, as though he was tired, facing the approaching train, and he stood up as it came nearer, still waiting. Nothing remarkable in any of that. Then the train was almost there and he took a leap. This is what the driver said. He did not fall under the train, he did not slide onto the rails, he took a leap, almost like someone trying to jump across, all the way to the other side. The grassy embankment. Except the train was there already. There was no way he could make it across. But the leap may be important. It could also be that he had spotted something or someone, that he gave chase. Those wartime instincts die hard.'

'He took a leap,' I echoed. 'Except the train was there.'

How do you live after that?

They did bring Albie back. On a plane. I went to Croydon to see him return to England in a small, grey aircraft. I watched it, like some distant bird, a grey falcon, getting bigger as it approached to land. It touched the ground, then made a barely visible jump, as though it was about to take off again. There were men at the airport, men in uniforms, men in suits, shaking my hand, saying things, waiting for Albie. A zinc box, a Union flag. There was a salute but no other ceremony; that still lay ahead. They took the box away. I sat in an official black car with men I did not know, and we moved through South London while everything around me took on the shape of a coffin: carriages and lorries, the new power station by the river, buildings and barges, brown and khaki and grey, boxes and boxes full of bodies.

'Did you have any idea that he was so unhappy?' Abercrombie had asked the afternoon he had delivered the news.

Yes, I did, of course I did, but not unhappy in the way that makes people want to jump under, no, to leap at, to throw themselves at an approaching train.

'No,' I said, for that was the easiest answer. 'Did you?'

'Yes,' Abercrombie said. He was the more honest of the two of us.

'We had an idea that he was unhappy, Peter and I. We talked about pulling him out. Recalling him from the Berlin business, I mean. Do you remember that evening here? The Klipdrift we drank together? We were trying to persuade him to do something different, stop travelling, move out of London even. Bristol, for example. You could have got yourselves a lovely house in Clifton, or out in the countryside. One forgets how beautiful England is, here in Earl's Court.'

'One does,' I said, although my knowledge of England, beyond the metropolis, was almost non-existent.

'Everything seemed to get to him suddenly,' Abercrombie continued. 'He was a great soldier, Albert was, but he had underestimated the peace, the effort it took. Did he tell you much about his work?'

'No, not really. I thought he was not supposed to,' I said and cried again. Tears came in spasms, returning every time I thought they would stop. Perhaps this was how it was going to be from now on.

'Do you have anyone who could be with you?' Abercrombie asked. 'You might find it impossible to cope on your own. Shall we send someone, at least until the funeral? Please tell me, Albertine. Just say the word.'

'I have no idea,' I said. 'No idea, Brigadier Abercrombie.'

'The family is being informed about Albert's death. He was a hero and he died like one. We will tell them, Albertine. We will advise his sister not to travel. There will be a memorial service for Albert at the garrison church in Darjeeling, while there is still a garrison, because of her. Your in-laws will be on their way here very soon. I know they were not close, Albert and his parents. I've known them almost as long as I've known him. Jolly decent people. There was no obvious reason for their estrangement. Albert wanted it that way, perhaps more than they did.'

He paused.

'That was how Albert was, I'm sure you know. He would push you away when he needed you most. He told you that you'd be better off on your own.'

'He told you to pull your socks up,' I said, thinking of Abercrombie's thin, child-like ankles.

'Yes,' Abercrombie said and gave a little smile. 'Yes, precisely.'

The day before Albert's funeral Peter Stanford met Albie's parents at Liverpool Street Station and brought them over to Earl's Court. They arrived in a strange car, a big black wagon with a double door at the back. I watched it park from the drawing-room window. I did not think it was them until the driver jumped out, opened Peter's door, then the back door. An old man came out of the near side with painful slowness, obscuring my view, so that the next thing I saw was Peter Stanford holding a woman, cradling her in his arms like a baby. He carried her out of the car so that she barely touched the ground with her feet before the driver handed her two walking sticks, strange tripods, and she leaned on them and turned towards the house slowly, hunched, like some small sad arthropod. I went out to greet them.

'Albertine,' she said, pressing deep into my ribs at the back with a bony hand as we embraced. Albie's father stood several paces away, his neck and his head protruding out of an unseasonal black coat like a tortoise's head out of its shell. This could have been unbearably sad, except that I had already lost any calibration for the unbearable.

The driver took a folded wheelchair and two suitcases out of the back of the car and carried them into the hall. I pointed straight upstairs, to the open door of Albie's and my bedroom. I had, notionally, moved into the spare bedroom just to its side, but was spending every night in an armchair, facing my marital bed through an open door. I pretended to read Albie's copy of *Days and Nights*. The beginning of his letter to me, the letter I found inside it, now haunted me: the words were like the musical notes you know to be the leitmotif of a composition only when you hear the entire piece to its end.

Albie's mother and father followed slowly, pausing at every step. The driver helped her; Albie's father took me under his arm.

'I had imagined this day differently,' I said. 'No, not this day, I mean. I mean our meeting.'

He took the last couple of stairs slowly, as if trying to gauge the level to which he had to lift his foot each time. He was an old soldier too. You could see that in the vestiges of his step, in his shoe polish, in his tie, in the white cuffs which emerged from his coat sleeves when he grabbed the banister before taking the next step. He gripped my arm with his other hand, above the elbow, like a rope someone has thrown to a drowning man. He was taller than me, considerably taller than his wife, but he was broken and I could not tell if he could ever be mended.

I did not want to ask why they had refused to meet me, why they had refused to come to see Albie, if indeed they had. I no longer knew anything for certain. I should have thought this through. They should not have to climb all these stairs. Except I never thought anything through, I realised.

Elsewhere, people were busy, things were being taken care of. In our house, Albie's house, there was little conversation and less movement. There were sandwiches on the table, delivered by Albie's people, picnic food for the saddest picnic imaginable.

'We are so sorry, Annabel,' Albie's father said.

I did not correct the name. They seemed defeated as it was. Annabel was Albert's sister.

'He spoke fondly of you,' I added. What was one more lie? They returned the courtesy.

'You're a lovely girl. Albert loved you a great deal,' his mother said, her posh voice breaking, barely audible. She patted her lap with a small, dry hand. She could not have known it, could not have known how much Albie loved me.

'Your English is excellent,' she added finally, unexpectedly, 'truly excellent.'

'Thank you,' I said. I was so eager to keep the pretence of a conversation, I almost added, So is yours.

I played with my bracelet, the one Albie had given me for our eighteen-month anniversary, turning it around and around my wrist, waiting for the chain to snap. It held: it was stronger than it seemed. The Prince of Wales, invisible doubling, I remember Albie explaining, it can take more strain than you would think possible. His voice echoed in my head. I wondered which faded first – the touch, the smell, the sound.

The telephone rang. It rang and rang, ten, twenty times, before I stood up to answer it.

'Albertine,' Alex Carr said. 'You've had us all worried. You didn't come last week. My father called you. Then he asked me to call. Is everything all right?'

'Albie has died,' I said and put the receiver down. I stood next to the telephone for two, three minutes, wondering if it would ring again. Then it did. I saw Albie's parents through the open door of the sitting room, in my and Albie's armchairs, facing each other, saying nothing.

'Albertine,' Alex Carr said, 'please forgive me.' The voice was not his own. 'I am not sure if this is some kind ... I am not sure what to say. That is devastating news. You never mentioned he was ill. Was it a heart attack?'

'No,' I said. 'Nothing to do with Albie's heart. I am sorry, but I can't speak now.'

'Don't put the receiver down,' he said. 'Albertine, I beg you, please.'

I did.

I went back to the drawing room, sat with Albie's parents as darkness fell outside. There was a pile of unopened telegrams and letters of condolence on a tray on the ottoman between them. We could have done a million things differently, his parents and I. I was not sure which, if any, of these things could have saved Albie.

The following morning, the morning of the funeral, it felt as though they had always been there with me, the old man and the old woman, sleeping in my marital bed. I hadn't slept at all, and at four in the morning, with the first whisper of light, I went into Albie's study. In the past, I had looked at things he happened to have left on his desk, if there were any, less out of curiosity and more as a way of feeling his company. I had never looked through his things in search of evidence. I had not been that sort of wife, a small blessing perhaps, given the sort of wife I turned out to have been.

I loved his hairbrush with two ivory combs tucked into it, a hideous leather box, the outline of the Corniche in lurid green on the lid, that contained paper clips and pencil sharpeners, Albie's monogrammed, silver-topped inkwell. There was a picture of me, in a silver frame, on a boat, leaning against the railings, my hair half obscuring my face, and behind, on the upper deck, several soldiers smoking. I held a pair of sunglasses in my right hand. If you looked closely, you could see Albert in the dark lenses, holding the camera, taking a picture. I stared, trying to discern Albert's expression. I took a magnifying glass to the photo. The image was too small. Enlarged, it became a blur.

I unlocked his desk drawers, one by one, something I had never done before. I felt I was invading his posthumous privacy. I found them empty, as though – impossibly – someone had already been through them. The paper linings smelled of ink and tobacco and old documents. I lifted them, one by one. There was nothing, absolutely nothing underneath.

I sat in Albie's chair and felt exhausted beyond any power I had to describe the feeling. The spines of books on the shelves were so familiar that I could close my eyes and list the titles correctly. One day, not now, I would go through them one by one, looking for my husband.

I took Albie's shoes into the back garden and started polishing them with black parade polish, the way I remembered him doing it, standing on our small lawn, working the polish in with a cloth, brushing then polishing again, until the toecaps shone as though they were made of patent leather. I saw the outlines of Albie's feet on the pale insoles, the feet that took the leap. I pushed my hand deeper inside, and carried on polishing.

'Good morning, Albertine.' There was something in Albie's father's voice that reminded me of his son. He took no obvious notice of what I was doing. 'Have you slept at all?'

'No,' I said, 'not at all. I took the pills the doctor gave me, but they made no difference.'

'I was thinking, Albertine. I was thinking of him. He was always such a sunny, uncomplicated child when he was growing up in India and then we sent him to school in England and we never really knew him properly again.'

'This happens,' I said. 'The price of Empire.'

'I'm glad that he had you,' Albie's father said. 'That he found happiness with you.'

He was now standing next to me, wearing Albie's tartan dressing gown over a pair of ancient pyjamas. His clavicles rose above tufts of white hair on his skeletal chest. His skin was parched, like a mummy's, and his face was criss-crossed by deep lines. There were scaly patches on the outline of his jaw, damage inflicted by years of Indian sun.

'We were happy when the war ended, on the boat coming here,' I said. 'I did not like London to start with, but I got used to it. I wish I had known more about Albie. I wish I had asked more questions. I don't think I was as good a wife as he deserved.'

'Don't be hard on yourself. He might not have told you more than he did,' his father said. 'Perhaps he was not free to tell you more, anyway. In his line of work, loyalty to one's country is more important than loyalty to one's wife. I don't mean this badly, for, ideally, one should not test the other. A man gets used to keeping secrets; secrets breed other secrets, until there are so many that you don't know where to begin, even when they are secrets no more.'

'Do you mean to say that Albie was a spy?' I asked.

'Oh no.' He was visibly startled by the word. He put his hand on my shoulder. 'I am not even sure what that word means. A spy, I mean. He would undoubtedly have been reporting back from Germany, but is that the same as spying? We always see much more than we say, that is the Borders trait. But he would not, ever, have lied to you. I am sure that you knew as much about him as he knew about you.'

'Do you mind the fact that Albie is being buried in London?' I asked. 'It suits me, of course, but wouldn't East Anglia, or Scotland, have been more appropriate?'

'We agreed to London with his regimental colleagues,' he said. 'He was theirs, if he was anyone's. India might have been appropriate from the family point of view, but it would hardly have been possible now. We belong to so many places that we don't really call anywhere home.'

'Then London is as good a place as any,' I said.

'That's it,' he nodded in agreement. 'Although we don't call London home either. It feels like a foreign city. Especially since this last war. Strange to think that my son's body will rest in it.'

The day of Albie's burial turned out gloriously sunny. I need not have worried about its unfolding. If it involves a ceremony, it will be something that the army does well. Albie's funeral did the army proud. There were dozens of people I had never met before, men dressed in black or in uniform, wearing stripes and ranks I could not read, and men I knew, the faces of the young gods from Alexandria. They were a little older than when they had confronted Rommel, a little greyer, but they saw the Desert Fox off, didn't they? The women, elegant young women from Albie's office and wives standing next to their husbands, threw furtive looks in my direction. They made me hate being there for I did not know what to do with myself, other than at those times when people came to shake my hand, to say words I failed to catch.

None of it mattered. I knew what the words were. I was sedated, literally so, the world was swimming around me, yet something was stirring amid the elemental numbness, something that was four parts pain to one part anger. When the coffin was lowered, this angerpain shot up my shoulders and squeezed my ribcage, so that I could not breathe at all.

We had been driven to the cemetery, barely half a mile from home, but the drive seemed never-ending while we progressed along the colonnades in a slow cortège. The ceremony seemed never-ending too. There were speeches, prayers, the rifle salute. There was a choir of boys from Albie's school, a trio of priests whose vestments shone silvery and purple in the afternoon sun. There was a lone piper, his tune so primeval that it seemed to grab and squeeze my innards, as though the bagpipes were made of them. Someone carried a cushion with Albie's decorations. He had more than you would expect for a man of his age. There were flowers, headily fragrant in the morning, the whiff of decay discernible as the day progressed. There was stateliness and dignity and just enough pomp about it all to reassure a casual passer-by that we were interring someone important. It was the most complex ceremony Albie and I had ever attended together, yet he was not there to explain the details to me.

The open grave seemed raw and physical somehow, like a suppurating wound in the middle of a green lawn. At one point I observed, with the corner of my eye only, the arrival of the Karenins. Alex and Diana and Gigi, with a huge bunch of white roses, sixty or seventy roses, tied with a purple ribbon, then Monsieur Carr in an ancient dark suit. They stood at the back, waiting for the moment to come forward, to lay the flowers. They looked different from everyone else, marked by an intangible foreignness that was difficult to define, yet it was there even in Diana and the boy, as though they had come not just out of another country but from another era. The father and the son looked broken. When they approached and took their place in the gathered ranks, I felt something move, deeper than my angerpain, no more than a flutter of a feeling. That is when I knew.

15

You, Anna

'And how are you, my dear? Is it all becoming more or less bearable?' Monsieur Carr asked.

A whole year, almost, had passed since I started coming to him. It was four o'clock, yet the evening was already settling in, darkness defied only by an occasional flurry of bright yellow leaves. Some hit the windowpanes with the gentle sound of a child's tapping finger. The crowns of the lime trees in Queen Anne's Grove had thinned again, and the first stars shone through the branches. There was something eerie in the cries of the magpies: the sound of approaching winter.

Monsieur Carr looked out, then returned his gaze inside the room. It flitted across my face, and settled on my stomach, hard and round over my lap, like a tethered balloon. I felt movements inside, no stronger than the flutter of a quail's wing in the charred stubble of a cereal field after the harvest. They went on, these movements, at regular intervals, all day and into the night. I spoke to them in the evenings when I was alone, and that now meant every evening. We got to know each other well, the little bird and I. Everything else was a mystery yet to be unravelled.

'I am not sure about bearable, Sergei Alexeievich.'

He had insisted on, and I was finally getting used to, this informality. I still called him Monsieur Carr when I thought about him. We continued to converse in French. I had insisted on not being paid for my visits any more. He took a lot of persuading, but Albie's pension was sufficient. The greater intimacy came with the absence of transactions; the clarity of friendship and devotion.

'I must confess something, Albertine. I have given you a whitewashed version of our family history,' Sergei Alexeievich said, looking at a slim folder on the coffee table. It now had a morocco binding that nearly matched that of his mother's book. Nothing produced in these austere times could quite rival the Art Nouveau craftsmanship of the Angevins.

'I am not sure whether to regret it or not. You've written it all down, given it back to me and I have reread my story to Gigi and to Korda, but now I feel guilty, after everything that has happened. You deserved better from me, Albertine.'

'What do you mean, Sergei Alexeievich?'

'I told no lies, certainly no lies, but I left so much ugliness out, and I don't mean just the ugliness that followed my mother's death. That was as nothing compared to this century of ours, yet now I feel old and I have no stomach left for ugly things. But you may be like me. I now know that you asked me about Tonya only after you had completed your manuscript. You too – consciously or unconsciously – wanted to keep my story as sunny as possible. I should have trusted you more, Albertine. We could have cooperated, edited *Karenin's Winter* together.'

'But for that I would have needed to have the confidence to tell you about my project much earlier. Does it matter, Sergei Alexeievich? I was not thinking about my writing as editing, as leaving things out. I suppose I was writing the story down as I would for Gigi, or my own child. Would you want them to know? I left out some other things you said, but I remember everything.'

'I know,' he said and leaned over, patted my knee. 'But thinking about Gigi makes me wonder how much I knew when I was his age, how much Alexei knew. What do we do when we sanitise our history thus for our children? I loved my mother more than either her husband or her lover could, and I needed her more, but a son's love is never enough. Or at least was never enough for Anna. You are about to find out, and I hope you'll find out differently.'

'They are different, those kinds of love, and we are greedy, we want them all. I don't know why, Sergei Alexeievich, but I am convinced it is a girl. It is not long now.'

He had never asked who the father was. Perhaps the question was unthinkable.

'Remember how you and I began, reading *Madame Bovary*?' he asked. 'It seems like a century ago. There is a story about reading books I have wanted to tell you all this year. Soon after the Revolution, they moved dozens of peasants from the countryside into our house in St Petersburg, starving families looking for work in the city, four or five to a single room. We were left with one single room too, but it was just the three of us, a luxury, almost. It was as cold as last winter. Winters always seemed like that then. Our new tenants dug up the parquet flooring to feed the stoves. They started from the corners, replacing chevrons of cherry and mahogany with cardboard. I did not complain. I call them tenants but they had as much right to our property as we did. Wood was now too impractical anyway; it perished under the nails of our cheap boots, under the snow melting from the bottoms of coal buckets, or the brine leaking out of pickle barrels everywhere.

'I wished they would take it all up, as fast as possible, burn it away. But once they had, they started feeding the fires with books from the family library. The sight of that broke my heart. No one understood my grief. Latin letters, French and German verse, they might all just as easily have been witchcraft. I sneaked around when these people were out – no one bothered with keys then – stealing my own books from faraway corners of my own house, hiding them in nooks only I knew, in the wine cellar, which was now full of broken glass and mounds of useless furniture waiting to feed the fireplaces. I was caught, and arrested. One of the women found me in her quarters, thought that I was trying to steal a side of bacon. I was one of the former people; nothing was too far-fetched.

'I was arrested and beaten, and cross-examined so many times by different people that everyone forgot the original charge. I ended up in solitary confinement and stayed there for seven months, in a basement cell barely big enough to stand up in, tormented by the thought of my wife and my son. Gradually I worked out that there were identical cells, with prisoners like me, all along the corridor. For some reason the wall which faced the corridor was immensely thick, the metal door we had come through so heavy that the guards delivering our rations – and that happened all too rarely – had to lean against it and push it in with their backs, using the full force of their weight. The dividing walls were much thinner. We could not talk to each other, but we could drum, fingers and palms against the damp brick. Slowly, we developed a kind of alphabet and we used it to communicate late into the night, compulsively, as though we would stop existing if we stopped being heard.

'The man in the cell next to me, a religious philosopher I had known, distantly, for many years, was allowed to keep his

Bible when he was arrested. I am not sure why they allowed the Bible. The Bolsheviks may have been more tolerant in those early days; even Stalin had trained to become a priest, had been an intending ordinand, testing his vocation. Or they thought that it made no difference if the man was never going to leave the place. Well, it turns out, in his hurry he brought the wrong book with him. One of his sons, he guessed, must have taken the dust jacket and wrapped it around a volume just as thick, perhaps to read it furtively, in the church even. It was my mother's story.

'The man now offered to read *Anna Karenina* to me. He had no idea who I was. You won't believe this, Albertine, but I had not read the damned volume before; at first because my father would not let me, then because I did not want to. I had heard stories about it, of course, the many stories about the way its author adapted the truth to suit the needs of his fiction. Real life is too untidy, too improbable. The old Count had added things that were patently untrue, that – even if they were true – he could not possibly have known about my mother. Contraception, for example. I am sure that Anna would not have known how to go about that. She would have thought women who used contraception dishonest before God. But that is the nature of fiction. And of people. If you write a memoir, everyone looks for lies; if you write fiction people search for the truth, assume that you have invented nothing.

'Even Tolstoy became fed up with all the gossip, protested, played down the level of veracity, avoided us. That was all right. My father had not a single kind word to say about him. Father had been dead for almost a decade when Tolstoy was excommunicated from the Orthodox Church, but he would not have been in the least surprised.

'And now, in the basement cell, it took my neighbour two months to read *Anna* to me by tapping the novel, letter by letter, on his prison wall. I could barely sleep during those two months. I would not say I forgot Tonya and Alexei, how could I, but I kept wanting to hear what happened next, or, rather, how it happened, for I knew all too well the doomed moment the story was racing to. Two months. Tap, tap, tap, tap. The novel was much more complex than anything I had imagined, much more nuanced. Tolstoy understood my mother better than she understood herself. The only person he did not quite manage to grasp was my aunt Dolly, Uncle Stiva's long-suffering wife. Stiva treated Dolly abominably, but Tolstoy had no ear for the nature of her willing martyrdom. Dolly provoked the worst in the novelist, I think. He captured all the others. His writing was so great, it was, almost, worth all our misery.'

He turned and looked up to the portrait of his parents on the wall above.

'You know how Marx says – and I know a thing or two about Marx – ' he continued, 'that writers of genius are capable of rising above their epoch and class. So Tolstoy transcended his gender to understand something about Anna that none of us who had claimed to love her had understood. She was an orphan who needed to be held. My father possessed her, but would not hold her. The failure of their bond was not necessarily sexual, although one does wonder why she had only me – until her affair, that is. Father might have been withholding his husbandly duties too, but the withholding of a human touch was more important.

'In my cell, I dreamed of holding Tonya in my arms, all night, of holding Alexei. I woke up with his boyish smell in my nostrils. I could have killed a man to experience it just once more. Anna created two orphans in her desire to be held. An affair was an acceptable thing in St Petersburg and in the circles I was growing up in, for men and women alike. So long as you observed certain rules, obeyed certain hypocrisies. Anna's sin was not that she had wanted an affair. I know this will sound sentimental, but it is no less true for it. Her sin was that she needed to be loved.

'I had just one conversation with your husband, at our film party, and he admitted that he had never read *Anna Karenina*. "I never wanted to read it," he said. "Though I did read *War and Peace* when I was at school, and I loved it. I just wasn't that interested in *Anna*."

'"We obsess about adultery," your Albert said, "as though it matters so much more than any other betrayal, more even than the betrayal of our deepest-held principles." I liked that. Your husband was a good man, a noble man.'

'He was,' I said. 'Of course he was. You forgot to tell me what happened in that prison after you heard the novel to the end. How did you escape?'

'I did not escape,' he said. 'I was freed. Let go. Just like that. They never explained their reasons, the Bolsheviks, never apologised. Tonya and Alexei had left for the countryside. They were never allowed to visit me and there was no other reason to stay in St Petersburg. It took two months to find them. They were living in a village on the Oblonsky estate, in a house which belonged to one of their former serfs. Tonya thought that she was seeing a ghost when I appeared. My hair had turned completely white in prison.'

'That happens, I know. Overnight sometimes.' I touched my temple where I now had a lock of white hair.

'Much later, in Istanbul, one of the Russians I saw at Pera Palace, when I went there begging for work, one of Wrangel's men, told me what he had heard. That I was released, together with several others, at the behest of Evgeniy Levin, my cousin Constantine's son, who was high in Bolshevik ranks, Leon Trotsky's right hand man. I had never set eyes on Evgeniy, but I could tell that I was a little suspect in the eyes of my Pera Palace acquaintance. Why would a Bolshevik vouchsafe for me?'

'Blood ties,' I said. 'Surely even the Communists must have them?'

Sergei Alexeievich lifted a card from his side table. It was a photograph from the film of *Anna Karenina*, Vivien Leigh in front of a painting depicting an urn brimming with flowers. The star looked like a flower herself, wearing a ruched dress in pale silk, with garlands of silk flowers around the skirt, a posy on her waist, even a hat made of posies, like a human doll, or a poodle. There was something so manipulatively coquettish about the dress, so disingenuously innocent, that the image seemed more suited to vaudeville than a great tragedy. But perhaps the true tragedies all have an element of vaudeville. I no longer knew.

'I like the painting,' I said. 'Does the painting appear in the film? All those ruins in the deep background, beyond the flowers; they remind me of London.'

'You make me laugh, Albertine,' he said, although I wasn't trying to elicit his laughter. 'Do come, sit with me.'

I went over and sat down next to him. My body took its time to move, its time to settle. He raised his right hand and placed it on my stomach, as if waiting for the flutter of the quail's wing. Waiting for you, Anna, to give him a sign.

He tapped with his fingers against the hardness of my skin.

'A code?' I asked.

'An old Russian poem.'

We sat like that and he tapped on, slowly, inaudibly, finger then palm, letter by letter, for a long time. It was the most soothing thing anyone had ever done to me.

'Almost there, my dear. Almost over,' he said, in Russian, and leaned in, closer, as if to await a reply. Your reply.

When Albie's parents had returned to East Anglia, I started tidying up the house. I had no idea what I wanted to do with it. It sometimes seemed that I had to stay put, just in case Albie returned. He needed to be able to find me, I thought, insane with grief. The mortgage was paid off after his death. It had not been a big loan; property in London was cheap in those days. I had no financial worries, but I had problems of every other kind. A combustible mixture of pain and anger and guilt did not go well with morning sickness. Eventually the sickness and the angerpain died down; there was just the guilt and the waiting.

One summer's day a letter came from Albie's sister. The stamp depicted the crowned King-Emperor in profile, in an oval. 'Postage one and a half annas, registration three annas', it said. Things failed to make sense that summer. I saw Annas everywhere. I read everything two or three times, found meaning where there was none, and failed to understand the simplest of things. I believed that my English was deteriorating.

The British were leaving; India was being partitioned. Annabel was on her way to England. I didn't think she knew that I was pregnant. The envelope was flimsy, the onion-skin airmail paper Annabel's letter was written on almost transparent, but there was another, thicker letter tucked inside.

Deutsche Post, this one was: its stamps had pictures of hands in chains releasing white doves into the air. 'Dear Albertine', Annabel's letter said:

> Forgive my long silence. After I sent you a letter of condolence, a letter which no sister should ever have to write, I had what I suppose you could call a nervous breakdown. I could not get out of bed for days, and it was a bad time to stay in bed. During that time this arrived. A letter from the dead.

There were blotches all over the sheet of paper, right across Annabel's neat handwriting. I could almost touch the fine salt on the rims of each smudged circle.

> I'm now back on my two feet, moving. What can I say? When we were children, I used to be jealous of my younger brother. He was the golden boy who had escaped to our beautiful England to have fun, leaving me with Ma and Pa, to their aridity, the suffocating months and years of home tutoring. But, he grew up to be a wonderful, handsome man. No one stayed angry with him very long. Forgive me for not sending you this letter before. The one I'm writing and the one I'm enclosing. It arrived several weeks after Albert's death. I'm still not sure why he sent it to me. I think it would mean even more to you than it does to me, but I could not surrender it for such a long time. I've never met you but I remain,
>   your loving sister-in-law,
>   Annabel

'Darling Bella', Albie's letter said:

The winter's finally over and I'm in Berlin again, in a residence near Lake Slaughter. Yes, Schlachtensee. The Germans have a predisposition for the morbid, but the lake's anything but. There's a path around it. It takes a good hour and a half to walk. The view changes with every step and it's invariably magical. Otherwise, things here are dire. I can't tell you much in a letter. There's a coffee house on the shore where I escape the horrors to miss my Albertine in peace. She has been quiet lately. She has a secret she's hiding from me. I think – I'm convinced – she's pregnant. I'm not sure how to react when she finally chooses to divulge the news. I love her more than she'll ever know, but I worry. This world's not a good place for a child, not yet, and perhaps it'll never be again. It was my duty – British duty, for we created the vastest empire this world has ever seen – to build a world fit for a child. We did not. To that extent we have – I have – failed. But I mustn't be morbid, I'm not German (a feeble joke!). I'm rushing to catch the last post now, then the train (you'd love our little railway station, a fairy-tale thatched cottage, like something in Berkshire, with primitive wooden figures on the platform) to hear the Berlin Philharmonic in rehearsal. Beethoven. Can you imagine them, rehearsing Beethoven after all that's happened recently? I'm a lucky man, I've my moments of panic about this child, but I'll be a good father, and that's all there is to it. I hope you're well. I hope the second flush is coming on. God, how I miss India, how I've missed it all my life. You were so lucky, *bellissima,* so lucky to have had years and years of it while I suffered in the rain.

Your loving brother,
Albie

'It seems selfish to me, what Albert did,' Alex said one day while he was seeing me off from his father's house to the train. 'But I would say that. Leaving you the way he did, he took you away from me.'

He was the only person I had told about Albie's death. I knew I could trust him. I had to be able to talk to someone.

'No more selfish than what we did,' I said, reacting to the only part of his statement I managed to grasp.

'But he did not know about that. His ignorance was *your* choice. When he made *his*, he knew that you would know, that you would suffer as a result of his impulse, if impulse it was.'

'It looks as though I will never find out,' I said. 'He must have suffered.'

We met from time to time, Alex and I, sometimes by accident, sometimes by design, pretending to need to talk about his father, yet we always ended up talking about that afternoon. Talking about it, that is, without ever referring to the most obvious event. Sooner or later, I guessed, he would ask for my permission to tell Diana, because he was too honourable to keep withholding the truth. I hoped that Diana would forgive him. In a strange, confusing way, I now loved this man and I did not know what to do with that love, any more than I knew while Albie was alive.

It is possible to love two men at once. Most people cannot, or so they say. I very obviously could. I hoped I could be forgiven for it.

I saw 1948 in alone – not quite alone – listening to the BBC Theatre Orchestra on the wireless, playing music for *An Ideal Husband*, the film version Korda had released that November. I was making a shirt with a ruffle collar, no darts at the waist, out of that fine silk fabric that could best be described as challenging. I was beginning to get out of my widow's weeds. It was confusing for others, to be visibly in mourning while so heavily pregnant, so unbearably alone, going to the doctor alone, listening to your heartbeat. The colour of my clothing changed nothing, but it allowed some privacy for my pain. I no longer felt angry with anyone.

The silk, with its red petals like bloodstains, had been languishing in the back of the wardrobe since spring. Albie had seen it the day I bought it. I remember undressing for him. He wrapped the silk around my breasts as we pretended to care about ruffles and cuffs, and he tugged my carefully layered curls and plaits, until the complicated weave unfurled down my back. There were those moments when he knew exactly what to do and say; knew the vocabulary of tenderness so well that you had to assume that at other times he held back. We walked to our bed – me backwards, he facing me, like a couple in a dance – and as he fell over me he reached for the drawer in the bedside chest.

'No, Albie, please not. Let's carry on as we are.'

His face darkened for the briefest of moments, or perhaps I imagined this, but we carried on, exactly as we were. By the following morning I had forgotten the shadow, the split-second refusal to contemplate a child, like a cloud that passes over the sun.

That second body, gaunt and gentle, I almost forget it now because I saw it only once, some hundred hours earlier – the distance between a Monday and a Friday – and in the advancing darkness, perhaps while at the same moment Albert sat in some dull meeting in Bristol. I am not sure if I imagined this, but Alex's Russian was as tender as the falling snow, and he held me, for a long while, afterwards. To take a lover to your marital bed: is there a worse trespass?

I thought of it all as I stitched, of those five days.

It may have been foolish of me to set out to Korda's party alone the evening before the night I went into labour, but I had to see the film, had to be there.

The cameras turned to me because I was alone and because I must have been a strange sight. Sergei Alexeievich waited at the top of the stairs, holding his grandson's hand. Gigi beamed with a sense of importance. He was one of the stars at the premiere.

'Oh, my dear Mrs Whitelaw,' Duvivier laughed as I walked the length of the red carpet, my first red carpet ever, 'I almost failed to recognise you. We have been productive since our last meeting, but not nearly as productive as you, I see. I realise why you failed to call.'

'Oh my,' Elizabeth Montagu echoed when she saw my bulk. 'You were meant to be my assistant, you know, an assistant's assistant.' She laughed too, a lovely, throaty chime.

'I'd love to work with you in the future. For you. If there is still a vacancy after this,' I said.

'Oh yes,' she said, 'I'm sure there will be. Very much so. I've just fired a girl. Just so you know that I'm not a shrinking violet. We are the future, we film people; everyone says so. We can afford to be ruthless. We'll be filming in Vienna, if I'm right, by the time you're up and running again.'

She looked at my figure.

'I'm all for working mothers; that's the future too,' she added. 'But wouldn't the father mind?'

'No, the father wouldn't mind,' I said. It was not a moment for explanations.

Then Leigh and Olivier arrived. They had become Sir Laurence and Lady Olivier since I had seen them in person for the first time. People surged around them, whispering about Vivien's dress, about her pearl choker, the dark velvet ribbon in her hair. She kissed Elizabeth on both cheeks, then held my hand in hers, fishnet-gloved and cold, and seemed to take in our likeness for the first time.

'When is the baby due?' she asked. She was beautiful, much more beautiful than me, but she wasn't Anna.

'Any moment now,' I said. Just then, I could not guess how right that was.

She turned to wave at the gathering crowds. A camera flashed and there I was, my forehead and eyes caught above her right arm in a thousand newspaper clippings.

I see a man's face almost obscured by her waving hand, and I recognise Alex's forehead and I now know that neither of us would see *Anna Karenina* that evening. Because in the end, when I felt the first contractions and had to leave the cinema, he was the first to notice, and he was the only one to follow.

I searched for Sergei Alexeievich across the vast space of red plush and gilt. He nodded and gave me a little wave as I got up. That was the last time I saw him. By the time you and I came out of hospital, he had suffered a second, fatal stroke.

I saw Alex whispering something in Diana's ear. He followed me out, summoned a taxi.

'I can't believe you were planning to do this alone,' Alex said inside the car, while my face contorted and the driver cast worried glances at me.

'I was going to walk,' I said. 'Charing Cross Hospital is only ten minutes away.'

He went there with me and stayed, pacing the lobby, that whole night and the following morning. The midwives must have wondered at the man in a dinner jacket and the woman in an over-the-top ruffled shirt and a long, black, forgiving skirt, who stepped out of a taxi as though she had gone into labour at some glittering event. Everyone knew that he was not my husband. But it did not matter. I needed to have someone to hold me when it was all over. Someone to hold me so that I could hold you.

Afterword

I spent most of 2016 with a calendar for 1947 on my desk savouring the pleasure of time travel. I won't offer footnotes or a bibliography here, and of course I took my own liberties, but I would like to register three moments in the gestation of the story.

The youngest Count Karenin – Gigi – was inspired by Patrick Skipwith who played Sergei in Alexander Korda's version of *Anna Karenina*. Patrick's mother was a Russian princess exiled in London, and she worked at one point as an assistant to Laurence Olivier. Her life story is the subject of Sofka Zinovieff's excellent biography *The Red Princess* (2007).

Readers of *Monsieur Ka* may recognise many names, either from Tolstoy's work or from the history of British film. However, Prince Nikolai Rodionovich Repnin, the main character of Miloš Crnjanski's *The Novel of London* (1971), one of my favourite Serbian books, will probably pass unnoticed unless I mention him. He is that unnamed East European who looks mournfully at Albertine from the top of a double-decker bus on Piccadilly in Chapter Two. He sits above an advertisement for Emu wool. I am not sure why I thought it important, but I went to great lengths to find the slogan for the ad which is mentioned only in passing by Crnjanski.

Halfway through writing, when I already knew that Monsieur Carr was going to read *Anna Karenina* for the first time in a revolutionary prison, but I still had no idea how this was to be achieved, I heard a Radio 4 programme about Adan Abokor. Abokor did just what I describe. It took him two full months to complete the reading of Tolstoy's great work in this way.

I hope my readers take less time than that to read *Monsieur Ka*. For advice and encouragement, I am grateful to Clara Farmer and Charlotte Humphery at Chatto, my agent Faith Evans, Neal Ascherson, Simon Bradley, Laurence Colchester, Simon Goldsworthy, Alan Hollinghurst, Roderic and Mandy Lyne, Peter Mudford, Graham Swift and Sofka Zinovieff.

penguin.co.uk/vintage